A Pinch of
MAGIC

Also by Michelle Harrison

A Pinch of MAGIC

BY MICHELLE HARRISON

HOUGHTON MIFFLIN HARCOURT

BOSTON NEW YORK

hmhbooks.com

The text was set in Berling LT Std.
Map illustration by Michelle Harrison
Chapter opener illustrations by Celine Kim

Library of Congress Cataloging-in-Publication Data
Names: Harrison, Michelle, 1979–author.
Title: A pinch of magic / by Michelle Harrison.
Description: Boston : Houghton Mifflin Harcourt, [2020] |
Summary: Three sisters—adventurous Betty, curious Charlie,
and proper Fliss—go on a quest to break the curse that has
haunted their family for generations.
Identifiers: LCCN 2019020306 | ISBN 9780358193319 (hardcover : alk. paper)
Subjects: | CYAC: Sisters—Fiction. | Blessing and cursing—Fiction. |
Magic—Fiction.
Classification: LCC PZ7.H256133 Pi 2020 | DDC [Fic]—dc23
LC record available at https://lccn.loc.gov/2019020306

Manufactured in the United States of America
DOC 10 9 8 7 6 5 4 3 2 1
4500799603

In loving memory of Elizabeth May Harrison

1943–2017

The boldest, bravest Betty there ever was

Prologue

THE PRISONER GAZED OUT HER WINDOW. It was one of four in Crowstone Tower, the tall stone cage in which she was being held.

Here, if she kept her eyes up, she could pretend that the prison walls far below did not exist, and that she was looking upon the world from a castle, or perhaps a mountain.

But today she was done with make-believe; pretending she was in a dream, pretending someone was going to save her. The girl wrapped her arms more tightly around herself, against the cruel wind that whipped through the bare windows. It smelled of the marshes: briny with a whiff of fish. The tide was out, leaving only a vast expanse of mudflats stretching before her. In places she could see gulls pecking at stranded fish, tussocks of marsh grass, and a battered, abandoned rowing boat. A tendril of her long, tawny hair flew in between her lips. She tugged it free, tasting salt, and leaned over the cold, scratched stone sill as far as she dared. The windows were not barred; they didn't need to be. The height of the tower was deterrent enough. The noise of the crows circling outside was constant. At first she had thought of the birds as friends, chattering to keep her company. Sometimes, one would land on the sill. Pecking, watching, unblinking. The caws began to sound less friendly. Accusing, mocking. *Marsh witch*, the crows seemed to croak, in the voices of the villagers. *Came in off the marshes, she did, killing three of our own.*

She had never meant to hurt anyone.

The scratches in the stone stretched the length of the windowsill, one for each day she had been imprisoned. Once, she had known how many there were, but she no longer counted.

She walked a lap of the circular tower room, tracing her fingers over the stone. There were more scratches in the wall's surface: some shaped into angry words, others deep gouges where she had thrown things. Chipping away, but never breaking free.

A pale red moon had appeared in the sky yesterday, which had set all the warders' tongues wagging. The moon being visible in daylight was a bad omen at any time, but a red moon was worse still. A red moon was a blood moon, a sign that wrongdoing was afoot.

The girl explored the rough stones until she found the small gap she had discovered in the mortar when she hadn't long been in the tower, assessing the walls for possible footholds. When she had still had hopes of escaping. In the crevice she had wedged a broken chunk of stone, hidden from the prison warders. It was too small to be used as a weapon, but the warders would no doubt confiscate it if they knew about it.

She worked the stone loose and held it in her palm, hardly recognizing her own hand. Her skin was dirty and gray, her nails ragged. Using the stone, she scratched on the inside walls as if she were writing with chalk. With each letter she focused, thinking dark thoughts. She wrote a single word: a name . . . the one who had wronged her. When she was finished, she let the stone fall from her fingers. She didn't need it anymore. This was the last thing she would write.

She stared across at Crowstone. At high noon, a boat was to take her across the water, to the crossroads. There the gallows were being prepared at this very moment. It would be her first and last journey to the mainland. Her last journey anywhere.

It was there she was to be executed.

She wondered how the warders felt about transporting a supposed witch across the marshes. She would be shackled in irons, of course, which reputedly rendered witches powerless, but even the most fearless warder would be unsettled to be near her once she was out of the tower. Especially under a blood moon.

Her eyes drifted to the marshes, where it had all begun on a little boat one stormy night. Where three lives had been lost.

"I never meant to hurt anyone," she whispered, gripping the sill with numb fingers. It was true, she hadn't wanted to cause anyone harm then, but now, revenge was all she could think of.

And she would have it, even though she knew it would not save her.

Chapter One

Trick or Treat

BETTY WIDDERSHINS FIRST LEARNED of the family curse on the night of her birthday. It was her thirteenth, a number considered unlucky by some, but Betty was too practical to believe in all that. She liked to think she was too practical to believe in most superstitious nonsense, despite having grown up surrounded by it.

It was a Saturday, always a busy night in Betty's home, which was the village inn. The Poacher's Pocket was the rowdiest place on the isle of Crowstone and had been in the Widdershins family for generations. It now belonged to her granny, who was also named Betty but whom everyone called Bunny to avoid confusion. They lived there with Betty's sisters, Felicity (known as Fliss), who was the eldest, and six-year-old Charlotte, who would only answer to "Charlie."

Betty's birthday also happened to fall on Halloween. As she and Charlie galloped downstairs, their trick-or-treat costumes billowed behind them in a satisfying, villainous way. In fact, Betty's outfit was helping her to feel rather daring, which she was glad of, as she and Charlie were about to break Granny's biggest rule. Only, Charlie didn't know it yet.

As they threw open the door to the lounge bar, warm beer-scented air hit Betty's nostrils through the holes in her skeleton mask. She picked up Granny's favorite horseshoe, which had clattered to the floor, and placed it back above the doorframe. Charlie did her best witch's cackle to announce their entrance and swished her cape. Grabbing Granny's broomstick from the corner, she began dancing around the scuffed tables and mismatched chairs, chanting as her eyes sparkled in her painted-green face.

"Trick or treat, trick or treat . . . the marshes are misty and sugar is sweet!" She twirled and hopped like an imp as the regulars looked on in amusement.

"Careful, Charlie!" Betty called, eyeing her sister's cape near the crackling fires. She had lit them earlier, after she and Charlie had carved pumpkins into jack-o'-lanterns. She adjusted her long black cloak and motioned impatiently to Granny, who was wiping down the bar.

"We're off now, Granny," she said, thankful her face was hidden. She had been planning this evening for weeks, feeling only excitement, but now that it had come to carrying it out, she couldn't quite believe her own disobedience. She hoped her grandmother would put the tremor in her voice down to excitement, and not to the nerves that were buzzing inside her like marsh midges.

Granny stamped over. She stamped everywhere instead of walking, slammed doors instead of closing them, and mostly shouted rather than talked.

"Off out scrounging?" she said, blowing gray hair out of her face.

"It's trick-or-treating," Betty corrected her. "And everyone does it."

Granny tutted. "I'm well aware of what everyone does, thank you. And it looks like scrounging to me, when you could be useful here."

"I've been useful all day," Betty muttered snippily. Under the hot mask her bushy hair itched against her neck. "So much for birthdays."

Granny snorted. Birthday or not, all the Widdershinses had to help run the place, even Charlie.

3

"Only go around the green," Granny ordered. "No further, do you hear? And I want you back by—"

"Suppertime," Betty finished. "I know."

"Well, mind you are—remember what happened last year." Granny's voice softened. "There's birthday cake for later."

"Oooh," said Charlie, pausing her imp dance at the mention of food.

Betty caught Fliss's eye as Granny was called away to serve a customer.

"Are you sure you won't come with us?" Betty asked, a note of pleading entering her voice. It had always been such fun, the three of them getting into their Halloween costumes each year. "It won't be the same without you."

Fliss shook her head, her dark, glossy hair swishing over her shoulders. There was a faint smear of green on her perfect upturned nose, from when she had painted Charlie's face earlier. "I'm too old for all that. Besides, I'm needed here."

"Or maybe you don't want to miss Will Turner coming in?" Betty joked. "Or is it Jack Humble this week? Who's getting the Fliss kiss? I can't keep up, Flit."

Fliss glared. "I've told you not to call me that!"

Betty rolled her eyes, deciding to keep quiet about the paint on her sister's nose. Since her birthday, Fliss hadn't been herself. She was quiet, even moody at times, and clammed up whenever Betty asked what was troubling her.

"Betty?" Fliss said, glancing warily at Granny. "You will stay by the green, won't you?"

Under her mask, Betty gulped. She crossed her fingers within the folds of her cloak and fibbed. "Yes. We'll stay by the green."

Fliss's expression was unreadable as she gazed past Betty to the window. "It's best you stay close, anyway. It's looking a bit foggy out there. Taking a ferry over the marshes could be dangerous." She turned away to serve as a hoity-toity regular named Queenie rapped on the counter impatiently.

Betty rolled her eyes at her sister's back. "Mustn't do this, can't do that," she muttered under her breath. What had happened to Fliss since her birthday? True, she was as vain as she'd always been, often staring broodily into an old mermaid-shaped mirror Granny had given her, but all her fun had been blown away with the candles on her cake. In fact, she had started sounding exactly like Granny.

Increasingly, Betty felt as though her life at the Poacher's Pocket was a corset tightening around her, with Granny pulling one string and now Fliss yanking the other, lacing her in so she couldn't breathe. Tonight, Betty was determined to cut those strings, if only for a little while.

She called to Charlie, who had interrupted a domino game to proudly show off the gap where her front teeth had fallen out. Together, Betty and Charlie headed for the doors, weaving past tables of familiar faces that Betty knew as well as her own. They were almost at the door when Charlie's foot tangled in Betty's cloak and she tripped, bumping into a table where a sour-faced fellow named Fingerty sat alone. He made an unfriendly noise between a grunt and a growl, scowling as his drink slopped against the side of the glass.

"Sorry," Betty mumbled, hurrying past.

Icy air snaked around her ankles as she and Charlie squeezed past more customers who were piling inside. Then they were out into the freezing night. But, oh— what a night . . . freedom! Or at least, it would be, once they were firmly on the ferry in a few minutes' time. Betty silently cheered, shivering as much from anticipation as from the cold. She felt a flutter of anxiety, too. Fliss had been right: it was looking a little misty out here. As far as Betty knew (for she had been checking), there was no fog forecast. Yet she also knew the marshes were unpredictable, and that sometimes the forecasts were wrong.

Charlie's breath came in white puffs as she ran ahead, shaking her empty cauldron, the cold not bothering her. Betty strode after her, her eyes sweeping Nestynook Green. There were a few costumed people going from door to door, and she counted five jack-o'-lanterns glowing on doorsteps. Most of the houses, however, were in darkness. Many people had no wish to be disturbed by masked strangers—for good reason.

Last year, the Halloween fun had been cut short when the bell of Crowstone had started clanging. It was an alarm and meant that across the marshes the prison beacons had been lit, signifying danger. Calls of "Trick or treat!" had been replaced with cries of "Prisoners on the loose! Everyone inside, lock your doors!" Betty and her sisters had raced back to the Poacher's Pocket and sat upstairs, their noses pressed up to Betty's window. While Fliss nervously chewed her nails and Charlie complained about losing out on sweets, Betty had fizzled with excitement, secretly hoping the prisoners might stay on the run for a few days just to shake Crowstone up a bit. Escapes were rare, and growing up in the prison's shadow meant they could almost forget how close it was—and how dangerous it might be. The girls had watched and waited, but apart from two prison warders searching with lanterns, they saw no one. By breakfast the excitement was over, for they'd heard the felons had been caught on the marshes. Betty had always followed any tales of escape with interest, as she sometimes felt like a prisoner herself. Unfortunately, the story of inmates on the loose had been added to Granny's collection of reasons for preventing the girls from wandering too far.

Snapping back to the present, Betty glanced back at the Poacher's Pocket. Fliss had once described it as a tired old racing pigeon, with its loose tiles and shutters flapping like ragged feathers. It perched at the edge of Nestynook Green, its weathered bricks a patchwork of the years gone by. Time had nudged it like an elbow, and now the whole building slumped drunkenly to the left. The light from the windows glowed amber, broken by moving figures within and a few hagstones and other lucky charms Granny had strung up. No one was outside; no one suspected.

Good. The possibility of being hauled back by an enraged Granny was both scary and humiliating. Sure, Granny had a foul temper, but it was the consequences Betty feared most. If Granny found out what Betty had planned, she would never let her take Charlie out alone again . . . and any chance of adventure would vanish. The corset laces would tighten, squeezing the life out of her.

Already Charlie had knocked at the first house, chorusing "Trick or treat!" before sweets were popped into her cauldron. She skipped back to Betty, unwrapping a sticky-beak toffee from Hubbards, the sweet shop. "Didn't you bring anything to put your treats in?"

"Nah, I'll just pinch a couple of yours," said Betty, poking through the cauldron until she found her favorite: a marsh-melt. A plume of powdered sugar wafted off it as she stuffed it into her mouth, crunching through the wafer shell into the whipped center. She checked the clock on the craggy old church as they neared the lane beside it. Seven minutes. Under the mask, her temples prickled with sweat and her pulse began to race. *We can't get caught, not now . . . not when we're this close.* With another glance back at the inn, she took Charlie's sleeve and urged her toward the lane. "This way. I've got a surprise for you."

"A surprise?" Charlie looked up at her, wide-eyed. "But you told Granny we were only going around the green. You said—"

"I know what I said." Betty shepherded Charlie in

front. "But you and I are about to have a little adventure, which is why I need you to keep this our secret. Can you do that?"

Charlie gave a mischievous, gappy grin between chews. She nodded, her pigtails bobbing. "What kind of adventure?"

"We're going to Marshfoot."

"Jumping jackdaws!" Charlie's huge green eyes suddenly looked even huger. "Marshfoot? But that's . . . that's on the ferry!"

"Yes, it is." Betty patted her pocket, feeling the weight of the three coins there. It had taken her weeks to scrape together the return ferry fare, at a cost of a silver Raven each. She had managed it by saving the small amount of pocket money Granny allowed them, as well as whatever she came across when sweeping the floor of the Poacher's Pocket. She'd hoarded every coin, Rooks and Feathers. They'd all added up, and now that Fliss wasn't coming, there was money to spare.

"But, Betty, we'll get caught!"

"Not this time."

"That's what you always say before something goes wrong."

Charlie had a point here, but Betty wasn't to be deterred.

"I've got it all figured out." She was so confident that she had even thought up a new motto, but she was saving that.

"What if Granny finds out?" Charlie whispered, half gleeful and half afraid. "We'll be in for it then!"

"She won't," said Betty. "Why do you think I chose tonight? Everyone's going to be dressed up or wearing masks. It's perfect! If no one knows it's us, no one can rat on us to Granny."

"What's in Marshfoot?" Charlie asked. "Bigger houses? More sweets?"

"Better than that." Betty shooed Charlie farther down the darkened lane. "There's a fairground. Bobbing apples, and soul cakes, and a prize for the best costume . . . and cotton candy!" *And adventure*, she added in silent defiance. She didn't care where they escaped to, as long as it was out of Crowstone. Marshfoot was both far enough to feel satisfyingly daring and new and close enough to get away with. Sneaking off to the unknown like this felt like scratching an itch that had been there all her life.

"Cotton candy!" Charlie breathed. Since she'd lost her front teeth, her sweet little voice had a slight lisp to it. She slipped a hot, sticky hand into Betty's. "But it's so far away. What if we don't make it back in time for cake?"

"We'll easily make it back," said Betty. "I've got it all

planned. And they're not going to eat my birthday cake without me! But hurry—we've only got a few minutes before the ferry leaves."

They slipped farther down the lane, rounding the corner. Beneath the mask, Betty grinned triumphantly, her heart racing. They were really going to do it! They would finally get to see what life beyond Crowstone was like, and all because of her.

Betty loosened the cloak around her neck and they started to run. Beside her, Charlie counted glowing jack-o'-lanterns and carved turnips in windows, pointing out one she had made yesterday that was on the school steps. They followed the girls along the cobbled streets like wraiths leading them to the Misty Marshes.

Soon the houses became fewer, and then the crossroads were in sight and there were no houses at all. Instead, some distance away across the marshes, rows of tiny prison-cell windows glowed yellow, like watchful eyes in the blackness. Rising even higher, another light flickered from a solitary tower that loomed over the rest of the building.

Charlie slowed to a walk, and they sidestepped to allow a couple of people, hurrying for the ferry, to pass. "How long has Father been in there now?" she asked.

"Charlie!" Betty scolded, hoping those in front hadn't heard. She lowered her voice. "Two years, eight months." She paused, rummaging through dates in her head. "And four days."

"How long till he gets out?"

Betty sighed, feeling a familiar mixture of emotions at the thought of their father: sadness, frustration, disappointment. Like their mother's death, his absence had hit Betty and Fliss harder than it had Charlie. Even if Barney Widdershins was, in Granny's own words, a useless toe rag, Betty couldn't help but feel some sort of loyalty toward him. He wasn't much of a father, but he was the only one they had. "Two years, three months, and twenty-six days," she answered finally.

"Why you whispering?" Charlie asked. She had been only three when their father was taken away, and the lack of contact since meant she had never been close to him, merely curious. "You're always telling Fliss there ain't no point getting 'barrassed about him being in there."

"*Em*barrassed," Betty corrected her sister. If they'd lived anywhere else, she would have squirmed about it, but almost everyone who lived near the prison did so because they were related to someone on the inside. "No, there isn't. But don't blab about personal stuff when we're meant to be undercover. You never know who's listening. Now get a move on. I can see the ferry waiting."

"Oh!" Charlie grinned and pulled her witch's hat lower on her head, clearly enjoying being up to no good.

Betty ran ahead, with Charlie scampering behind. Her gaze fixed on the prison. Which cell was Father's? From here it was impossible to tell. Prisoners often moved. He might not even be in the same cell now, not that Betty would know. It was six months since Granny had last taken Fliss and Betty with her to visit. Apparently, their father had claimed he was too miserable and ashamed to see his daughters or even respond to their letters.

Betty glared at the prison. He should have thought of that before he got himself arrested. She gave the prison a last scowl before looking away, determined not to let her father ruin tonight like he ruined everything else. They reached the ferry, running the last few steps. Evidently, the fog warning hadn't changed for the worse, as the ferryman appeared unconcerned about the wispy mist that was wreathing around the boat. Already onboard was a group of costumed people who also appeared to be heading for the Halloween Fayre. Betty paid her own and Charlie's fares, then squeezed onto the narrow seat next to Charlie.

She glanced gleefully back the way they had come. Had they really gotten away with it? It had been so easy! Still, she tapped her toe impatiently until the ferryman pushed off, and then they were gliding over the water.

"Adventure awaits the audacious!" Betty whispered in excitement. (It was the first time she had spoken her new motto aloud, and she had been dying to say it all day.)

Charlie was unimpressed. "What color cotton candy do you think they'll have?"

"Green, perhaps, or orange . . ." Betty trailed off, staring back to shore. A little way along from the ferry was the harbor. Somewhere among the other boats was their own, a ramshackle ensemble of rotting wood that their father had won in a bet and had been trying to fix up ever since, without success. Perhaps he never would. For once, Betty didn't care. She didn't need Father, or his boat, for adventures. Here, on the marshes by night, she wasn't just the middle Widdershins sister, plain and blunt against Fliss's prettiness and charm and sensible next to Charlie's cuteness and mischief. Here she was Betty the Brave; Betty the Explorer! She could go anywhere, do anything!

Everything looked different, eerier and more mysterious, and in the distance she could see strange flickering lights, like magical orbs hovering above the water's surface. People called them will-o'-the-wisps. Some said they were the souls of those who'd died on the marshes; others believed they were mischievous sprites, trying to lead travelers astray.

She stared toward the prison. They would pass this first, located on the island of Repent, which was one of three nearby craggy isles on the marshes. The second, smaller island, where all of Crowstone's dead were buried, was known as Lament. Betty had been there only twice, most recently when her mother died shortly after Charlie had been born. A pang of sadness crept over her at the memory, still raw even now.

The final island was called Torment. It was out of bounds for those who lived on mainland Crowstone. Those on Torment had been exiled: people who had been released from the prison but still had punishment to serve by not being allowed to return to the mainland, or those who had committed crimes not serious enough to be locked away for but enough to warrant being banished. Collectively, the three places were still part of Crowstone and were known as the Sorrow Isles. Along with mainland Crowstone, they were all the girls had ever known—and the farthest any of them had ever traveled.

Tonight, after all Betty's longing, that was about to change. It was her birthday gift to herself, she decided. A step toward the life she wanted: one of opportunities and adventure, one where she would have golden sand crusted under her fingernails instead of coal dust.

The boat had not gone far when Betty became aware that something was happening. The Misty Marshes were living up to their name: the prison's lights had vanished. Instead, all that could be seen was thick, swirling gray mist, and it was curling around them, chilling their bones. Her scalp prickled with dread. A mother sitting opposite drew her small son closer, muttering in concern.

"Betty?" Charlie tugged at her sleeve. "What if the boat gets lost, or we can't find our way back from Marshfoot—"

Betty swallowed. Granny had used many excuses over the years to avoid taking the girls too far, and now those warnings came flooding back. *We could miss the return ferry . . . Lost boats have struck rocks and sunk into the marshes . . . People say there's still pirates in these parts, just waiting to snatch people away and sell them . . .* Suddenly, Betty didn't feel so smart or brave. She felt rather silly, and worried.

"It's getting hard to see!" the lady with the young boy called to the ferryman.

"Aye," he grunted. "May just be a pocket. If it don't clear in a minute, we'll have to turn back."

Charlie's bottom lip wobbled. "B-but my cotton candy . . ."

Betty didn't respond, fighting to appear calm for her sister's sake. Perhaps Granny hadn't been too cautious. Perhaps she was right to be afraid . . .

The temperature plummeted as thick, freezing fog wrapped around the boat frighteningly fast. This wasn't a pocket. It was all around them. The ferryman stopped rowing and lifted his lantern. Betty felt Charlie's small hands reaching for her. She wrapped an arm around her sister's shoulders and raised her free hand in front of her face. It was almost touching her nose before she could see it.

A huge bump shook the boat. There were screams and gasps as they rocked dangerously on the water.

"What's happening?" Charlie's voice was high-pitched with fear. Her fingers dug into Betty's arm painfully.

"I don't know!" Betty gasped, clutching the side of the boat. Freezing water slopped up her elbow. "Did we hit a rock?"

"I want to go home!" Charlie wailed, all thoughts of cotton candy forgotten.

The boat lurched again as a familiar figure loomed over the two girls. Betty gave a squeak of surprise as someone pushed their face to hers, almost nose to nose.

"Good!" said Granny. "Because home is exactly where we're going!"

Chapter Two

Prisoners

BETTY SAT RIGID WITH SHOCK and confusion. Next to her, Charlie was also frozen, her hand clamped around Betty's arm.

Bunny hadn't been on the boat when they'd left; Betty was convinced of it—but now she had doubts. Could Granny have disguised herself? It was impossible that she could have boarded without them seeing her otherwise . . . but then why would she have let the boat leave? It made no sense.

"Granny?" Betty whispered. Already, through the folds of her disbelief, she knew what this meant. Any future glimmers of freedom were in tatters, as impossible to grab as the swirling mist. "How did you . . . Where did you come from?"

"Never you mind." Granny glowered down at her. She looked half mad, with her gray hair flying loose from its bun and her shabby coat and shawl and Wellington boots horribly mismatched. Worse still, Granny had brought the ugly old carpetbag she insisted on carrying everywhere, though goodness knew why. Betty began to feel grateful for the fog. It was, at least, a screen against curious eyes. Clearly the only things that awaited her audaciousness were embarrassment and confusion, not adventure. She needed a new motto.

"Return this boat!" Granny demanded. "We're getting off!"

"That's what I'm trying to do," the ferryman snapped, not looking up from the wind rose compass he was bent over.

Other passengers squinted, their eyes flickering over what they could see of Granny's strange appearance as though they were trying to work out what kind of Halloween costume this was. Betty cringed.

"Hurry up, please," Granny repeated loudly. "This is no place for children!"

"You're the one who brought 'em!" the ferryman said,

annoyed. Then he frowned. "Although, come to think of it, I never saw you get on . . ."

"Nonsense. I've been here all along!"

But she can't have been! Betty thought, bewildered. *Or she would have said something sooner.* She bit back a frustrated growl. All that sneaking about, all that effort, for nothing! She didn't feel like a big adventurer now. She felt like a silly little girl. And the worst of it was there was a tiny part of her that was relieved, because in those misty moments before Granny had appeared, Betty had been scared.

"But, Granny," Charlie whispered. "You haven't!"

"Shush," said Granny, in a not-at-all-quiet voice.

The ferryman peered closer at Bunny. "I remember the girls getting on, but not you. You didn't pay your fare!"

"I most certainly did." Granny's voice cooled a few degrees. "Or do you suppose that I swam out here fully clothed and boarded the boat still dry, by some miracle?" She narrowed her eyes. "And don't get lippy with me, young man. I know your father!"

The ferryman looked more alarmed about that than he did about the fog.

"He's in for it now," Charlie said in a small voice.

"No," Granny snapped. "You two are in for it when

you get home. And this time you'll be getting more than you bargained for."

Betty gulped. She should have known better than to try to trick Granny—after all, she'd never managed to before. And now some other unpleasant thing was in store, to add to her already ruined birthday. "What's that supposed to mean?"

Granny didn't answer. Instead, she said to the ferryman, in an even sterner voice, "Now, I suggest you stop quibbling and get these cold, damp people back to safety. I expect many of them will want to know why the ferry was permitted to leave in the first place if a fog was expected."

"B-but it wasn't . . ." the ferryman objected.

"Then you must be terribly inexperienced," Granny said coldly. "Or too fond of money." She looked away pointedly.

The ferryman stopped protesting and, after consulting the wind rose once more, began rowing meekly. No one said a word for the entire journey back to shore, but Betty could feel the tension building in Granny. She might be silent now, but once they were off the boat, she would have plenty to say. Well, so did Betty. Something extraordinary had just happened, and neither Granny's temper nor her punishment was going to stop Betty from asking questions.

Just how had Granny gotten on that boat? True, she had always possessed an uncanny knack for tracking the girls down. If they spent too long on an errand or wandered farther than they should while out mushroom picking, it was a running joke that Granny would pop up like a sniffer dog. But this time Betty found nothing funny—or logical—about it. Instead, she felt a creeping sense of uneasiness.

When they docked, Betty and Charlie were shivering, both from the freezing air nipping at their ankles and from the shock of being caught. Granny looked the opposite: hot and cross and a bit dragonlike, with her breath coming in quick bursts that misted the air. She made them wait until everyone else had gotten off before they clambered ashore and headed for the lanes leading to the Poacher's Pocket. Betty looked back at the Misty Marshes. Sometimes the fog would come all the way up onto the land, wreathing its way through the streets. Tonight, however, the fog stayed at the fringes of the water, hovering like a marsh creature protecting its lair. When she was certain the other passengers were gone and the Widdershinses were alone, Betty spoke.

"How did you do that, Granny? How did you get on that boat without us seeing you? It's not possible."

"I was on it the whole time," Granny answered shortly.

"But you were so caught up in your little adventure you didn't see me."

Betty stared, trying to read Granny's face. All she saw there was anger, something that normally stopped her from asking too many questions or answering back . . . but tonight wasn't normal. Her hopes and plans had all been dashed. She had nothing else to lose by saying what she really thought, even at the risk of being punished with extra chores. "I don't believe you. You wouldn't have waited all that time before saying something to us."

"I wanted to see if you'd actually do it," Granny snapped, but she still didn't quite sound truthful. "Or whether you'd come to your senses and turn back."

"Come to my senses?" Betty's face grew hotter as her temper rose—or perhaps it was the sting from Granny's harsh words.

"Bringing Charlie out here like this was stupid and irresponsible. Anything could have happened!"

"Exactly," Betty muttered. She ignored the prickle of shame, unable to hold her tongue now that she had begun. "We might have even had some fun."

Granny ignored Betty, pulling her shawl tighter around her. She jabbed a finger between Betty's shoulders, prodding her along the lane. "I thought I could count on you,

Betty Widdershins. I thought you could be trusted, but it looks like I was wrong."

"That's not fair!" Betty's voice rose, carrying through the night. "All right, I shouldn't have gone behind your back. But, come on, Granny! Wanting a bit of freedom . . . that's not a crime, and you know I'd never let Charlie come to harm—"

"I know that's what you think," Granny cut in. "But you're thirteen years old! You know nothing of the world. There's plenty out there that could harm you, things you don't know about . . ."

"I never will if you don't let me." Betty spoke quietly now, but with as much defiance as she dared to show. Granny's fierceness was normally enough to stop her from answering back, as well as a feeling of not wanting to be a bigger burden than she and Charlie already were —but enough was enough. She waited for her grandmother to protest, to make the usual promises about taking the girls on trips or holidays . . . but this time Granny didn't. She looked terribly tired, then, and even older than usual.

A guilty, worried lump rose in Betty's throat. Granny was, after all, the one who had looked out for Betty and her sisters. If she hadn't been there to take them in, the girls would have ended up in the orphanage or worse, split up and homed with strangers. Betty pushed the thought away. Being grateful shouldn't stop her from getting some answers.

"You say you can't trust me now, but you never have—not to go out of Crowstone, anyway."

Granny stamped over the cobbles. "Leave it, Betty. This isn't the time or the place." She set off at a pace, one hand clutching her shawl and the other carrying the traveling bag. Betty grabbed Charlie's hand and hurried after Granny, determined not to be brushed off so easily. "How did you find out?"

"The flyer," Granny said brusquely.

Betty closed her eyes in dismay. Earlier that day, Fliss had seen a hidden flyer fall out of Betty's cloak and had picked it up, frowning.

"What's this? A Halloween Fayre in Marshfoot?"

"Oh," Betty had said, her heartbeat quickening. "I asked if we could go, but Granny said no, of course."

"Of course," Fliss had echoed, holding the flyer a fraction too long before handing it back.

"Fliss snitched on us, then?" Betty fumed. "Or did she just leave it for you to find?"

Granny avoided the question, pausing to hitch up her stocking. "It's lucky you didn't cover your tracks more carefully."

"Lucky?" Betty stopped in the middle of the road. Lucky was the last thing she felt after having her adventure snatched away. Why didn't Fliss want to escape the everyday drudgery, or care about Granny controlling them anymore?

Granny halted up ahead. "Stop dawdling!" she scolded.

"Come on, Betty," Charlie begged. "I'm cold!"

Betty released her sister's hand, her own slowly forming a fist at her side. Keeping the Halloween Fayre flyer had been careless, and now it would be harder than ever to plan any secret trips, with Granny watching her every move. But plan she would, and next time the scheme would be flawless. Heck, next time she might not come back at all.

Footsteps cut across the silence; then Granny was in front of her.

"Stop sulking. And I don't want any trouble when you get back. None of this is Fliss's fault."

"No." Betty uncurled her fists. "It's yours."

"I beg your pardon?" Granny said. Her voice was dangerously low, but Betty persisted. All her pent-up resentment and frustration, all the times she'd been told to stay close to home—the way Fliss had shut her out recently —it all came pouring out.

"Fliss used to want to explore as much as I do," said

Betty. Cold air hit her cheeks as she pulled off the mask. "She used to plan all the places she was going to visit . . . but not anymore. She's sixteen! She should be allowed to go wherever she wants. But she's given up, because of you."

All of a sudden Granny seemed to shrink in her baggy clothes as the anger went out of her. "That's not fair."

"No, it's not." Tears pricked Betty's eyes. "All your stories and what ifs have stopped Fliss from trying. You've squashed the adventure out of her. I won't let that happen to me, or to Charlie."

Granny shook her head, a strand of hair unraveling as if Granny herself was coming undone. "It's not like that."

"Then explain," said Betty, hardly believing the words that were pouring out of her. "Why all the broken promises and excuses? You act so tough, but maybe you're the one who's too scared to leave!"

Granny lowered her eyes, unable to meet Betty's. "We've been out of Crowstone plenty of times. You were just too young to remember."

"I don't believe you," Betty said. Her voice hardened as she became more certain. Now that she really thought about it, there had always been something odd about Granny's reluctance to let them go anywhere. And her hold only seemed to tighten as the girls got older. It felt all wrong. "I'd remember. And wouldn't there be pictures, memories of special days out? There's nothing!"

Granny didn't answer.

"Betty," Charlie whispered. "Please stop it. I want to go home."

"Why?" Betty said bitterly. "What's the big rush? Home is all there ever is!" She jabbed a finger in the direction of the prison. "We're no better off than the prisoners in there." She glanced around at the crooked little streets, hating them. "And it might not be tonight, but I'll escape this place. There's more to life than Crowstone."

"No, there isn't." Granny's eyes were haunted. "There's no leaving this place. Not for us." Her words dangled in the air like sharp little needles. Charlie began to cry.

"N-not for us?" Betty echoed. Surely Granny was just trying to scare them again. How could they not be able to leave?

"You think you're ready for the truth?" Granny asked sadly.

Betty stared back helplessly. She wasn't sure, not now that Granny was as good as admitting that Betty had been right all along. But all she could do was nod.

"Very well." Granny nodded slowly. "I'll tell you. No more secrets." She shuffled closer, resting her hand on Betty's cheek. "But I warn you, it's nothing good."

Charlie huddled closer into her, crying harder. Betty's mouth went dry. Was this somehow linked to their rat-bag father? Were they being punished along with him, forbidden to leave, like the people on Torment? It was all she could think of.

"What is it? Tell me!"

"Not here." Granny lowered her hand, her jowls wobbling as she glanced about. "This'll only be a short journey, but I need you both to keep your wits about you. We mustn't be seen."

"Not seen? Granny, I don't—"

"You don't need to understand. Just hold on." Granny hooked her arm through Betty's, the carpetbag dangling from her wrist. "Link your arm with Charlie's. That's it —nice and tight. Whatever you do, don't let go."

Betty wondered if she had finally sent her grandmother loopy. Why else would she be acting so peculiar? "Granny, you're scaring me."

"Yes, well. I can't help that, and you were going to find out sooner or later." Granny tightened her hold on Betty's arm. The familiar smell of her, of tobacco and beer, was warming in the chilly air. "Ready?"

"For what?" Betty asked, bewildered, as Granny opened her bag.

Her grandmother didn't answer. Instead, she reached

into the monstrous carpetbag and turned it inside out, saying in a crisp voice: "Poacher's Pocket!"

Betty's insides gave an enormous lurch, like she had fallen from a great height. Her ears were popping and her eyes were forced closed as a huge gust of icy air rushed past her, knocking her off her feet. She heard Granny gasp and Charlie do a funny little moan, but kept hold of them both as tightly as she could. Her balance was gone, her feet finding nothing but air.

"Granny!" she wailed, her eyes flying open as she toppled backwards. She landed with a bump, arms still locked with her grandmother and Charlie. Hard cobbles bit into her bottom, and the whistling wind had been replaced with rowdy voices and laughter. Betty looked up in amazement to see that the three of them were sitting in the doorway outside the Poacher's Pocket.

"Not one of my better landings, I admit, but I'm not used to passengers." Granny released Betty's arm and got to her feet. "Oof, me hips." After dusting herself off, she checked over the carpetbag and then snapped the clasp shut with a nod. "Home."

Chapter Three

The Three Gifts

"UP YOU GET," GRANNY TRILLED, peering out of the darkened doorway across the empty village green. "Good—no one saw us."

Stiff with shock, Betty clambered to her feet and hauled Charlie up beside her. They stared at their grandmother. Though Betty was too stunned to speak, her mind was jammed with questions. What in crow's name had just happened . . . How was it even possible? And how could Granny be acting so matter-of-fact about it? Next to her, Charlie had stopped crying, but her face was grubby and tear-streaked, her little body trembling.

"Come on." Granny guided them toward the door. "Inside, out of the cold."

The door opened to warm air; jumbled, merry talk; and music. Betty stepped in, clasping her arm tightly around Charlie's shoulders. It was dimly lit, with the glow of the jack-o'-lanterns turning everything and everyone golden. There were so many people it was difficult to move through them all, but Granny nudged and jostled, clearing a path to the bar, where Fliss and another girl, Gladys, were serving drink after drink.

Granny pushed the carpetbag at Betty. "Take this up to the kitchen. Put the kettle on."

Betty held the bag at arm's length, afraid it would swallow her up and spit her out again in some unknown place.

"Oh, for crow's sake." Granny snatched it back, tucking it under her arm. She touched the horseshoe above the door. "Fliss!" she called. "Upstairs."

"Now?" Fliss blurted out in surprise.

"Now."

A look passed between them, and Fliss's face became grave. She nodded, wiping her hands on her apron, glancing at Betty. Betty stared back, her gaze dropping to something sticking out of her sister's apron pocket. Fliss hastily tried to poke it back in, but Betty recognized it immediately: it was the corner of the Marshfoot flyer. So

Fliss had ratted on them. Yet all that had just happened had cooled Betty's temper, leaving more questions. Did Fliss know what Granny's old carpetbag could really do, as well as the big secret Granny was about to tell them? Little threads of envy knitted together in an unfamiliar pattern. It used to be Betty and Fliss who had shared secrets; now Betty was the one being locked out.

"Where are you going?" Gladys shrieked. "I'm ankle-deep in beer, here! I can't manage on my own!"

"We won't be long, and I'll double your wages tonight." Granny touched the horseshoe again.

"That's not going to help," said Fliss primly.

"What would you know?" Granny snapped, turning to Betty. "I thought I told you two to go upstairs?"

Numbly, Betty placed her hands on Charlie's shoulders and steered her to the stairs. As they climbed them, Betty eyed the peeling wallpaper and threadbare carpet, trying to focus on normal, everyday things. This was their world, not one where smelly old carpetbags transported people. Perhaps there had been snuff powder in the bag, she decided. Something that had momentarily befuddled them. It was the only practical explanation.

Once in the kitchen, Betty and Charlie sat down at the table. Charlie drew her knees up and peered over them, wide-eyed, like a frightened little mouse. Granny pulled out a chair and tutted, shaking a scruffy black cat off the table.

"Scram!" she snapped at the hissing creature. The cat hated everyone; only Charlie persisted in trying to befriend it. It had mysteriously wandered in some months before (though Betty suspected Charlie had enticed it with scraps) and now they couldn't get rid of it. Despite Granny's strict instructions not to name it, brandishing her broom and yelling "Oi!" every time it took a swipe at Charlie, the cat always returned and did as it pleased. And thanks to Charlie, it did have a name.

"Poor Oi," she murmured as the cat skulked away downstairs.

Fliss filled the kettle and put it on to boil. Granny sat at the head of the table, took out her pipe, and began stuffing it with tobacco.

A minute later, Fliss put cups of tea in front of them, stirring in mounds of sugar. "It's good for shock."

"And rotten teeth," muttered Granny.

Fliss gave an injured sniff. Then Charlie burst into sobs.

"There, there, I know." Granny reached out to pat her arm. "You've had a bit of an upset. Have a good cry and get it all out."

A bit of an upset? And yet Granny was about to reveal something else, some explanation of why they were trapped in Crowstone. Well, it had better be good, Betty decided. A real, solid reason to crush her dreams and not just flimsy fears.

Charlie continued to cry, her shoulders shaking with huge gasps. "Granny? I don't understand what just happened. Are you a . . . a witch?"

"A witch? Dear me, no!" said Granny.

"B-but your b-bag . . ."

"Yes, yes, I know. We started in one place and ended up in another. It's a traveling bag, not a broomstick. And guess what? One day it'll be yours!"

This only made Charlie cry harder.

"But how . . . ?" Betty began, for despite Granny's denial, she couldn't help wondering. Witches were make-believe, weren't they? Or did Granny use more than beer to bamboozle?

"I don't know." Granny lit her pipe, sucking on it deeply. Thick smoke billowed around her, strongly scented with cloves and spices. "I don't know how it works, only that it does."

"Must you smoke?" Fliss chided, moving her chair away. "You know it stinks, and we don't like breathing it in."

"I don't want you breathing it in, either," said Granny. "It's my smoke. I paid good money for it."

The familiar squabble seemed to set Charlie more at ease. Her sobbing reduced to sniffles. Eventually she reached out and snatched her tea like a mouse taking a piece of cheese back to its hole.

Betty gulped her tea, grimacing. It was weak and too sweet, as lousy as everything Fliss attempted in the kitchen. "How long have you known, Fliss? You don't exactly seem surprised by all this."

"A few months." Fliss fiddled with a tiny braid she'd woven into her hair. "Granny told me on my birthday."

So Betty hadn't imagined the change in her sister. All this time, Fliss had been hiding things. Guarding Granny's secrets. The threads of envy tightened, tangling with feelings of betrayal. Why hadn't either of them trusted her?

Granny huffed out another cloud of cloying smoke. "There's more."

Betty remained silent. She'd thought as much.

"That . . . that mirror Granny gave me on my birthday," Fliss continued. "It does something, too."

Charlie peered over her teacup. "The mermaid mirror?"

Betty found she was gripping her cup so tightly it

made her knuckles ache. She set it on the table. "What does it do?"

Fliss glanced at Granny, her cheeks flooding red. "It . . . it lets me talk to people . . . who aren't there."

"Who aren't there?" Betty echoed. Before tonight she would have scoffed at this—before Granny's jiggery-pokery with the carpetbag, that was. Part of her longed to believe this was all an elaborate trick to pay her back for sneaking off, but she knew Granny would never neglect a pub full of thirsty customers, and Fliss was as useless at lying as she was at cooking. "Like . . . like ghosts?"

Charlie gave an alarmed squawk.

"No!" Fliss said hurriedly. "Not like that. People who are somewhere else. On the other side of the island, perhaps, or even the next room. On one of the Sorrow Isles—or farther away."

The Sorrow Isles. Immediately, Betty thought of their father. Had Fliss used the mirror to speak to him? She opened her mouth to ask, then changed her mind. Barney Widdershins could wait. Too many other questions about these strange objects were forcing their way to the front of her mind, demanding answers.

Betty sipped her tea again. Some of the shock was leaving her, and she was beginning to tremble. There was no such thing as a magical object, not outside of dreams and stories . . . but however practical she was, Betty couldn't deny what she had experienced moments earlier—and she knew she wasn't dreaming. How was it possible to travel from one place to another in a few seconds simply by turning an old bag inside out, or to talk to people through mirrors? There was only one way to describe it: magic. She remembered other times when she, Fliss, and Charlie had tried to sneak away and been outfoxed by Granny at the last moment . . . and how Granny never seemed to be late—for anything. Now it made sense.

"Where did they come from?" she said at last. "The bag and the mirror?"

Granny puffed on her pipe some more, coughed, then hesitated. "I'm not sure, exactly. No one is. But they've been in the family for decades. Passed down through generations of Widdershins girls. It's always been that way . . . for as far back as I know, anyway."

"How long is that?" Betty asked.

Granny's mouth puckered as she was thinking. "About a hundred and fifty years."

"And when were you going to tell Charlie and me?" Betty added. "If you were planning on telling us at all?"

"I was," Granny answered. "When you were sixteen. Just like I did with Fliss."

"And you?" Charlie asked. "Were you sixteen, too, when you got the bag?"

"No," said Granny. "I was given the bag on my wedding day."

Of course, Betty thought. Granny wasn't a Widdershins by blood. She had married into the family, like the girls' mother.

"Some wedding gift," she remarked.

Granny smiled thinly. "I suppose it made up a little for the rest—" She hiccupped and broke off, like she'd said something she shouldn't have, but Betty pounced.

"The rest of what?"

"I'll get to that in a minute."

Betty glanced at Fliss, her chest tightening. Whatever it was, she could tell by Fliss's expression that she knew, and it wasn't good.

Granny took a break from her pipe. "There are three items . . . three gifts, if you like. Each of them is an everyday object. Each of them holds a different kind of power. I call it a pinch of magic."

Fear or excitement—or a mixture of both—began to tingle in Betty's tummy. Something about Granny saying the word "magic" was rather wonderful. And yet . . . Granny's snuffed-out sentence smoldered uneasily in

Betty's thoughts. What had this to do with the Widdershinses being trapped in Crowstone? Was the magical gift simply a sweetener before something more sinister? She leaned forward. "You mean . . . when Charlie and me turn sixteen, we'll both get one of these . . . these gifts, too?"

"That was the plan, yes."

Betty frowned. "'Was'?"

"After what happened tonight . . . with the two of you going off like that, I've seen that some plans have to change."

"Oh, Granny, please . . ." Betty said. "I know I was wrong to break your rules, and I know I don't deserve whatever magic thing you were saving for me . . . but please don't punish Charlie." She slumped back in her chair miserably. "It's not her fault. It was all my idea."

"I know." Granny's voice was soft. "I don't intend to punish either of you, though. It's never been about that, only about wanting to keep you safe. But tonight, I realized that keeping secrets from you only puts you in more danger. And that's the reason I've decided to bring everything out into the open." She placed her pipe in her ashtray, then rose from the table. "Wait here."

Granny vanished into the hallway. Betty reached for Charlie's hand. It was ice-cold. "There's nothing to be scared of," she told her, although already she wondered if

Charlie was ready for this. Guilt gnawed at her, but it was too late for regret now. Whatever was about to happen had been brought on by Betty alone. Still, she couldn't imagine a way Granny could convince her not to leave — or make her accept giving up her dreams.

Granny returned, carrying a wooden box. It was dark, with a curved lid and curling iron embellishments. There was a large padlock on it, and carved into each side of it was a large ornamental "W." It looked like exactly the sort of thing that held secrets, and excitement, or treasure. Yet as Granny unhooked the ring of keys from her belt, Betty felt a tremor of dread. Did one lock opening mean another was about to snap shut around her? Was the price of these objects their freedom?

Despite this, she found she was leaning forward as Granny removed the lock and lifted the lid. A musty smell drifted out. Betty peered inside. There was a small package in the box, wrapped in plain brown paper and tied with string.

"Like I said," Granny said. "As the youngest, Charlie will be the last to inherit, so it stands that she'll get the traveling bag from me. This, Betty, is yours. But before you open it, let me tell you that each item will be bound to you, and you alone. There's no swapping with each other."

Hesitantly, Betty reached for the package. *I don't have to accept it,* she told herself. *Not if it means staying in Crowstone forever.* Not even magic was worth that. Even so, she felt a thrill of wonder and anticipation. The item was lighter than expected. She pulled the string, releasing it from its knot.

"Wait," said Granny. "Before you open it you must all promise to keep these things secret. Do you understand? You're not to tell anyone outside this family about these objects and their powers."

"You mean . . . Father knows?" asked Betty.

Granny's expression darkened. "Yes. As far as I'm aware, it's the one secret he's managed to keep."

"I'm surprised," said Fliss, in a tight voice. "I'd have thought something as big as this would be the first thing he'd blab about." She struggled to talk about their father much. When he had gone to prison, it had taken Fliss the longest to accept it.

Betty would never forget his arrest: Fliss tearfully insisting it was all a mistake; Granny holding her head in her hands, calling their father terrible names, no doubt wondering aloud how she was going to bring up three young girls alone. Even Charlie, too young to understand, had picked up on the mood and eaten twice as much as usual. Betty herself had felt betrayed. She couldn't have felt it more if he had rowed them out to sea and abandoned them. How dare he leave them like this, after Mother?

Granny sighed. "Yes, I thought so, too. Still, he proved me wrong, and I'm glad about that. Your father is a fool and a braggart, and that'll never change. But for all his faults, this was a secret he kept, and he did it out of love. You girls remember that."

"Wasn't it difficult to hide?" Betty asked. "The magic?"

Granny shrugged. "I hid the bag's magic from you three all this time, didn't I?" She fell silent, nodding to the unopened package.

Finally, Betty tore off the paper.

Inside was a set of wooden nesting dolls, the kind that hid away, one inside another, getting smaller and smaller until the last tiny one, which did not open. Using her thumbnail, Betty eased the first doll open and took out the next, then the next, setting them in a line. They were beautifully painted, each one similar and yet different from the next. There were four in total, each with wavy auburn hair and chestnut-brown eyes, so detailed that tiny freckles even dotted their cheeks.

Each doll had a circular area at its center, painted with the same little cottage, meadow, and river. With each doll the season changed: The largest showed blossoms on the trees and a clutch of eggs in a nest. The next showed ducklings on the water, and the third, fully grown birds flying south as russet leaves fell from the trees. The final doll depicted a wintry snow scene painted in pale blues. Each doll held an ornate key, painted and engraved into the wood's surface in such a way that when the dolls were taken apart, each half had part of its key.

"They're beautiful." Betty touched the key on the outermost doll with her thumb.

"I want the dolls," Charlie complained. "The bag is ugly!"

"Too bad," said Granny, with a shrug. "Anyway, it's not what they look like, it's what they do that counts."

"So what do they do?" Betty asked.

Granny's expression lightened. "Something rather splendid," she whispered, rubbing her hands together and chuckling mischievously. "Take something of yours, something small enough to fit inside the second doll."

A thrill of anticipation shivered up Betty's back. She glanced at Fliss, but her older sister seemed as puzzled as she felt. Clearly Granny hadn't told her of the dolls' powers. "Something small, like . . . like a coin?"

"No, no." Granny's hand waved around like an excited wasp buzzing over a jam jar. "Something personal . . . some small item of jewelry, perhaps?"

"I don't have any jewel— Ouch!"

Granny had leaned over and plucked a frizzy brown hair from Betty's head. "This'll do."

Betty rubbed her scalp and stuffed the hair into the bottom half of the second doll.

"Now put the top on," said Granny. "And—this is important, or else it won't work—you line up the two halves of the key exactly, then put that into the largest doll and repeat."

Betty did so, wondering what on earth was about to happen. As she twisted the two halves of the outer doll together, Fliss gasped and Charlie squealed.

Betty frowned. "What?"

Charlie leaped off her chair. "Betty? Where are you?"

"Nowhere," said Betty, confused. "I'm still here!" But neither her sisters nor Granny were looking at her anymore. "Granny? What's happening?"

"You've disappeared," said Granny with a cackle. "None of us can see you."

"Disappeared? Don't talk marsh rot . . ."

"Look in the mirror if you don't believe me."

Betty turned to the small looking glass on the wall. As usual, it was covered in Fliss's fingerprints. What wasn't usual was that only the kitchen behind Betty was reflected there. Betty herself was nowhere to be seen.

She had vanished.

Chapter Four

By Sunset

STUNNED, BETTY LIFTED HER HANDS in front of her face. She could see them, but the mirror showed nothing . . . and it was plain no one else could see her, either. Just to be certain, she made a rude gesture at Granny . . . but her grandmother continued to stare straight through her.

A gleeful thrill bubbled inside her. She grabbed a tea towel from the back of a chair and flapped it. In the mirror she saw it reflected, flying through the air as if it had a will of its own. "Woooooooooooo!" she said in a deep voice.

"Oooh!" said Charlie, evidently thrilled.

Fliss shuddered. "Betty, stop that! It's creepy!"

"Oh, don't be a spoilsport," said Betty. "It's about time there was some fun around here!"

"It's not a laughing matter," Granny said. "These aren't toys to play with."

The tea towel slipped through Betty's fingers and landed on the floor. "Then what's the point of them?"

"They're for protection. To help us out in a sticky spot."

"Not likely to get used much, then," Betty said sulkily. "The only sticky spots around here are when Fliss hasn't washed the dishes properly."

"Hey!" said Fliss indignantly.

"Or when Oi gets shut in all night," added Charlie.

"How do I make myself visible again?" Betty asked. "Just take the hair out of the doll?"

"Not quite," said Granny. "You twist the top half full circle counterclockwise, then pull the halves apart and remove the hair."

Betty did so, checking her reflection. Sure enough, it returned.

"Now," said Granny. "You can make other people vanish, too. You do exactly the same thing, only this time, you use the third doll. Remember that. The second doll is for you, and only you."

"Me!" Charlie begged. "Make me disappear!" She

reached into her pocket and dug out something tiny and white, flinging it across the table. "Here, use Peg."

"Meddling magpies!" Fliss exclaimed. "Are you still carrying that tooth around? And since when does it have a name?"

Charlie flashed her gappy grin proudly. Since losing her first tooth and waking to find a bright copper coin under her pillow the next morning, she had decided to carry her second offering in her pocket at all times in the hopes of catching the tooth fairy. It had been three weeks now, and neither Granny nor Fliss had managed to extract it from her pocket without raising suspicion. Charlie was becoming frustrated with the tooth fairy's apparent lack of effort, and had even taken to leaving disgruntled notes to illustrate her feelings. Betty picked up the tooth and placed it in the third doll, twisting it closed before nesting it in the outer dolls. Instantly, Charlie vanished from sight.

"Am I invisible yet? Am I?" Charlie demanded.

"Well and truly." Betty reached out, expecting to find air, but her fingers came into contact with warm flesh.

"Ah, yes," said Granny. "While you can't be seen, you can be felt."

Betty removed the tooth, much to Charlie's disappointment, and hid the dolls away inside each other.

Charlie pouted jealously. "Why does Betty get the dolls? She's the one who wants to go on adventures! The bag would be better for her!"

"The bag's just as good, Charlie," Betty pointed out. "Better than the dolls, actually." The bag would have been perfect for her, she realized wistfully. How easily it could whisk her away, to anywhere she chose . . . and back again before Granny could stop her. The dolls could be just as useful for sneaking off unseen, though. The thought was as guilty as it was delicious. She still had the feeling that Granny was hoping the magical gifts would buy their obedience, and here Betty was dreaming up ways to be anything but obedient.

"Don't care," Charlie went on sulkily. "I want them 'cause they're like us." She pointed to the largest doll. "See? That one is Granny, looking after the three smaller ones."

"Yes," said Fliss, smiling faintly. "I suppose they are like us."

"The dolls go to Betty," said Granny. "Fliss has already chosen the mirror and, until you're old enough, Charlie, the bag will stay with me. Each item goes to a Widdershins girl on her sixteenth birthday or, like myself and your mother, on their wedding day." She ran a finger around the rim of her glass. "Once an item is yours or meant for you, it's the only one you'll be able to use."

Charlie looked up, suddenly less huffy. "Does that mean the bag would work for me . . . now?"

All three girls looked at Granny expectantly, and Betty got the impression from the way Granny's mouth was puckering that she didn't want to answer the question.

"Yes," Granny said at last. "It would. But that doesn't mean you can try. Not until you're sixteen!"

"Sixteen?" Charlie spluttered. "That's not fair! Betty's only thirteen and she's getting the dolls now!"

Granny closed her eyes, looking pained. "All right, thirteen. You can have it then."

"Yes!" said Charlie. She counted on her fingers, her expression growing glum. "That's still an awful long time."

"Not as long as it could have been. Don't push your luck."

"So all this time," said Betty, who had been thinking during Charlie's little bout of bartering, "only the bag has had an owner? What about the mirror and the dolls? How long have they been waiting for another Widdershins girl?"

"A while." Granny struck a match and relit her pipe. "I never had any daughters, only your father, as you know.

But he had a cousin, Clarissa. The mirror went to her. She died shortly after your parents were married, before any of you were born." She gestured to the old wooden box, her eyes dark and distant. "And so the mirror went back in there to wait for its next owner."

"What about Mother?" Betty asked. "You said she would have gotten one of these on her wedding day?"

Granny nodded. "The dolls. Though as far as I know, she never used them."

"Why not?" asked Fliss.

"She never had reason to," Granny replied. "She was warned, same as all the women before her, not to use them flippantly. And she didn't like them—not knowing where they came from or how we got them."

"No one knows?" Betty asked faintly.

A haunted look passed across Granny's face. Once again, Betty got the feeling the old woman wasn't being entirely truthful. "If they do, they've chosen not to say," Granny said.

The kitchen went quiet, so quiet that the ticking of the old jackdaw clock on the wall could be heard. Betty eyed the dolls uneasily. There was something spooky about enchanted family objects that no one had answers for being passed down. But the lure of them was almost too much to resist.

"All this magic," Betty said wistfully, "and you're telling us we shouldn't use it?"

"I'm telling you," said Granny, "that it's meant for times of need, not to amuse yourselves with parlor tricks."

"Why would we need it?" Betty asked.

"You never know," Granny mumbled, suppressing a hiccup. "There might come a time when you girls need to hide or escape quickly. Just like I did one night, before you three lived here. There was a break-in after hours, when I was alone. I used the bag to get out safely with the night's takings and raise the alarm. Without it, I'd never have escaped." She reached for a nearby glass, then realized it was empty and discarded it crossly. "I'm not saying you will need them. But you must never use these objects without care, especially in a place like Crowstone. Most people here are connected to the people in that prison. Dangerous people, who'd go to any lengths to get their hands on these things. Imagine if they knew of a bag that could transport them outside the prison walls . . . or a set of magical dolls that could sneak them past the warders unseen. So you listen to me, and you listen good: Your magic must only be used when it's truly required. Anything otherwise is a risk."

"But you did," Betty pointed out. "You used your

traveling bag to find us tonight, to land right on the boat, when you could have waited for the next one."

"That's the point—it couldn't wait. I'd never have found you in time."

"In time for what?" Betty asked. "To stop our fun before it even began?" She waited for a remark about being lippy, but it never came. Dread uncurled in her stomach. All the talk of the dolls and magic had distracted her from her biggest question. "None of this answers what you promised to tell us earlier . . . about why we can't leave Crowstone."

Granny sighed. "I thought I'd get the nice part out of the way first." She took a deep drag on her pipe, as though she were filling herself with courage. "The truth is, we're cursed . . . all of us. No Widdershins girl has ever been able to leave Crowstone. If we do, we'll die by the next sunset."

Chapter Five

The Widdershins Curse

BETTY STARED AT GRANNY. For a moment the kitchen was completely still, like a scene painted on a canvas. Granny's face was a mask of sorrow; Fliss's dark eyes were staring into her lap. Even the smoke from Granny's pipe appeared motionless, a choking cloud hanging over them.

A horrible noise caught in Betty's throat, something that was half groan, half sob. The room felt airless, as if the truth had sucked the breath from it, just as all Betty's dreams and hopes had been crushed out of her. This was it: the big secret. The answer she had been scratching for, like something buried in dirt. They were stuck here in Crowstone forever.

The practical side of her wanted to laugh, to blurt out how ridiculous the idea of a curse was. Only, Betty didn't feel practical now, not after everything that had just happened. Added to Granny's excuses and sudden appearances out of nowhere over the years, it suddenly seemed scarily possible that she was never leaving. Never going to sail off and be Betty the Brave, Betty the Explorer. She was just another Widdershins girl, destined to be a drudge in a life of endless gray routine. They were all as stuck as Father's ramshackle boat rotting in the harbor: bobbing, with no hope of ever going anywhere.

She blinked as Granny's pipe smoke hit her eyes, making them water. Next to her, Charlie began to cry softly. Betty was too numb to comfort her.

"Cursed . . . ?" Betty asked, her voice hollow. "How? Why?"

"I asked myself the same questions, when I first found out." Granny puffed on the pipe, her eyes glassy. "I thought it was just a story, invented to keep curious girls from wandering too far. But even I had to admit that the deaths of eight Widdershins girls stretching back over the past hundred and fifty years couldn't be by chance. Strange, unexplained deaths of otherwise healthy girls and women."

"When did you find out?" Betty asked, chilled. "Was that on your wedding day, too?"

"No." Granny smiled faintly. "Before then. Your grandpa warned me a long time before, when we were just sweethearts. He gave me plenty of chances to change my mind."

Betty gaped. "And you still went through with it?"

Granny shrugged. "People make all kinds of sacrifices for . . ."

"For love," Fliss finished. She placed her hand over Granny's old, wrinkled one.

"I-I'm sorry," Betty spluttered. "But I can't understand any of this . . . It's just too strange." *And confusing and unfair*, she raged silently. All the possibility the enchanted objects seemed to offer had been cruelly snatched away, and seeing the magic for herself made it harder to doubt the rest of what Granny was saying. "Are you certain?" she asked weakly. "Couldn't it just be . . . bad luck?"

"I was a lot like you, once," Granny continued. "At first I refused to believe it. Then, one day, I saw it for myself. The day the death toll rose to nine."

The air in the room seemed to thicken, and not just with smoke. Betty suddenly had difficulty breathing. "Nine . . . nine girls died?" she said faintly. "I mean . . . I know you said it happens by sunset after leaving Crowstone, but what exactly happens? They . . . *we* . . . drop dead?" She searched Granny's face, waiting for more horrible revelations and imagining tales of freak accidents. A vision of falling from a great height, of the ground rushing toward her and wind roaring in her ears, floated before her eyes, and a wave of terror and grief washed over her. She blinked it away, trembling with adrenaline. Where had that come from?

"It's always the same," Granny said. "It starts with birdsong. The crows' chorus."

Betty frowned. "But that happens anyway at dawn, doesn't it?"

Granny nodded. "The difference is, no matter how hard you look, you'll never see them. The sound exists only in your head."

From the corner of her eye, Betty caught Fliss shuddering.

"It gets louder," Granny continued, staring into the distance, as though remembering. "As the sound grows, you become cold, and colder still. And even though your skin is like ice to the touch, the last thing you feel before the end is a cold kiss."

The hairs on Betty's arms stood up. "How could you . . . know that?"

Granny's lips quivered. "Because I saw it with your father's cousin, Clarissa," she said finally. "I was there."

"Did she know about the curse?" asked Betty. "Or was it an accident?"

Granny's fingers tightened around her glass, then slid to the tabletop, almost lifeless. "Yes, she knew. She thought she could undo it. She'd heard of a place where, legend has it, wishes can be made. Horseshoe Bay, across the marshes. She thought making the wish could uncurse us all, but it didn't work. Whatever magic exists in that bay—if it even does—it's not strong enough to undo the Widdershins curse. And when she came back, she already knew it had failed. The crows were rasping in her head; her skin was like ice. We couldn't get her warm . . ."

"She came back to Crowstone?" Betty asked. "But wouldn't that stop the curse, if she returned before sunset?"

"Nothing stops it," Granny muttered, glassy-eyed. She linked her thumbs and fanned her fingers like birds' wings over her heart in the sign of the crow.

"Tell her about the stones," Fliss croaked. Her skin was waxy pale.

"Stones?" Betty pressed.

"Every time the curse is triggered, a stone falls from

the tower wall," Granny said, in an uncharacteristically quiet voice.

"You mean, Crowstone Tower . . . ? The prison?"

Granny nodded.

"But what does the prison have to do with the curse?" Betty asked. Fliss's ashen face wasn't helping with the image of a freezing, dying Clarissa haunting Betty's thoughts. How brave Clarissa had been to even try to break the curse, risking everything. To do that, she must have wanted to leave as much as Betty did, and believed there was a way . . . even if she had failed.

Granny shrugged. "The tower is ancient, older than the rest of the prison. As for its link to the curse, well . . . there are stories. But none that tell us how to break it."

Betty swallowed the lump in her throat, trying not to cry. Tears solved nothing, but her leaking eyes didn't seem to care. Before tonight, she'd been able to dream of leaving Crowstone and living a different life. She'd never known that being kept there was more than Granny being overprotective; that leaving was actually impossible. She could see why Fliss had given up, but Betty couldn't accept it. Not yet. "There must be a way to break it. There has to be . . ."

Granny gave a hollow laugh. "Oh, that's what they all

say. You think girls like you haven't had the same thought for generations? Of course they have. Clarissa was as determined as they come! Everything you can think of has been tried, from marrying to lose the Widdershins name, to taking something of Crowstone with you, to leaving something of yourself in Crowstone. Nothing has worked. So now you know why I can't let it happen, not to any of you."

She grasped Betty's hand suddenly, startling her. "Please, Betty." Her shrewd old eyes were haunted. "I'm begging you . . . don't try. I couldn't go through that again, not with one of you. Not . . . not like Clarissa. It'd kill me."

Betty felt as though her heart were being wrung out. The last time she had seen Granny vulnerable like this had been when their father was taken away. It was easy to pretend this side of Granny didn't exist when it was so well hidden.

"And Father?" Betty asked. "Surely he knows about the curse?"

"Yes." Granny's voice was grave. "Something like this . . . the whole family has to know, it's too dangerous not to. I often wonder if it was guilt, as well as your mother's death, that pushed him down the wrong path."

"Guilt?" Fliss asked. "You mean . . . for passing the curse on to us?"

Granny nodded. "He hated the unfairness of it, that no Widdershins woman could ever leave. Yet, because of his own foolishness, he's now as trapped as we are."

"And Mother?" Betty asked. "Was it really an accident, like you said, or was . . . was it the curse?"

Charlie had been just a baby, but Fliss and Betty both remembered the morning they'd learned their mother was gone. Granny and Father had been sick, though their father had been the worse of the two. It was Granny who'd broken the news that their mother had gone to fetch a doctor in the night while a dense fog had lain over the island. On the way she had become lost, wandered onto a frozen pond, and fallen through the ice.

"I was telling the truth about that." Granny rubbed her ruddy nose. "I'm not sure whether that makes you feel better or worse, but your mother . . . It wasn't the curse. It was bad luck."

Bad luck: the unwanted guest Granny was always trying to ward off with her charms. Nothing ever worked. Their parents were gone. The inn never made enough money to clear its debts. Fliss ruined everything she cooked. All Betty's travel schemes had failed miserably, and Charlie was always getting nits. Yes, thought Betty. It was fair to say that Lady Luck crossed the road when she saw the Widdershinses coming.

They were interrupted by a low, rumbling chant accompanied by a rhythmic thudding from downstairs. A moment later came the sound of a door being flung open. The chanting of "Beer! Beer! Beer!" was followed by a shriek from Gladys at the foot of the stairs: "Bunny! If I don't get some help right now, I'm leaving!"

"They're thumping on the bar, the louts!" Granny said, outraged. She leaped to her feet with a fresh burst of energy, her knees clicking. "Get yourself together, Fliss," she said. "Then come downstairs. We've already been gone too long." She left the kitchen, and a moment later the noise downstairs surged as Granny rushed through the door into the bar. Momentarily, the spell over them was broken and things felt almost normal.

Normal? How could any life carry on as it always had, when for Betty, everything had changed? All this time, she'd thought she was in control of her destiny, but if what Granny said was true, Betty's only destiny was this. One there was no escape from.

Betty glanced at her sisters. Charlie had been struck dumb and had one thumb lodged firmly in her mouth, a habit Betty had thought was long broken. Fliss was silent, brooding.

"You should have told me about the curse," Betty said at last. She felt heavy, as though the revelations of the evening were crushing her like stones fallen from the prison tower.

Fliss looked up, her dark eyes weary. "I wanted you to still have hope that someday you'd leave this place."

Betty felt herself getting prickly now. "What's the point if it can't ever happen? Wouldn't it have been kinder to tell the truth?"

"Yes, I mean . . . no, oh, I don't know!" Fliss bit her lower lip. "I wanted to, but Granny made me promise."

"It never stopped you before," Betty said, hurt creeping into her voice. "We used to tell each other everything."

Fliss's cheeks went pink. "Do you remember when you were little?" She glanced meaningfully at Charlie. "The thing that I told you?"

Betty nodded, scowling. When Fliss was eight and Betty just five, Fliss had discovered that the tooth fairy wasn't real, and had in fact been Granny putting a copper coin under the pillow. She had immediately told Betty. Granny had been furious and had never let Fliss forget it.

"I never forgave myself for that," Fliss said quietly.

"Spoiling it for you, when you could have had the magic a while longer."

"This is nothing like that," said Betty. "That was a silly childhood belief. A family curse is not the same!"

"I think it is. It comes down to the same thing, which is innocence." Fliss tried to smile. "I wanted that for you, just for a little longer. To not have this be the first thing you think of in the morning, and the last thing at night. Because once it's there, that's it." Her eyes shone suddenly. "This is the rest of our lives."

The rest of our lives. Betty stared into her sister's desperate eyes and saw her own mirrored there. She had felt smothered before, but that was nothing compared to now. The curse had snared her like an invisible bindweed, strangling the hope out of her. And not even magic could make up for it.

Hours later, Betty lay awake in bed with Charlie snoring softly next to her. It had taken ages for Charlie to fall into a restless sleep, hours of fidgeting and thumb-sucking as Betty told every story she knew to try to settle her—but none was as strange or as dark as the one they had just heard. Eventually Charlie dozed off, but Betty was wide awake.

Voices burbled beneath them. How odd, she thought, to live the way they did. Even though the Poacher's Pocket was theirs, it never truly felt it. It always hummed with other people's voices, creaked under other people's feet.

Even the bedroom was shared, a jumble of Charlie's stuffed toys, rag dolls, shells, and pebbles, and then novels, jam jars of buttons and other useful bits, and a sewing kit of Betty's. Her most treasured items were her book of stamps and her map collection, which she had pored over on many a quiet afternoon, jotting down the names of places she planned to explore.

It had all begun when her father had been haggling down at the harbor one morning. Betty had wandered off with a mapmaker's daughter from one of the ships. Her name was Roma, and she had smooth brown skin and braided hair, as well as a thousand memories of clear turquoise waters, arid deserts, and snowcapped mountains. Betty had listened, spellbound, wishing more than anything that she could see them herself. Later, as Roma helped pack up the maps, Betty had begged until her father had relented and bought her one: her very first map. She had cradled it like treasure as the mapmaker's ship set sail, becoming a speck in the distance. They never saw Roma again, but the spell she had cast over Betty remained.

Her eyes lingered on her maps, a whole world she'd longed to explore rolled within them. Now the curse had ruined them for her, like a tempting but poisoned box of chocolates. She could look, but a single taste would kill her. Her gaze slid from the maps to a flicker of moonlight on the cracked ceiling, and a tear trickled down her cheek. She couldn't imagine a world she was forbidden to explore, just as she couldn't imagine that there wasn't an answer, somewhere out there, to make it possible.

And then she sat up in bed, realizing something. Granny hadn't said it wasn't possible. She had said that nothing the other girls had attempted before had worked. Which meant that Granny still believed there was a way the curse could be undone, even if she was too afraid to pursue it.

"I'm sorry, Granny," Betty whispered determinedly in the darkness. "But if there's a way to break the curse, I have to try."

Chapter Six

Leechpond Latchdown

BETTY LISTENED FOR ANOTHER half an hour, until she heard Granny and Fliss creaking up the stairs. There followed the sounds of running water, bedroom doors clicking closed, and the groan of beds being slid into. Then silence.

Betty waited until Granny's snores were rumbling through the wall. Then she slipped out of bed, shivering as her bare feet met the chilly air. Quickly, she hopped into her slippers and crept out to the hall. Her arms prickled with goose pimples as she approached the dank, creepy cupboard on the landing. It was full of cleaning things and junk, and was the one part of the building all three girls disliked. After getting locked inside once during a game of hide-and-seek, Charlie especially hated it. Betty shivered, hurrying past. The snores were regular and deep now. She pushed Granny's door open a little way and slunk into the darkened room.

The scent of pipe smoke lingered in the air. Granny was down for the count, all right. Betty remembered Granny's plea and felt a moment of guilt.

Please, Betty . . . don't try. I couldn't go through that again . . . It'd kill me.

The idea of hurting Granny was even worse than the thought of angering her. *But I have to do this*, Betty reminded herself. *As much for Granny as for us.*

She moved to the wardrobe and, opening it, retrieved an old cookie tin from the shelf. Then she tiptoed into the kitchen. She didn't want Charlie waking and asking questions, and if Granny woke up she could easily hide the tin and say she'd come to get a drink.

She sat at the table, easing the lid off the tin. She wasn't doing anything particularly wrong: all three girls had seen this tin many times. Granny had often amused them with its family keepsakes and knickknacks, such as the girls' cards and drawings, a couple of old photographs, and a pair of baby shoes that all three of them had worn. There was also a sheaf of papers Granny had always whipped away "in case something got mislaid," but tonight, that was exactly what Betty was looking for. She lifted them out and spread them over the table. First she found a stash of letters their grandfather had sent to Granny during the war, each one brittle and yellowed with age. They were all Granny had left of him now. Betty set them aside. They were not hers to look through.

She passed over the girls' birth documents and her mother's death papers. A quick glance confirmed what Granny had said: their mother had drowned. Betty slipped the papers back into the pile—then froze as a light creak sounded from the hallway. Granny's rumbling snores had stopped! Desperately, she gathered up the papers, but the pile of letters teetered, scattering on the floor as someone stepped into the kitchen. The glow from a candle flickered over a heart-shaped face and a mass of dark, shiny hair.

"Jumping jackdaws!" Betty hissed, heart thumping.

"Betty?" Fliss whispered, rubbing her eyes. "What are you up to?"

Betty pressed a finger to her lips, beckoning. In silence, Fliss came closer, setting the candle on the table. Both girls kneeled down, retrieving the letters. Moments later, another loud snore assured Betty that Granny was still asleep.

"I was just looking for something . . . anything that

might help us find out more about the curse," Betty said. "Something Granny might have missed."

"But, Betty," Fliss began worriedly, "Granny said—"

"I know what she said." Betty shot her a warning glance. "But there's no harm in looking." She gathered up another handful of letters. "I hope there isn't an order to these." She frowned, lifting an envelope to the light.

"What is it?" Fliss whispered.

"These letters . . . I thought they were all Granny's, but there was another pile underneath. Look." She pushed the envelope at her sister, pointing to the familiar scrawl on the front. "It's Father's writing, and it's addressed to us, but . . ." She turned the envelope over. "It's never been opened."

Fliss snatched up another envelope, stricken. "But . . . Granny said Father had stopped writing. That he'd been too ashamed, too miserable. Why would she lie? Unless . . . what if he's sick? Dying?" She slid her thumbnail under the seal. "We have to open them!"

"No!" Betty snatched it away. Something was very wrong here; she felt it as much as Fliss did. Granny was brutally honest most of the time, especially when it came to their parents, so why would she conceal these letters? The only things she had hidden were connected to the curse . . .

"But they're ours!" Fliss insisted. "We've every right to see what's in them!"

"I know," Betty answered. "But there must be a reason why Granny's kept them from us. We need to be smart—she's planning on giving them to us at some point. Otherwise why keep them at all?"

"When, though? Look . . . the postmark is from three months ago!"

Betty squinted at the envelope, trying to work out what was different. Then she saw it. "There!" She jabbed at the paper, where a slightly smudged emblem had been stamped. "See that? I can't believe I didn't notice it right away!"

Fliss peered closer. "Wait . . . that's not the Crowstone Prison emblem. It's different."

"Too right it's different." Betty could recall the Crowstone emblem perfectly: an ornate etching of the prison tower surrounded by a flock of crows. This emblem was unfamiliar: a heavy padlock entwined with what appeared to be writhing eels.

"He never stopped writing to us," Betty murmured, suddenly ashamed of how readily she'd accepted the idea of their father cutting off contact. Of him letting them down, again. He hadn't. A surge of love lifted the grudge inside, lightening it. "He's been moved to a different prison away from Crowstone, and Granny didn't want us to find out."

Fliss read the tiny words under the stamp. "Leech-pond Latchdown?"

"Doesn't sound pleasant." Betty eyed the emblem in distaste. Not eels, after all, but leeches. She leafed through the other envelopes. On others the postmark was clearer.

"Lostmoors . . ." Betty read. It sounded familiar. "Wait here."

She left the kitchen and crept back to the bedroom. Charlie was breathing deeply, huddled under the covers like a dormouse. Betty pawed through her maps before settling on the one she wanted. She brought it into the kitchen and unrolled it on the table. The waxy paper was crinkled with time and wear, but the inky lettering and tiny hand-drawn details were as beautiful as ever. She quickly located Lostmoors on the map, slightly off center. It was surrounded by valleys, mountains, and not much else. A lump rose in her throat. Just how far away was he?

Her finger traveled down the paper to four craggy marks at the bottom: Crowstone and its three Sorrow Isles within the Misty Marshes. A crescent of deadly rocks known as the Devil's Teeth curved around Lament. And there, inked on the island of Repent, was Crowstone Tower, the oldest part of the prison.

"Granny was protecting us," Betty said, understanding. "She couldn't risk us leaving Crowstone to try and visit Father. It was easier to hide the letters and pretend he was still here, but . . ." She trailed off as a thought pricked her like a thistle.

Fliss frowned. "She could have told me . . . I knew none of us could leave. Why would he be transferred in the first place?"

"Maybe it was simpler if none of us knew," Betty replied, speaking in a rush now that the thistly thought had taken root. "There's probably lots of reasons why prisoners get moved, but why would Granny still have been visiting if he's not there? Unless she's been pretending—"

Fliss shook her head. "She was there."

"How can you be sure?"

"Because I do the washing," Fliss answered. "And Granny usually forgets to empty her pockets. Wait here." She vanished, leaving Betty alone in the darkened kitchen to creep back to her room. Moments later she returned with a scrap of paper bearing the Crowstone emblem. "See? A visiting slip from last week."

"Why did you keep this?" Betty asked. "Surely you didn't already suspect . . . Oh." Turning the paper, she found a soppy love poem in Fliss's looped handwriting, embellished with doodled hearts and flowers. "Ugh!"

"Don't read that!" Fliss growled. She snatched the paper back, blushing. "The point is, this is proof Granny has been visiting the prison recently."

Betty felt another ripple of unease. "But if it's not Father she's been seeing, then who is it?"

Chapter Seven

The Prison on the Marshes

THE MORNING DAWNED to a thick fog sweeping in off the marshes. It sprawled over the streets and seeped into the Poacher's Pocket in damp, salty drafts.

Betty woke with even frizzier hair than usual. She shivered into freezing clothes and wriggled into a pair of Fliss's hand-me-down boots, which were a smidge too big. Stamping into the kitchen to try to warm herself, she found Fliss at the stove.

"Morning," Fliss said.

"Morning." Betty suppressed a yawn, gritty-eyed. She watched as her older sister ladled porridge into a chipped bowl for Charlie, who was waiting impatiently. The scene was so reassuringly familiar that Betty fleetingly wondered if she had dreamed the events of the previous evening, and there was no curse or magical family heirlooms . . . but then she saw that Fliss's smile was tight and heard the tapping of Charlie's spoon on her dish, which was more of a nervous tremble than a merry jingle. Betty's stomach lurched. No, everything that had happened last night was real, all right. A curse . . . and three magical objects. Stones dropping out of tower walls. She replayed the powers of each item in her head, then thought about the curse again. Though Granny hadn't said as much, Betty couldn't help wondering if the magical objects and the curse were connected.

"Granny's still in bed," said Fliss distractedly. "She said she's got a stinker of a headache."

"I'm not surprised," Betty muttered. When she had crept back to replace the tin last night, her grandmother had been frowning, even in her sleep. Betty's eyes watered a little to think of how hard it must have been for poor Granny to be responsible for them all while keeping such a terrible secret.

Fliss gave the pot another stir. The smell of singed porridge floated past Betty's nose. "Want some?"

Betty eyed the gray gloop. "Er . . ."

"I'll have it if Betty don't want it," Charlie interrupted, scraping out her bowl.

Charlie was always hungry and would eat practically anything. She had been the same ever since she was a baby; so much so that Granny always said she must have worms. Father, who always had to exaggerate, said they were eels, not worms.

"You have it." Betty ignored the rumbling in her tummy. This was easier than usual now that her thoughts were occupied by the curse—especially since she'd made up her mind to break it.

Fliss gave Betty a meaningful glance. "Granny said she's not visiting Father today."

Betty's ears pricked up at once. "Oh, isn't she?"

Granny had missed a couple of visits recently, with flimsy excuses. However, last night's discovery made this all the less surprising, seeing as their father hadn't been there for months. The only other thing connecting the Widdershins to the prison was the stones falling from Crowstone Tower. Could Granny's recent visits be linked to the curse, and not to their father? Perhaps they could find out—if they dared.

Fliss glanced at Charlie, who was still shoveling down her lumpy breakfast.

"What about church?" Betty asked.

Fliss made a face. "Doubt it."

Granny only went to church to stay on the right side of

her customers. Given what a sinful place Crowstone was, everyone on the outside of the prison was eager to prove how law-abiding and repenting they were. Betty didn't enjoy going, either. It was bottom-numbingly cold, and Granny often dozed off and embarrassed them by snoring.

Fliss, on the other hand, was always looking for ways to be a nicer person. At times her attention wandered, however, only to be caught by whichever lad was the latest to take her fancy. Charlie was simply there for the warm bread rolls handed out to the poorer folk at the end, and would loiter around looking mournful until she was taken pity on.

"I wonder if that means we don't have to go to Sunday school, then?" Fliss mused. "Seeing as Granny's not going to the prison today." She scraped some porridge into a bowl for herself, grimacing as she forced a mouthful down.

"But I want to go," Charlie piped up, licking her bowl. "We're finishing the blankets for the orphans this week!"

"You can still go, Charlie dear," Fliss soothed her. "We know you enjoy it."

"You know," Betty said with a sidelong glance at Fliss, "now that you're sixteen, we wouldn't need Granny to come to the prison with us to see Father. If he still wanted to see us, I mean."

"You're right," Fliss replied. She lowered her voice and looked thoughtful. "But surely being alone is only making him gloomier. Perhaps what he needs is a nice . . . surprise."

She caught Betty's eye, and the two sisters shared a look—the kind of look that used to pass between them often but hadn't in a long time. It was a secret look, and it was one Betty had missed. And they both knew, without any words, exactly what they were going to do.

They left after church a couple of hours later, moving briskly through the cobbled streets, ducking their faces from view whenever someone came the opposite way. Delicious smells of roasting meat wafted through cracked windows. Betty's stomach rumbled, but as they neared the marshes, briny air dampened her hunger.

"I'm not sure about this, Betty. What if Charlie lets slip to Granny?" Fliss's voice was low and nervous. Damp air blew their hair around their faces: Fliss's like a long silk scarf and Betty's like a mass of dry wool. They drew their shawls more tightly around their shoulders, shivering.

"Charlie will be too busy yapping about what she did at Sunday school to care about us," said Betty. "Anyway, it won't matter if she does." She thought of their father's hidden letters. "By the time Granny hears about it, we'll have found out who she was visiting and why. We can play dumb and say we wanted to surprise Father. We're not doing anything wrong, exactly."

The prison came into view in the distance. Farther away to the left were the other Sorrow Isles and beyond, a smear of gray on the horizon.

"The next town along from Marshfoot is Merry-on-the-Marsh," Fliss said softly. "Do you suppose we'll ever see what they've got to be merry about?"

"We will if I have anything to say about it," Betty answered, more bravely than she felt. Yesterday, crossing Crowstone's boundaries had simply been an adventure. Today she knew it was something that would kill them. Yet, Betty couldn't deny an undercurrent of excitement. For so long she had wished for something to happen, and now it was happening . . . or at least, it could happen. Whatever Granny said, there had to be a way to change things.

They arrived at the ferry point shortly before the boat docked at the platform, the only passengers aside from a wizened old woman. They paid their fares and clambered on. The early morning mists had cleared, and patches of blue sky were peeking through thick cloud. In the distance, a tiny ship bobbed on glittering water, reminding Betty of the day she had spent with the mapmaker's daughter. Where was Roma now? How much more of the world had she seen, while Betty had been stagnating here?

"Do you remember those stories Father used to tell?" Betty asked. "The ones he heard from the merchants and sailors, about beaches with golden sand as fine as sugar and water so clear you could see to the bottom?"

Fliss nodded, her mouth twisting as she looked over the soupy water stretching away from them. "I used to love those stories. But they just became harder and harder to imagine."

Betty gazed toward Repent as a troubling thought occurred to her.

"What if Granny's just been coming here to appeal? To get Father moved back?" Suddenly, doubts were pressing in on her. Already she had known the chances of a link to the curse were slim, but they had no other leads.

Fliss frowned. "I don't think so. The visiting slips have a prisoner number on them."

"A prisoner number? But we'll need that!"

Fliss grinned, patting her bag. "Good thing I brought it, then."

Betty sagged against the side of the boat with relief. "I'm surprised Charlie didn't insist on coming with us," she murmured, once they'd pushed off from land. Her warm breath misted the air, which was even cooler out on the water.

"Why would she?" Fliss said, through chattering teeth. "Better to stay in the warm than freeze her cockles off for someone she barely remembers outside of the prison walls."

There was a bitterness to Fliss's tone that Betty rarely heard. She felt it, too, but less sharply since the discovery of their father's letters. The letters meant he still thought of them. He still cared.

"You've never forgiven Father for leaving us, have you?"

Fliss huffed out a long breath. "I've tried. I'm still trying. But it's hard. He should be here, with us, not in there . . . especially after losing Mother. I know he was trying to look after us in his own stupid way, but . . ." She trailed off, looking over Betty's shoulder. Betty became aware that the ferryman was listening with interest. Fliss didn't need to say more, anyway. They both remembered how it had all happened.

After their mother had died, Barney Widdershins had drunk and gambled, spiraling out of control. By the time any of them knew how much money he had frittered away, the Poacher's Pocket was deep in debt. Still, Father had insisted that he had a solution: selling smuggled goods. Only he'd boasted to the wrong people and been rewarded with a five-year prison sentence.

"It's Charlie I feel most angry for," Fliss said, ashen-faced. She had never been good at traveling over water. "She didn't really have a chance to miss Mother, but she could have known what it was to have a father. Even a fool like ours."

Privately, Betty disagreed. Charlie seemed happy enough, not missing what she'd never had. It was Betty and Fliss who remembered and felt the loss strongest. And Betty thought, a little enviously, that as the first-born daughter, Fliss had been their father's favorite. A daddy's girl.

Fliss gave a little moan as the boat lurched.

"If yer gonna throw up, do it over the side," the ferry-man said without an ounce of pity.

"Keep your eyes on the prison," Betty told her. "Granny always says it helps to look at something in the distance."

Granny. It was the first time either of them had made this journey without her, or with the knowledge of the curse that ran through their veins. It was a grim thought that the ferry was plunging toward the edges of Crow-stone—where their world ended.

The prison looked worse by day. When Betty had

seen the lit windows and flickering will-o'-the-wisps on the water the previous night, she could almost have imagined that it was a fairy-tale castle in the distance.

In daylight, there was no pretending. The stone building was squat and gray, hulking over the land as if consuming it. The rows of tiny windows were like mean, empty eyes, and as the ferry drew closer, the bars on them came into view. Only one part didn't fit: the high stone tower. It didn't look as though it belonged or was part of a prison at all.

Betty gazed up at it, shielding her eyes from the brightening sky.

Every time the curse is triggered, a stone falls from the tower wall . . .

Without warning, the vision of falling from a great height flashed through her mind again. Her breathing quickened. What was that? A memory bobbed to the surface: a story of a girl who had fallen to her death from the tower. She tore her gaze away as the ferry docked. Betty stepped off and held out her hand to steady Fliss. They wobbled past the ferryman onto dry land, past the line of people waiting to board.

"I feel a bit better now," Fliss muttered, color returning to her cheeks. "Looks like I'll hold on to my porridge after all." They headed up the path to the prison, crunching over pebbles and cockleshells. Up ahead, just outside the prison walls, was a seafood stall.

"Urgh . . ." Fliss moaned as the fishy smell wafted around them. Impatient, Betty urged her on, doing her best to block her sister's view of the jellied eels and winkles. Then they were past the stall, with the huge prison doors ahead.

Betty stiffened, aware that the sentry was watching them—Fliss in particular—with interest. Betty rolled her eyes: Fliss could hardly go anywhere without being gawked at, even when she was green from seasickness. There was no question she was pretty. Her silky hair and dark eyes had always drawn admiring glances, but it was more than that. Her goodness and willingness to see the best in things was something people seemed to sense. Today this was the last thing they needed, drawing unwanted attention when they were trying to find things out.

"Names?" the sentry asked, smoothing his uniform like a bird preening its feathers.

"Widdershins," said Betty, in the same clipped tone Granny used when she wanted to hurry things—or people—up.

"Visiting?"

"Our father," Fliss replied, before Betty could interrupt.

Betty could have kicked her. What if the sentry knew that Barney Widdershins was no longer in this prison? She held her breath, hoping that there were more prisoners than the warders could keep track of—or that admiring Fliss was enough of a distraction.

"Brrr!" said Fliss. She blew into her hands and gave the sentry a beseeching look, and like his boots had been buttered, he slid back and ushered them through.

They stepped into a vaulted stone walkway. The dark, shadowy shapes of rats scurried along ahead of them, squeaking and causing Fliss to squeak even louder.

Below a rusted sign saying **VISITORS** was another door.

Through this lay a large room with wooden benches and a line of somber people waiting to sign the visitors' book.

"Oh, no," Fliss muttered. "Look over there!"

Betty searched the line, smiling tightly at a couple of Poacher's Pocket regulars farther on who were looking their way. It was inevitable that in a place as small as Crowstone, they'd see someone they knew.

"What if they tell Granny they saw us?" Fliss asked, pulling her shawl up further.

"I doubt they would," said Betty. "Everyone knows how cross she gets if they dare to mention Father being in prison. Anyway, if they did, Granny would have more explaining to do than us about who she's been visiting all this time."

As they waited, the girls' pockets and bags were searched for contraband and their scalps inspected for fleas with a long-toothed comb.

"The indignity of it," Fliss blustered, rearranging her hair.

Moments later they reached the front of the line, and the visitors' book lay open before them. Fliss lifted the pen, dipping it into the inkwell on the counter. Under "Visitor Name" she simply wrote "Widdershins," followed by the date, time, and visitor number.

"Five-one-three," Betty read, trying to recall what Father's number had been.

"Father's was four-four-nine," Fliss said softly, not looking up. "In case you were wondering."

Under "Prisoner Name" she scrawled an unreadable squiggle, then tore off the slip. They squeezed their bottoms into a small space on one of the hard benches and waited. Minutes later the word "Widdershins!" was barked.

They stood up, glancing at each other nervously. It was time to find out who prisoner 513 was.

Chapter Eight

Prisoner 513

THE GIRLS WERE LED THROUGH a stone courtyard that stank of gutters and sewage. They hurried
after the warder, dodging rat droppings and traps. Fliss
pulled her shawl over her nose and mouth, squeaking as a
furry shape scuttled past their feet.

"Did you see the size of that? It looks like it eats prisoners for breakfast!"

Betty found that her own lips were clamped into a
revolted line. At the center of the courtyard was a large
wooden frame with steps leading up to a trapdoor set into
a platform. Above it swayed a long rope noose.

Betty gulped, her fingers flying to her throat. She had

seen the gallows on previous visits, but it was never any less disturbing. Thankfully, the one that used to be at Crowstone's crossroads had been torn down years ago, and executions were no longer public. Instead, they took place here, within the prison walls. It was a stark reminder of exactly how grim the jail was, and Betty suddenly, desperately, wanted this not to have been a wasted journey.

Please let us get some answers, she thought. *I don't know where else to start.*

Crossing the courtyard they were shown into a wide, high-ceilinged room. Its only windows were high up and barred. A long bench ran the length of it, set before a wooden counter. The bench was occupied by visitors, and the counter was partitioned by iron bars. On the other side sat the prisoners, in identical clothes: distinctive loose tunics and trousers that bore the same marks all over them. At first glance the markings looked like tiny arrows, but as Betty continued to stare, they came to look more like birds' footprints. The image of crows clawing the dirt went through her mind.

Betty scanned the prisoners' faces. All were men or boys; the prison had stopped housing women some years ago. She felt Fliss's cold fingers wrap tightly around hers and knew what was going through her sister's head: some of these inmates were little more than children, perhaps only a year or two older than herself. Yet the haunted look in their eyes made them appear far older.

It was now that Betty felt the first stirrings of unease. Who was this prisoner Granny had been visiting, and what had he done to end up here? Would he even talk to them, or were they clutching at straws?

She felt Fliss's grip tighten. Her sister was attracting interest. Though the prisoners appeared too cowed to do or say anything in the warders' presence, the way some of them were eyeing Fliss—like dogs around meat—made Betty glad of the bars between them. From the way Fliss kept her eyes lowered, Betty knew she was glad, too. One prisoner in particular caught Betty's attention, for he was different from the rest. He looked around Fliss's age, and his black hair had been cropped close to his scalp. Yet it was more than his appearance that made him stand out.

His black eyes did not share the resigned look of the other prisoners. There was a spark of something behind them. They were lively, questioning, and they were regarding Betty and Fliss not with the same wolfish look as the others, but with a fierce, open curiosity. Somehow, before she had even read the numbers sewn onto his tunic, Betty knew—and suddenly felt that this was all a big mistake. He was barely more than a boy! Surely he couldn't know much about an ancient curse. Perhaps Granny had another reason for visiting him, but Betty couldn't imagine what it was. Now that she was here she might as well try to find out.

"That's him," she whispered, nudging Fliss. "Five-one-three." Gently, she pulled her hand free of Fliss's, and moved toward the bench in front of him. Fliss followed closely, ducking her head. It was so unlike her not to want to be looked at that it was almost amusing, and ordinarily Betty would have poked fun at her. But today wasn't ordinary.

The young man shifted and sat up straighter as they squeezed onto the hard bench side by side. He had been interested before, but now he was alert and watchful, too.

Betty cleared her throat. Not because she especially needed to, but because she couldn't think of anything to say, and it didn't appear that Fliss would take the lead. She waited, hoping that the surprise of them sitting might make him speak first, but he continued to stare in silence. Betty leaned closer to the bars, suddenly aware that the elbow of the visitor next to her was touching her arm. There was so little space, so little privacy in here.

"You must be wondering who we are," she began awkwardly. Still he said nothing, so she continued.

"I'm Betty, and this is my sister, Fliss. We understand our granny, Bunny Widdershins, has been visiting you?"

The prisoner's expression remained unchanged, but he leaned forward. For a horrible moment Betty thought he wouldn't speak.

"Where is she?"

His voice was disappointingly ordinary. Betty had been hoping he was from one of the faraway lands she had read about . . . but his accent was every bit as common as her own.

"She's . . . not well."

The prisoner looked from Betty to Fliss, then back again. She caught a glimpse of amusement in his dark eyes and felt a flare of annoyance. He found the idea of Granny being unwell funny?

"She doesn't know you're here."

It was a statement, not a question. From his tone, Betty understood that it was this he found amusing, not Granny being unwell. Already she could tell he was sharp. Like he had them all figured out. It made her feel wrong-footed, like she had already lost control of where the conversation was going.

"Who are you? And why has our granny been coming to see you?"

"I'm prisoner five-one-three. Names don't mean much in here."

"Well, we'd like to know it anyway," Betty replied evenly, trying to sound bolder than she felt. "So please don't waste our time."

He shrugged. "Colton. My name is Colton." He said it slowly, as if he was savoring it. Betty wondered when it was that he had last been asked, instead of being referred to as a number.

"And why has Granny been visiting you?" she repeated.

Colton lifted his hands onto the counter, drumming his long fingers on the wood. His wrists were shackled, and his hands looked like they belonged to someone much older. They were dry and calloused, the hands of someone who knew hard work. She wondered what hard work in a prison might involve. Then she wondered again about the crime he had committed—what those hands had done—for him to end up in this place. There were all sorts in Crowstone Prison: thieves, smugglers, and murderers. According to Granny, it had once held suspected sorcerers and witches, an idea Betty had always dismissed along with Bunny's other superstitions. Given everything she had learned in the past day, the thought didn't seem quite so silly now.

"Why don't you ask her yourself?" he said.

Betty stared at him. Was he being obnoxious, or genuinely curious? It was difficult to say. "We could," she said stiffly. "But seeing as she hasn't been honest about her recent visits here, and, well . . . about a lot of things, actually, we wanted to see what we could find out for ourselves."

Colton nodded slowly. "So you're smart. Just like the old lady."

"Are you going to tell us or not?"

"Impatient, too." Colton grinned infuriatingly. "That's another thing you share." He glanced Fliss's way. "How about you, princess? You always let your clever sister do the talking?" He peered at her. "Can you talk?"

Fliss glared, her cheeks flushing pink. "I can talk."

"Hmm," said Colton. "Maybe just too law-abiding to talk to the likes of me, then."

"I'm here, aren't I?" Fliss's voice was prickly. "Which would suggest not."

Colton's gaze lingered on Fliss a moment longer before returning to Betty.

"All right, smart girl," he said softly. "Let's see how smart you are. Let's see if you can work it out."

Betty wondered whether Granny's visits to Colton

had been as frustrating as this. Had she also struggled to steer the conversation, and felt as helpless as Betty did now? The more Colton held back, the more she wanted answers.

"Why don't you stop playing games and tell us?"

"Because, in here, there aren't many games to play. Not for someone like me." Colton's dark eyes were wide, and serious, and Betty understood then. She nodded. She would play his game.

"Well, Granny's never mentioned you, so I'm guessing you only met after my father was moved out of here." She paused. "Did you have something to do with him being moved?"

"No." Colton clasped his hands together on the counter. "I saw him often, for a while. Our cells were directly opposite, but I barely spoke to him. Your father . . . well. He's not someone I wanted knowing too much about me, if you understand my meaning."

Betty did understand. She avoided looking at Fliss, but her sister was fidgeting, a sure sign she was uncomfortable. They all knew Barney Widdershins had a big mouth, but hearing it from outside the family stung.

"Do you know why he was moved?" Betty persisted.

Colton shrugged again. "To make space. This place is

overcrowded. But it's high security. The location makes it harder to escape from than other prisons, and old Barney isn't much of a threat compared to others here."

"What did you do to end up here?" Fliss blurted out. Betty looked at her in surprise. It was unlike Fliss to be so direct, but Colton seemed neither surprised nor offended.

"Nothing," he said. "I'm innocent. But in here, that's what everybody says. So I don't expect you to believe me."

Betty stayed silent, studying him. Colton wasn't making this easy, and she couldn't imagine Granny giving up her time to be here unless it was important. Really important. If Colton barely knew their father, then the visits must be about something else. Perhaps she had been wrong to assume Colton was too young to know anything about the curse. He certainly had something Granny was after.

"What is it my grandmother wants from you, exactly?"

"Not my place to say. Ask her."

"I've already explained about Granny hiding things," Betty said, impatient now. "And why would you care whether it's your place to tell us or not? What are we to you anyway? Nothing, that's what!"

"True," Colton said without a hint of emotion. "But it's not you I'm looking out for. It's me. And let me tell you something, nothing is given away in here. Everything is traded, and knowledge is valuable. You've gone to a lot of trouble to get here, haven't you? You want information badly. I can give it, but only in exchange for what you have."

Betty's mind whirred with excitement. So there was information! But what did Colton think they had to trade? She knew what she had to ask—at the risk of sounding foolish or mad. What did it matter? They never had to see Colton again after today. And if he knew something of value, it could be the start Betty needed to change her family's terrible legacy.

"Is this about the curse?"

Betty heard Fliss's breath catch and knew she had seen the trace of recognition in Colton's eyes.

"So what do you know about it?" Betty asked. Her insides were fluttering like a candle flame.

"How to break it."

Four tiny words, with such enormous power. Betty tensed, like a bowstring that had been pulled back, ready to fire. She had hoped Colton might know something, but she hadn't considered that he could have the solution. After the shock of having her dreams shattered only hours ago, the possibility of her freedom now felt tantalizingly close. But doubts still lurked. How could this . . . this stranger know of their sinister family secret? And how could he know how to undo it when generations of Widdershins girls had failed? She only realized she was holding her breath when Fliss squeezed her hand. She leaned forward, her nose almost touching the bars. "What?"

"You heard." Colton's voice was low. "I know how it can be broken."

"How . . . how could you possibly know that?" Fliss whispered.

This he didn't answer.

"If you know, then why haven't you told Granny?" Fliss asked. "I mean, you can't have, not if she keeps coming back . . ."

Still he said nothing.

"He's bluffing," Betty muttered. She felt suddenly sick and dismayed at how easily her hopes had been raised. "He must be. If there was a chance the curse could be undone, Granny would've taken it!"

"I haven't told her," Colton cut in, "because she hasn't given me what I want in return."

Bitterness spread through Betty, like water turning to ice. It would be so easy to reach through those bars and seize him by the collar, and she badly wanted to; to shake him until his teeth rattled . . . but of course, she wouldn't dare. For one thing, she hadn't forgotten that Colton was a potentially dangerous prisoner. For another, there were too many warders—they'd be right on her, like a ferret on a rabbit. "We don't have anything," she said through clenched teeth. "Everyone knows the Widdershins are poor. Our father left debts."

"I haven't asked for money," Colton replied. "What good would that do me, in here? No, what I want is something far bigger." He lowered his voice further, so that Betty and Fliss had to lean even closer to hear him. "I want to get out." The emotionless look in his eyes wavered. Betty glimpsed something else behind them: desperation —and fear. "I want her to help me escape."

"But . . . that's impossible!" Betty said, her voice rising. She lowered it, afraid of drawing attention. "How on earth do you think Granny could help you? She's an old woman!"

"And a law unto herself, from what I've heard," Colton said. "It wouldn't be impossible, not for her." He blinked, his eyes becoming calm and hard to read once more, but Betty couldn't forget how haunted they'd been just moments ago. Why did he believe Granny could help him? Surely he couldn't know what else the Widdershins possessed.

"Look," said Betty, troubled now. "Even if it . . . what you're asking . . . were possible, Granny couldn't risk it. She'd go to prison herself!"

"I know about that bag of hers," Colton whispered, never taking his eyes from Betty's. "And what it does. She could get me out, and no one would know until I was long gone!"

The words sent an unpleasant tremor through Betty, rather like a marsh eel had slithered down her back. This changed everything. If Colton knew about the bag, who else did? The thought of their secret being exposed made her fearful. Granny had stressed how much danger they'd be in if the knowledge of it was leaked. "How . . . how could you possibly know about that?" she asked at last.

"I know all about you Widdershins," he hissed, his eyes taking on a wild look. "The same way I know about the curse. How it began here, within these walls. In that tower. So if you want to escape Crowstone, you'd better listen to me!"

Betty froze, aware that Fliss's breathing was coming in gasps. Her sister was every bit as stunned as she was.

"Aren't you forgetting something?" she said, forcing the words out with difficulty. "If you know about the curse, then you know we can't leave. We're trapped! Even if we got you out, we couldn't take you beyond Crowstone's borders."

Colton leaned forward hungrily. "I'm not asking you to. I just want you to get me outside these walls—the rest I can handle myself." He dropped his voice to barely above a whisper. "All I need is to get to Lament. From there I can escape Crowstone once and for all."

Betty shuddered. The thought of the graveyard isle filled her with a creeping dread. It was a mournful, desolate place, perfect for someone trying to escape. There was little likelihood of being seen.

"Does anyone else know about the bag?" she asked.

Colton shook his head. "If they do, they didn't hear it from me."

"How do we know that's true?" said Fliss, her voice quavering.

Betty met Colton's eyes. They were even darker than Fliss's, and she couldn't imagine what was hidden in the depths of them. But she could imagine the bag from his point of view. It was his ticket to escape.

"Because he doesn't want anyone else getting their hands on it any more than we do," she said.

Outside in the yard a bell began to chime, signaling that visiting time was over. The prisoners rose to their feet obediently. Though Colton stood, too, his gaze never left Betty's face. The prisoners ahead of Colton began shuffling to the door like meek dogs. He turned to go, but Betty sprang up. "Wait!" she begged, desperate to know more before he was whisked away.

"Time's up!" a warder barked, rapping his baton harshly on the counter.

Colton lowered his head, but turned his face to Betty, delaying his exit by a mere moment. "Help me," he said, through gritted teeth. Again, the self-assured mask slipped, and his frustration and hopelessness were plain to see. "And I'll help you."

The delay earned him a hefty thwack on the arm from the warder's baton. Colton winced, hushing immediately before following the rest of the prisoners to the door like one in a line of ants. He gave the girls one last, pleading glance.

Then he was gone.

Chapter Nine

Ghosts

OUTSIDE THE PRISON ONCE MORE, Betty and Fliss waited at the marsh's edge, watching for the ferry to arrive at the jetty. Betty stared up at the foreboding tower. *Lost Widdershins lives,* she thought, searching its walls for missing stones. She was too far away to see any, but the vision of falling and the flashes of terror and grief she'd experienced were fresh in her mind. Was Colton right—had the curse all started there? And how could they persuade him to tell them what else he knew? Because if it meant changing their destiny, they had to.

It was a relief to be in the open air, despite the chill. Even the saltiness of the marshes smelled better than the stench of the prison.

"So, now what?" Fliss asked.

"Now we go home and decide what we're going to do."

"Do . . . do? You surely don't mean . . . ?" Fliss's eyes darted about, but there was no one close enough to hear them. "You're not really thinking of trying to get him out, are you?"

"I don't know what I'm thinking yet," Betty replied. "But it's obvious he knows things—things we thought were secret. Granny would never have told him about the bag. And what he said about the curse starting here . . . if there's a chance it can be broken, then we can't ignore it."

"But, Betty, helping him escape would be a crime! I know he says he's innocent, but if we were caught—"

"Slow down a minute," Betty interrupted. "We only have his word he's innocent. We don't know anything about him, except that he's smart. We certainly shouldn't trust him." She began walking toward the ferry as it docked, trying to order her thoughts. Last night she had vowed to change their future, and now Colton seemed to be offering that possibility . . . in exchange for a huge risk. The question was, were they brave enough to secure their freedom by giving him his?

"Granny must think he knows something, or else why would she keep visiting him? This could be it, Fliss.

If he's telling the truth, we could change things—for all of us."

"Big if." Fliss looked thoughtful.

The boat was waiting by the jetty, and people were boarding. Betty and Fliss joined the end of the line, feet sinking into the damp shingle. They handed over their return tickets and climbed on behind an off-duty warder. Unlike many of the other warders, he had a kind, but weary, face. His eyes were fixed on mainland Crowstone like he couldn't wait to arrive.

"Long night?" the ferryman asked him as they pushed off from the jetty.

The warder looked around, his eyes sunken. "Always a long night in that place. The days, too."

"Heard it's haunted," said the ferryman, his eyes glinting ghoulishly. "Ever seen anything?"

Betty leaned closer to listen. She had the feeling the ferryman would know of any tales of hauntings and was looking to amuse himself with his passengers' reactions. She glanced uneasily at the prison, relieved to see it slipping away. She had never believed in ghosts . . . but then, she hadn't believed in magical objects or curses, either.

The warder hesitated. "Not seen anything, exactly . . . but others say they have."

"Such as?" the ferryman asked, picking up speed. Fliss

was starting to hunch over, gripped by seasickness once more. "Come on. Tell us some ghost stories to pass the time."

The warder blew into his chapped hands. He looked like all he wanted was a quiet journey back. "Some say they've seen flickering lights up in the tower," he said eventually. "And a red-haired figure at the windows."

Betty stiffened at the mention of the tower. What was its link to the curse, and what of its crumbling stones? Once again, the memory of a story surfaced—one all the children of Crowstone knew—of a girl imprisoned there who had flung herself from the window. The Widdershins girls had heard it in the schoolyard rather than at home. Granny had never liked repeating the tale and was so superstitious that she refused to even say the girl's name, and now Betty couldn't quite remember it. Sonia . . . Sophia?

"They say she haunts the tower," the warder continued. "The marshes, too. Sightings, whispered words. How many of them are genuine, who knows? I daresay some stories are made up by bored prisoners, and others by long-serving warders looking to frighten the new ones. But a lot of them ring true . . . too many, for my liking."

"And you?" the ferryman asked. He wore an unpleasant little smirk, apparently enjoying the fear on the faces of some of his passengers. "You said you'd never seen anything . . ."

"I've heard things. Words being chanted in the tower when it's empty."

The rest of the boat's passengers were so quiet now that the only sounds were the oars cutting through the water, and Fliss taking deep, slow breaths.

"What words?" the ferryman prompted.

"The same words carved into the walls inside. 'Malice.' 'Injustice.' 'Betrayal.' 'Escape,'" the warder replied. The shadows under his eyes seemed to darken. "They say if you speak her name three times she appears." He ran his tongue over cracked lips. "Sorsha Spellthorn . . ."

Sorsha Spellthorn, Betty thought, her flesh prickling with goose pimples. Yes, that was it.

Silence hung in the air. No one repeated the name, or spoke again for the rest of the journey, but the warder's words were hooked into Betty's mind like little claws. Malice, injustice, betrayal. Were those the perfect ingredients for a curse? It seemed to fit. Because for Sorsha Spellthorn there had been no escape—but how, then, was she connected to the Widdershins? Betty's gaze slid to the tower as the idea churned uneasily, mixing with thoughts of Colton and his dangerous proposal like mud and seawater. When the ferry arrived on the other side of the marshes, the sky had darkened, with thick clouds gathering overhead.

Betty and Fliss were the last to get off, as Fliss was still shaky, sighing with relief as she stepped onto dry land. Ahead of them, the other passengers trickled away into the streets.

"Where's that warder?" Fliss asked. Her voice was still weak, but she looked less sickly now.

Betty nodded. "Over there, up by Thimble Street. Why?"

"Let's catch up to him. Perhaps he could tell us why Colton is in there."

Yes, thought Betty, pushing thoughts of the tower to the back of her mind. Here was a chance to learn how dangerous Colton really was, and whether they could trust what he said.

They hurried around the corner, just as the warder was about to vanish through the door of a cottage. He paused as Fliss called out in a thin croak, then approached, eyeing them curiously.

"Can I help you?"

"We wondered if you could tell us anything about one of the prisoners?" Fliss gave a wobbly smile, which still managed to be charming. "His name is Colton. Prisoner five-one-three."

The warder shook his head and then chuckled, not unkindly. "Do you know how many inmates are in that place? More than a thousand."

Fliss bit her lip, nodding. "Very well. Thank you anyway." She turned away, but the warder lingered by the door, watching them. Another idea occurred to Betty.

"What about Barney Widdershins? He was moved recently, to another prison. Do you know why?"

He gave them a sympathetic look. "Your pa, is it?"

Fliss nodded tightly.

"A lot of prisoners have been moved," said the warder. "More are being shipped out over the next few weeks."

"More . . . more prisoners are being moved?" Betty asked, her voice rising in alarm. If Colton was snatched away like their father, their opportunities to get more information—or make any deal with him—would vanish. "Who?"

He shrugged. "It's all kept hush-hush until the last minute. Has to be, for safety reasons."

Fliss tugged at Betty's arm, pulling her away. "You've

been most helpful, thank you," she called. The warder tipped his hat, retreating into the cottage, and the two girls hurried along the lane.

"Did you hear that?" Betty asked. "They're transferring more prisoners! What if Colton is one of them? If he knows how to break the curse, we can't let him slip through our fingers!"

"Maybe he won't be moved," said Fliss. "But we should try to meet with him again—"

"There might not be time." Betty's mind was racing. "Granny's been visiting him for weeks and he hasn't budged. I don't think he'll tell us anything else without us giving him what he wants." She glanced at Fliss. "Maybe he'd tell you, if we had more time . . ."

"Me? Why me?"

"Oh, come on, Fliss. People open up to you. Father always said you were born batting your eyelashes." Betty had tried it herself once, but Granny had only asked if she had something in her eye. "Me and Granny, we're blunt. Sometimes that works, but more often it rubs people the wrong way. If he is moved, we lose our chance. That only gives us one choice."

Fliss gulped. "You mean, g-get him out?"

"If we want to undo the curse, then we have to. And right now it looks like he's our best hope."

"What if he's lying?"

"What if he's not?" Betty shot back, then lowered her voice. "Yes, he could be bluffing, but he could just as easily be telling the truth. We can't ignore what he knows already. And if he's held on this long, then he must think he has something worth trading."

"How would we do it?" Fliss asked.

"Colton's right. We'll need the traveling bag."

Chapter Ten

Rats and Revelations

THE POACHER'S POCKET WAS QUIET that afternoon, but the girls had little chance to discuss their secret visit to the prison, or plan what came next. At first, Betty and Fliss snatched moments to whisper about their discoveries, but they abandoned their efforts with Granny buzzing around them like a marsh fly, nipping them with new chores every time they paused.

Despite this, Betty was determined that working time didn't have to be wasted time. Now that they knew of the risk of Colton being moved, every moment counted. Her grandmother had always said the inn was the gossip hub of Crowstone, so Betty decided to grab the opportunity to mine more information once the customers started arriving.

She stayed busy, keeping one eye on the door while topping up firewood, plugging the whistling gaps in the window frames with old rags, and even sweeping fresh sawdust across the floor.

"You'll need a lot more than that," said Granny. "Old Man Crosswick gets out of the pinch later today, so things are going to get pretty messy in here." Her smile faded. "I'll want you girls out of the way, with that leery lot coming in. You can all stay upstairs—Fliss, too. Though goodness knows, she's had enough time off this week."

Betty scattered more sawdust on the floor. Granny was right—they'd need it. The Crosswicks were always in and out of prison, and barely on the right side of what Granny described as hooligans. There would certainly be spitting and spillages, possibly even blood and teeth. More importantly, if Granny wanted the girls out of the way for the evening, Betty and Fliss would have time to plot. Or perhaps even more than plot . . .

Granny hefted a crate of mismatched bottles onto the counter, wheezing slightly. "Once you've done that, tell Charlie to sort these bottles into the right crates out back.

And make sure that spider she caught earlier has been put outside."

"Righty-ho," said Betty.

"You're being awfully helpful," Granny said suddenly, and her mouth went all shriveled up like a raisin. "You're up to something."

"I'm not!" Betty said indignantly, but she concentrated on the broom so she didn't have to look at Granny. Again, the feeling of being a burden weighed heavily upon her. Granny had done all she could to protect them, and had enough to worry about without Betty arousing her suspicions. The memory of her harsh words filled her with shame. "I'm sorry for what I said to you yesterday. About squashing the adventure out of us. I understand now."

"Ah." Granny's expression softened. "Yes, I know, poppet." She sighed. "We've all tried ways . . . to change things. But it's not meant to be. Sometimes you just have to accept your lot, and that's that." She turned away as the door opened, bringing in customers.

But I don't accept it, Betty thought. *I can't*. And whatever Granny said, her visits to Colton proved that deep down, she didn't accept it, either.

Betty finished sweeping and then lugged the crate of empties to the back door. The bottles clinked as she set them down in the cold air. To Betty's surprise, Charlie was already outside, sitting on an upturned crate with her back to the door. A bigger surprise was that Oi was sniffing at her in an interested, almost friendly way.

Charlie sprang up, stuffing something in her pocket as Betty approached. With that, the cat hissed and stalked off, slipping through the door just before it closed.

"What have you got there?" Betty asked.

"Nothin'," Charlie said defiantly, her pigtails bobbing.

Betty took one look at her sister's mischievous little face and knew she was up to something. "You've been acting strange since we came to get you earlier."

"So have you," Charlie said immediately. "You and Fliss, sneaking around whispering. I seen you."

"Don't change the subject!" Betty exclaimed, trying not to laugh. Evidently, she and Fliss had underestimated Charlie. "Come on. Out with it." She snapped her fingers, pointing at her sister's pocket, then blinked as it started to wriggle.

"Oh, Charlie. What have you gone and brought home this time?"

"You can't tell!" Charlie begged, her eyes huge and round. "Granny'll make me get rid of him!"

"Him?"

"Well, I think it's a him," Charlie said as a tiny, quivering nose edged its way out of her pocket. A pair of beetle-black eyes emerged, followed by a fuzzy brown body.

"Too right Granny'll make you get rid of it, it's a bleedin' rat! No wonder Oi wanted to be your friend, for once."

"You sure?" Charlie lifted the creature up, tickling its ears and stroking its wormy tail. "I thought it was a mouse."

"It's not much more than a baby," said Betty. "And you need to get rid of it before Granny finds out, or any of the customers, for that matter!"

"But look how sweet he is!"

"He might be now, but wait till he grows. Some of these rats on Crowstone end up the size of cats!"

"I know!" Charlie said excitedly.

Betty shook her head. "It's a wild animal. It wouldn't be fair to keep him."

"But he's hurt." Charlie lifted the rat, showing Betty his underside. "Look. It's his foot—there's something wrong with it. He walks funny, too, with a sort of hop. That's how I catched him."

Betty peered at the rat's feet. One of the back ones was no more than a toeless stump. Some of her hardness melted. "He must've been caught in a trap, poor thing."

"I've called him Hoppit," said Charlie. "Or is that mean? I don't want him to think I'm being unkind." She took out a bread roll she'd scrounged from the church and broke off a piece, feeding it to the rat. Betty raised an eyebrow. It was almost unknown for Charlie to save food —normally it was scarfed down immediately.

"I'm sure he won't mind what you call him, as long as he's getting fed," said Betty. Then, more gently, she said, "He's still got to go, Charlie. If Granny finds him . . ."

Charlie's bottom lip jutted out obstinately. "You won't tell, will you?"

"I won't need to. Granny will smell a . . . well, rat . . . *that* rat, sooner or later. So don't say you weren't warned." Betty nudged the crate of bottles with her toe, keen to get back inside. "These need to be sorted into the proper crates. Do it now before it gets dark."

She left Charlie sulking out in the yard and returned inside. A few more familiar faces had trickled in now, settling on tables close to the fire. Her gaze rested on the candy store owners, Henny and Buster Hubbard. In their spare time they were fonder of gambling than gossip, but they'd always lived in Crowstone and were friendly enough. Perhaps they knew of some clue in its history.

"Hello, young Betty," said Buster, emptying his

dominoes onto the table. "You playing? Hoping to rob us blind, are ye?"

Betty grinned. "Not today, Buster. Let's just play for fun." She helped turn the dominoes face-down on the table, before Henny dealt them out. "Actually, there was something I wanted to ask."

Buster nodded. "I'm listening."

"The prison tower," Betty said, trying to sound light and conversational, like she was simply looking for a story to pass the time. "Do you know much about it?"

"Let's see, now." Buster selected a domino and put it on the table face-up. "Before it was part of the prison, it was part of the old Crowstone Fortress, as you must know. That survived for, ooh . . . hundreds of years, and . . ." He paused. "Why are you asking us? Bunny's sure to know more than we do."

"Probably," Betty admitted. "But she doesn't like talking about the tower, the same as she won't go near the crossroads."

"Other than the tale of the girl who fell from the tower, there's not much to know," said Henny. "There's plenty that's been said, about her being a witch, but it was so long ago that only two things are certain: first, that she was locked in there against her will, and second, that she fell from the window to her death." She took out a tin of candy from the shop she and Buster owned and removed the lid, offering it to Betty.

Betty thanked her and rummaged through the tin, lingering over a jumping jackdaw before settling on a marsh-melt. Henny smiled and passed her the jumping jackdaw, too. Betty grinned, eating the jackdaw first. The popping candy crackled on her tongue.

"Why did people call her a witch?" she asked. There seemed to be plenty of ghost stories about the girl in the tower, but this was the first whiff of witchery that Betty had heard. She felt a tingle of fear mixed with excitement. Witches and curses went together like magpies and silver . . . Perhaps a piece of the puzzle was about to slot into place.

"It's said by some that the will-o'-the-wisps on the marshes are her doing," Buster said. Betty remembered the flickering marsh lights she had seen on the ferry, just before Granny had caught up with her and Charlie. She popped the marsh-melt into her mouth.

"Some suppose they're fragments of her memories, trapped on the marshland like she was in the tower. Others say they're curses, luring travelers to drown." Buster shrugged. "Me? I reckon they could be something as simple as marsh gasses letting off. But in a place like this, Betty, stories are never in short supply."

"Just as well," Betty said. "Seeing as there's not much else."

Buster chuckled. "You feel that way now, but you'll soon be old enough to go off on all those adventures you've been planning. You won't be stuck here forever."

A hard, achy lump formed in Betty's throat. She fussed with her dominoes, avoiding Buster's eyes. If only he knew . . .

"The tower itself is a mystery," Buster went on. "It should have collapsed when the rest of the ancient fortress was destroyed in the war, yet it survived. Something not right about that, if you ask me. But like I said, I'm not the best person to ask." Buster peered at his dominoes like a dragon hoarding its treasure. "But if you have more questions, there is someone else worth talking to."

"Who?"

Buster tilted his head. "Old Seamus Fingerty over there."

Betty groaned. Buster had indicated the thin, straggly-haired fellow who always looked as though he was plotting a murder.

"If anyone knows about that place, it'd be him," said Henny. "That's if you can get a civil word out of him."

"He was a prisoner, wasn't he?" Betty asked. There was no keeping that sort of thing quiet.

Buster nodded. "Did a long stretch, too. Because"—he lowered his voice—"before that, he was a warder. And no one likes a crooked warder."

"What was his crime?"

"Smuggling folk off Torment. They reckon he'd helped dozens escape before he was caught. I reckon that's the only reason he's not there himself now—too risky. Knows too much about escape routes."

Escape routes. The words sent a tremor through Betty as she thought of Colton. She watched Fingerty with renewed interest. Perhaps the old coot might be of use in more ways than one.

She thanked Buster and Henny, then abandoned her dominoes. Fliss was wiping down the counter.

"Where's Granny?" Betty asked as she drew level with her sister.

"Out in the office, making a start on the banking."

"Think she'll be back any time soon?"

Fliss shrugged. "She told me to call her if it gets busy. Why?"

Quickly, Betty recounted what she had learned about the tower and its mysterious prisoner. Fliss listened earnestly. "And Buster thinks he"—Betty nodded at Fingerty—"can tell us more."

Fliss looked doubtful. "Good luck with that. It's hard enough getting a 'please' or a 'thank you' out of him."

"That's where you come in," said Betty, giving her sister a meaningful look. "What's he drink?"

"Speckled Pig, usually. Port if he's especially grumpy. Why?"

"Give him his next two on the house."

"Betty!" Fliss protested. "Granny will be livid if she finds out I'm giving away free drinks, especially to a miserable old coot like him!"

"Then don't let her find out," said Betty. "If he knows anything, we need him."

Excitement crackled through her like the candy she had just eaten. Perhaps Fingerty could provide a valuable clue to breaking the curse. With luck, they might not even need Colton. *But he needs you*, her conscience whispered as she remembered his desperation. She ignored it. This was about the Widdershinses, not him.

Fliss pursed her lips, then filled a glass with frothy ale. "All right. But don't let anyone else hear or they'll all come scrounging."

"I'm going over," said Betty, taking the glass. "Warn me if you hear Granny coming. Ring the bell or something."

"I can't!" Fliss said, indignant. "Everyone would think it was time to leave!"

"Something else, then," Betty said, impatient. "Start singing. That old nursery rhyme: 'The Magpie and the Merrypennies.'" She pulled herself up to her full height, which, admittedly, wasn't very impressive. Then she walked over to Fingerty's table. She had never been this close to him before, and found that he smelled rather stale, like unwashed socks. His gray hair was long and straggly, draped like curtains on either side of his leathery face.

"Excuse me?" she said, when he continued to stare out the window. "Mr. Fingerty?"

For a moment he gazed ahead silently as though he hadn't heard. Betty's excitement fizzled out a little. Perhaps she should have sent Fliss over instead. A salty old grouch like Fingerty would need sweetening up, and Betty wasn't sure she had the charm or patience. He lifted his beer, sipping slowly, then banged it down on the table, startling her.

"Huh!" The sound was half chuckle, half snarl. "Long time since anyone's called me Mister."

"Oh," said Betty. "What shall I call you, then?"

Fingerty turned to look at her. He had dark eyes like gray shards of flint. The way they raked over her made her feel as though she were a pile of soggy leaves being poked with a stick, unearthing all the bugs and beetles hidden underneath. She gritted her teeth and stood her ground. If persevering with Fingerty meant she might avoid breaking Colton out of jail, then persevere she would.

"You're blunt, for one so young," he remarked.

Betty shrugged.

"Well, so am I," he said. "And my feeling is that yer want something. So yer can save your niceties and clear off."

"What?" Betty said in surprise. "I haven't even told you what I want!" The thought of having to help Colton escape nudged a little closer to becoming a reality, deepening her desperation. If Fingerty didn't talk, she had few options left.

Fingerty's mouth twisted unpleasantly. "I don't do favors for no one."

"What if there's something in it for you?"

Fingerty drained his beer, then drew his cuff across his wet upper lip. "Go on, then. What?"

Emboldened, Betty took a seat opposite and pushed the fresh pint of Speckled Pig toward him. "Two drinks on the house in exchange for a little chat."

"Huh," he said again, less nastily this time. "Sitting with a known felon? Won't do yerself no favors."

"My dad's a felon. I'm used to it."

He chuckled. "What d'yer want, then?"

"I want to hear what you know about Crowstone Tower."

Fingerty frowned deeply, carving lines into his already-wrinkled forehead. "The prison tower? Common knowledge, most of it."

"I know some of it," Betty said. "That it was part of the old fortress, and that they held a witch there, Sorsha Spellthorn. It's anything else you might know that I'm interested in."

Fingerty raked her over again with his eyes. "Why yer asking?"

Betty returned his gaze as boldly as she dared. "If I tell you that, then it'll have to be one drink, not two."

"Fair enough." Fingerty scratched his bristly chin with a too-long fingernail. "Sorsha Spellthorn. Some called her a witch, but a better word would be 'sorceress.'"

Something jolted through Betty's bones. "Sorceress." It sounded grander than "witch," and certainly indicated someone capable of a curse. Anything Fingerty knew about how—and why—might lead her to the breaking of it.

"See, rumors of witchcraft tend to be small," Fingerty continued. "Petty. Lotions for warts, potions for love or revenge. But Sorsha, she was different, or so I heard."

"Is that what got her locked up?"

"Depends who yer listen to. See, some say she was using her sorcery to make trouble. Others . . . well, they think she was imprisoned under false charges." He stared into the fire, and his sullen expression softened to something that became almost haunted. "And yer talking about something that happened a long time ago: well over a century. Think folks are superstitious now? It's nothing compared to back then."

"What do you think?" Betty asked.

"Don't matter what I think." Fingerty huffed out a long breath, his cheeks puffing out like a stuffed goose. "But I'll tell yer what I know, or at least what I've pieced together, if yer can stop interrupting for one pecking minute. I'm the one telling this story, and I'll tell it my way. And the best way is to start at the beginning, got it?"

Betty nodded, not daring to say any more.

"No one knew where she came from," said Fingerty, settling back in his chair. "Which is strange, considering that almost everyone knows where she ended up." He sipped his beer. "Sorsha Spellthorn was born on the Misty Marshes on a stormy winter night, in a little rowboat. There's no official record of her birth, but it's believed it was midwinter. The shortest day, the longest night. For three people, it was their last night."

A chill breeze blew around Betty's ankles as someone entered the Poacher's Pocket. She leaned closer to the fire.

"It appeared on the marshes out of nowhere," Fingerty went on. "The little boat, savaged by the storm and washed onto the mudflats, broken and leaking water. It got stuck, began sinking. Torment was the closest, but the boat was still far out, and the weather too wild to risk. When the islanders on Torment looked through their spyglasses, they saw a woman stranded.

"Three people took a boat out to save her: two men and a woman. Little is known about them, except that they happened to be a spy and two smugglers. When they reached the woman, they discovered that she had just given birth to a tiny baby girl. Somehow, they got them both into the boat with them, just moments before the damaged vessel was sucked into the marshes. Then came the grueling journey back to Torment. Along the way, one of the smugglers and the spy were lost to the marshes, and the next morning, after bringing mother and child safely back to land, the other smuggler died, too, his lungs having taken on too much water during the rescue." Fingerty paused, shaking his head. Betty took a breath, feeling a sting of tears pricking her eyelids, partly for the tale she was hearing and partly because somehow, she couldn't help think of the drowning of her own mother.

"They lived their lives on Torment in disgrace," she mumbled tearfully. "And yet they gave their lives to save two strangers."

"Yerp. And that's not all they gave. When people die like that—sacrificing themselves—the baby . . ." Fingerty glowered into his beer. "Even now, they're known simply by their crimes. Not by name . . . but for their mistakes. No one is wholly good, or wholly bad. Sometimes the best people are capable of doing the worst things, and the worst people can be capable of doing the best. The most honorable, and heroic. Despite whatever they've done in the past."

"The baby," Betty asked. "That was Sorsha?"

Fingerty nodded. "They stayed on Torment, out of gratitude for their lives. Sorsha grew, from a baby to a girl to a young woman. And people began to notice things about her, see? Odd things that made no sense."

"Like what?" Betty asked, sensing that Fingerty's pause, this time, invited an interruption.

He nodded at his glass. Somehow it had been drained without her noticing. She snatched it and hurried to the counter, tapping impatiently as she waited for Fliss to finish serving someone else. In her rush to get to Betty, Fliss slopped beer all over the side of the glass she was carrying and practically threw the customer's change at them.

Betty watched as the young man Fliss had served scrabbled to collect the coins rolling over the counter. "You're lucky Granny didn't see you do that. And that he's sweet on you."

Fliss waved a dismissive hand. Apparently, she'd forgotten that not so long ago she'd been sweet on him, too. Typical Fliss the Flit, thought Betty.

"What's Fingerty have to say?" Fliss asked.

"I'm still finding out. He knows things, about that girl in the tower," Betty said, experiencing a surge of adrenaline at what she was about to hear. She hoped she'd be able to carry the drink back without spilling it. "And he's not finished yet. Hurry up!"

Fliss held a fresh glass under the Speckled Pig and heaved at the pump. Frothy beer gushed out. "Is he as awful as folk say?"

"Yes and no," Betty answered. "He's a rotten old stick, but he took less coaxing than I expected." She said this with a measure of pride, glad that she, too, could be persuasive . . . even if it boiled down to bribery rather than charm.

Fliss set the full glass on the counter. "Maybe all he needs is a bit of kindness. Perhaps he's glad of someone listening to him, for once."

Betty snorted. "Or maybe you're drunk on beer

fumes. Soon as the free drinks dry up, so will the stories. Just you watch."

Betty returned to Fingerty's table, putting the beer in front of him. She sat down, aware that Fliss was lurking close by to eavesdrop. Fingerty took a slow mouthful of beer, leaving a creamy mustache of froth on his upper lip.

"Right," he said, settling back once more. "Now, listen." And so began the story of Sorsha Spellthorn.

Sorsha's Tale

SPLAT! THE EGG WHIZZED PAST Sorsha and hit Prue right in her middle. Somehow, it bounced off her and cracked as it landed on her feet, splattering the slimy white and golden yolk all over her shoes.

"Hey!" Sorsha yelled in fury, but the culprits had already dodged away into an alley at the back of the marketplace, their laughter ringing in the air. Sorsha considered chasing them, but her little sister's sobs kept her where she was.

"It's all right, Prue," she muttered, kneeling at her sister's feet with her handkerchief. She wiped the mess away as best she could, shaking fragments of white shell onto the dusty road. She sensed people were staring, but in the busy marketplace they didn't linger. Sorsha was used to stares. "There. Most of it's off. Did you see who it was?"

Prue hesitated. "The pig-keeper's lad, and a few others. They were shouting things, about us . . . about Ma." She sniffled, blinking away more tears.

"Don't cry," Sorsha said, more gently now. "I'll bet they weren't even aiming at you. They probably meant it for me."

Instantly, Prue stopped crying, looking brighter, and Sorsha was the one feeling unsettled, though she couldn't quite explain why.

"What were they saying?" Sorsha asked, even though she could already guess.

"They said we weren't proper sisters. That you and Ma are witches that came in off the marshes. That you sacrificed people with your bad magic so that you both survived. And that she witched my pa, and then—"

"Hush," Sorsha said softly, aware that Prue's shrill voice was attracting curious glances.

Prue stared at her, her strange eyes unblinking. They didn't look a bit alike. While Sorsha had their mother's looks—tawny hair and green eyes—Prudence mirrored the pale-skinned, mud-brown-haired islanders. And her eyes . . . they were so unusually pale it was hard to say whether they were gray, green, blue, or had any color at all. A word often used to describe them was "fishy," and although Sorsha felt it was unkind, she couldn't help but privately agree.

Sorsha sighed, collecting the basket and tucking the soggy handkerchief into her pinny. "Come on." She took Prue's hand and tugged her away from the marketplace in the direction of home. When she tried to release Prue's smaller, clammy hand a few minutes later, Prue held on stubbornly. At eight, she was only two years younger than Sorsha, but at times the age gap felt larger.

"We are sisters," Sorsha said, once they were in the quiet lanes. "Doesn't matter what anyone else says."

They fell into silence, walking briskly. Finally Prue released Sorsha's hand to wrap her shawl more tightly around herself. It was a chilly spring morning, and on the surrounding meadows patches of frost still sparkled. Cottages were dotted like breadcrumbs along the road. Their own was farther away than all the rest, an outsider just as they were. As the meadow opened out, a brisk wind blew up, reminding them that the cliff top was not far away.

"I wonder what it's like over there," Prue said, as she always did, nodding to the hazy land across the water.

"Better," Sorsha replied. Sometimes when they went walking with Ma, they'd gaze across to mainland Crowstone from a high point on the cliffs. On a clear day you could see the rooftops and church spire, and the little boats on the water. "People are free to come and go as they please. Not like here."

"My father's family is over there," Prue said, with a degree of pride. "Ma said so."

"Could well be true," Sorsha replied. "But you've never met them, and you probably never will."

Prue's chin jutted obstinately. "Sometimes people can get there."

"Sometimes, yes."

Ma had heard that in the past, people on Torment had "earned" their way across to mainland Crowstone with some good deed for the better of all. But in the ten years Sorsha had been on the island, the only ones who had left were those in boxes sailing over to their final resting places on Lament.

Their mother never spoke about Sorsha's father, or where they had come from before they'd arrived on Torment. Prue's father hadn't been around for long, either. Newly released from the prison and banished to Torment, he had been besotted with Sorsha's mother from the moment he arrived, despite warnings from other islanders. Sorsha had a hazy memory of bright blue eyes and a weathered face, but Prue did not recall her father at all. She had been just a year old when he'd gone fishing out by Lament and never returned after his boat was swept onto the treacherous rocks known as the Devil's Teeth.

The gossip hinted that this was their mother's witchcraft, too. But as the years had passed, the focus shifted to Sorsha — and things about her that couldn't be explained.

She hadn't realized she was different, at first. How was she to know that other children couldn't hide as well as she could? Or weren't able to see a person just by thinking about them? Or the . . . other thing, that couldn't be put down to slyness or imagination. Before she knew it, she was the one the villagers tugged their own children away from. The one no one wanted to play with.

Over time she grew skilled at hiding these gifts, but not before they had been noticed . . . and suspicion lurked in every pointed finger.

Lost in her thoughts, Sorsha's first clue that she had foolishly let her guard down was a clod of half-frozen earth that flew out of the meadow and skipped along the path. She gasped, grabbing Prue and ducking next to the hedgerow. The catcall followed moments later.

"Hide-and-seek!"

It wasn't a friendly request for a game, but a taunt. A jeer. A dare.

Come find us.

"Keep down," she told Prue. Slowly, she stood, gazing across the frosty meadows. The long grasses rippled in the wind, giving nothing away. She jumped as another lump of dirt cracked against the path. This time there was a large stone at its center.

Her skin prickled with fear, like a dog's hackles rising. She didn't know how many there were or where they were hidden, but she and Prue were alone out here. The nearest cottage was a way off, and knocking wouldn't guarantee help. Not for them, anyway.

"Sorsha?" Prue whispered. "Where are they?"

Sorsha ducked down again. "I don't know."

"Let's just go. If we hurry—"

"It's a long way. I'd be able to . . . outrun them but you won't. I need to do something."

Prue's pale eyes were fearful. "Ma said ignore them."

"Ignoring them doesn't work. It just makes them try harder." Another stone hit the path. This time there was no doubt. The stone wasn't a mistake, caught in a dense lump of dirt. It was large and rough, meant to do harm.

She had promised Ma she wouldn't, but Sorsha knew

now it was an eggshell promise, shattered by their missiles. She needed to stay safe. There was also a tiny part of her that wanted to teach them a lesson.

"Keep quiet and still," she told Prue.

"Sorsha," Prue began, but Sorsha squeezed her arm with a warning look and Prue quieted.

Sorsha closed her eyes, letting her mind roam. Already she could feel it crackling: a power ready to surge. Oh, but it felt good to use it again! Especially after suppressing it for so long. *Let me see them*, she commanded silently. And, like someone in a dream, she found that her mind's eye was looking down, as if she were a bird hovering above the field and searching out field mice. Quickly she spotted them, spread out in the high grass. There were two of them on either side of the path, and her and Prue on the path in the middle. They were surrounded.

Sorsha's face grew warm with rage. She wanted to give them something to really wonder about. Looking closer at each boy, she located Samuel, the pig-keeper's son. An oily-looking thing with a nose like a lump of squashed clay, he was the biggest and meanest of the group. There was a moment's hesitation—it had been so long since she had done this, but if anything, the unused power seemed to have strengthened rather than faded.

Her mind sharpened and flexed. Instantly, there came the sensation of weightlessness, of the ground slipping from under her feet and the whoosh of wind whistling in her ears. Adrenaline surged through her in a giddy, thrilling wave.

Her arrival at Samuel's back was announced with a rustle of brittle grasses. He whipped around, open-mouthed.

"H-how did you . . . ?"

He struggled for words, crippled by fear. His eyebrows curled into question marks. They both knew there was no way she could have sneaked up so soundlessly. Until now, he hadn't really believed the stories about her. They had just been an excuse to pick on someone, anyone. The easiest target.

"Found you," she said softly. Soft, but not like a baby dove or butter. Soft like a kitten's paw . . . just before its claws shot out.

This is a warning, pig-boy.

"My turn," she said, backing into the long grass, just far enough to hide herself.

Once again the ground whipped away from under her. She arrived back at her sister's side with nothing more than a light scratch of gravel under her heels.

Prue's eyes held the same awe Sorsha had seen in the

pig-boy's, but none of the fear. "You can still do it," she whispered. "I knew you could."

"It never went away. I just stopped doing it."

"Teach me," Prue begged, fingers clutching at her greedily.

"I've told you before, it's not something that can be taught," Sorsha said. "Even if it was, this wouldn't be the time!"

"What did you do?" Prue whispered.

"I gave the pig-keeper's son a scare he won't forget."

"Oh, Sorsha, Ma will be so angry!"

"Hush. I didn't do anything he can prove—just enough to rattle him."

They quieted, stepping back into a dip in the hedgerow as the pig-boy emerged from the meadow farther up the lane. Pale-faced, he gave a low whistle before stalking back toward the village, casting nervous looks behind him. One by one his friends scrambled out of the long grass after him. Mutters of "witch" and "fish eyes" floated back on the air.

When the boys were finally gone, Sorsha turned to Prue. Her sister's strange, light eyes were curiously bright. *Fish eyes.* The cruel comment echoed in Sorsha's head.

"What if they tell?" Prue said as they began walking the opposite way.

"Let them," said Sorsha. She glanced at her sister, afraid she had scared her, but if anything, her pinched white face looked thrilled.

"But people will talk."

"They've always talked. Maybe next time they might just leave us alone."

A shadow flickered in Prue's bleached eyes. "I wish I could do the things you can do."

"Probably best you can't." Sorsha sighed, starting to regret her hot-headed reaction now that her blood had begun to cool. "It only leads to trouble."

Hide-and-seek . . .

"Trouble," Prue echoed. "But you've never used your magic for—"

"Don't!" Sorsha hissed, looking about them fearfully. "Never say that word. You don't know who might be listening!"

"But you've never used it for bad things," Prue persisted.

Sorsha frowned. "Of course not. I've hardly used it at all, but if I could, I'd want to help people, not hurt them."

"Not even if they made you really, really angry?" Prue

breathed, her eyes wide and fixed on Sorsha's face. They glinted with excitement and longing.

"Perhaps," Sorsha admitted, to herself as much as to Prue. Her voice dropped to a barely audible whisper. "I've never thought about it before. No one's ever made me angry enough."

Prue looked up at her, slipping her hand into Sorsha's again.

She was smiling.

Chapter Twelve

The Traveling Bag

"The me-rry-pen-nies in the mea-dow, silver by
the niiiiiiight,
Were hopped upon by mid-night imps who
danced by pale moon-liiiiight!"

T HE SOUND OF FLISS'S SELF-CONSCIOUS
warbling snapped Betty out of Fingerty's story and
into the present. She stared at the leathery-faced man,
wishing she could stay immersed in his tale, but the
tuneless singing grew louder and more urgent, which
could only mean Granny was near.

"The mag-pie, oh that craf-ty crook, stole some
  to stuff his neeeest,
But dropped them in Ma's cook-ing soup, I needn't
  say the reeeeest!"

Betty stood up abruptly as Fingerty drained his glass. "I'm sorry," she said. "I have to get back to work."

"I was jest getting started," Fingerty said, outraged.

"I know." Betty was unable to keep the frustration from her voice. Clearly, Fingerty had merely scratched the surface of this dark chapter of Crowstone Tower. While it wasn't enough to confirm whether Sorsha's history was connected to the Widdershinses, the tower's link to the curse made it entirely possible. More than that, she felt she was on the verge of learning something crucial, although perhaps this was just wishful thinking. Either way, she had to hear the rest of the story. The question was, when?

Fingerty looked tipsy now and seemed to have one quizzical eye on Betty and the other on Fliss. He stuck one finger in his ear, grimacing. "This what Bunny calls entertainment?"

"Bang-bang! went the privy door! Bang-bang!
  for two days!

And cackle-cackle went the jackdaws at the
magpie's naughty ways!"

"Er . . ." Betty spied Granny behind the counter, just
as Fliss's rendition reached its earsplitting finale. There
was silence, then a few awkward claps before conversations resumed in their usual low hum. Betty made a pretense of wiping the table and collected the empty glass.
"Thanks," she told Fingerty, keeping her voice low. "Can I
talk to you again sometime?"

Fingerty squinted at her, evidently smarting at being
cut short. "Lips sealed tight unless the price is right."

Betty glanced at Granny, who was busy telling a red-
faced Fliss that her singing sounded like a cat being strangled. "Yes, of course. You'll get more drinks on the house."

She took the empty glass to the bar, Fingerty's tale
squirming in her mind like a nest of ants. She desperately
wanted to tell Fliss what she had learned about the girl in
the tower, but Granny was too close. She stood stoutly
behind Fliss, eyes narrowed.

"Where's Charlie?"

"Still in the yard, I think," said Betty. "Sorting the
bottles, like you said."

"She's taking her time," said Granny, looking suspicious. "I hope she's not burying more dead creatures.

There'll be more graves out there than there are on Lament at this rate!" She turned swiftly, heading for the back door.

"Great idea about the singing," Fliss said sarcastically, glowering with humiliation. "Next time I'll just break a glass to get your attention!"

"Your singing could do that anyway," Betty said, only half aware of Fliss's huff of indignation. She eyed Fingerty, wishing she could see into that gnarled head of his. There was no time to continue Sorsha's tale now, and little time to make a decision about breaking Colton out—not if there was a risk he could be moved. And if Fingerty didn't have the answers, they needed Colton. Yet perhaps Fingerty could help with that, too . . .

With Granny gone for another minute or two in search of Charlie, Betty decided to risk it.

"What now?" Fingerty said, scowling as she returned.

"One more thing," Betty said hurriedly. "I heard that you were . . . um, inside for helping folks escape from Torment."

"Oh, yer did, did yer?"

She ignored the meanness in his voice and rushed on. "I was wondering how . . . how you got away with it."

"Fact I got caught suggests I wasn't very good at it," he sneered. "No one gets away with it forever."

"I meant the ones before. I've heard there were lots, before you got caught—"

Fingerty's hand shot out and grabbed her wrist. "Now, yer listen, girly," he hissed. "I don't know what yer mixed up in and I don't care, but take my advice: Yer stay away from the Sorrow Isles. Ain't nothing but bad luck."

Betty twisted out of his grasp. "If you can't tell me how you did it, then tell me how you got caught."

He shook his head, chuckling suddenly. "Yer stubborn as they come, girl."

"And you're as mean as everyone says," Betty retorted, rubbing her wrist. She glanced at the counter. Fliss was pulling ale but watching nervously. There was still no sign of Granny.

"Meaner," Fingerty snapped. "But you've got guts, and I like that. All right, that I'll tell yer. Distraction. That's how. It was the one rule I always followed, and it always worked. Until the time I was careless."

"What kind of distraction?"

"Anything. A brawl in the prison, the ferry stuck on the marshes. Yer divert attention from what's really going on." He gave a cunning smile. "Folks have no love for the warders. They'll do anything if the price is right." The smile slid off his face as he settled back in his chair. "Now go away and leave me in peace. I've said enough for one day."

"Until next time, then," Betty said.

"Can't wait," Fingerty muttered sarcastically.

She returned to the counter just as Granny came back in from the yard, shooing Charlie upstairs into the warm.

"Well?" Fliss asked.

Betty went to sit on a barstool, then yelped and jumped away as five pinpricks pierced her bottom. She glared down into lazily blinking yellow eyes and realized she had almost sat on Oi. She remained standing, speaking quickly of what Fingerty had told her; about Sorsha and her half sister, Prue, living on Torment and the strange abilities of Sorsha's that marked her as different.

"But how does any of this link to the Widdershinses?" Fliss asked, eyeing Fingerty doubtfully.

"I don't know for sure, but somehow, all this is connected—I can just feel it. Sorsha ended up in that tower, which is where Colton says the curse began, too. And let's not forget she fell from it . . . just like the stones. Fliss, I really think he might have the answer we need."

"But what about Fingerty?" Fliss whispered. "If you think what he knows is connected, he's the safer option, where we're not risking our necks!"

"We need time to get to what he knows, time Colton might not have! And Colton seems convinced he knows how to break the curse."

Fliss's bottom lip wobbled. "And if he doesn't?"

Betty let out a shaky breath. "Then I guess we spend our days staring at these walls and stinking of beer."

"Maybe stinking of beer isn't so bad." Fliss sniffed herself and sighed. "Or maybe it is. So . . . how? And when?" She gulped. "Oh, cripes. We're really doing this, aren't we?"

"Fingerty said when he smuggled people off Torment he always used a distraction. That's what we need," said Betty. "So we won't be missed."

"What kind of distraction?"

"A rowdy night here, one where Granny wants us safely out the way, would be ideal."

"You mean . . . something like Old Man Crosswick's release?" Fliss said uneasily.

"Yes."

"But that's tonight!"

Betty nodded, anticipation thrumming in her chest like a second heart.

"I know. But if more prisoners are being moved soon, like that warder said, then we've no time to lose."

"What are you two whispering about?"

Betty jumped. Granny had appeared soundlessly at the door to the bar, her shrewd eyes upon them. The girls sprang apart guiltily.

"Nothing," they chorused.

"Hmm." Granny stamped over to them, lowering her voice. "I think I can guess."

Betty stiffened—surely Granny couldn't have heard much over the hum of conversations around them.

"As much as I'm sad that you both now have the burden of you-know-what on your shoulders, at least some good has come of it," Granny said, smiling wistfully. "The two of you huddled together and whispering, just like you used to," she continued. "I haven't seen that in a long time." There was a forced cheer in her voice, a looking-on-the-bright-side tone, and Betty thought she knew why. Speaking about the curse might have brought Fliss and Betty together again, but it was the reason for the distance between them in the first place.

"Now then," said Granny. "Betty, you can get the dinner on upstairs, and watch Charlie while you're up there." She glared at Oi, who was loitering on the counter, sniffing drops of spilled beer. "Fliss, feed that mangy cat before it starts eating the customers."

Betty glanced back as she headed for the stairs. Fliss caught her eye and the two shared a conspiratorial look that, despite the circumstances, sent a thrilling tingle through Betty. The Widdershins sisters had business to attend to.

It wasn't until later that they got their chance. Betty was scouring a stubborn pan when Granny emerged from the bathroom with a freshly scrubbed Charlie.

"Keep still, child!" Granny was saying. "I need to comb out that birds' nest of a head of yours before it dries!"

Fliss looked up from the sock she was mending. "Oh, Charlie, you look so sweet under all that dirt. Like a little pink piglet!"

Charlie stuck her tongue out as Granny chased her into the bedroom, brandishing a comb.

"My turn!" Fliss declared, throwing down the sock. Betty groaned. Bath day was only once a week, but Fliss took forever, and always left bits of dried lavender and rose petals stuck to the tub. She'd been hoping Fliss would wait until later to get her bath, for it would have been a chance for the two of them to plan while Granny was busy with Charlie, but evidently Fliss had other ideas.

Betty looked up to the shelf above the sink for some

salt to help her scrub, then jumped back with a scream, dropping the pan at her feet with a loud clang.

There, hovering in midair over the sink like an apparition, was a hazy, shimmering image of Fliss's face. "Boo!" it said.

Betty gaped, her heart smashing against her ribcage. Could this be something to do with . . . ?

"Betty?" Granny called. "What's all that racket?"

A finger appeared in front of Fliss's wavering face. "Shh! Don't tell Granny—I'm using the mirror!"

"Betty?"

"Er . . . everything's fine, Granny," Betty called. "Just me being clumsy!" She peered at the image of Fliss, suspended ghostlike before her. Now that she had recovered from the surprise, she could see soapsuds in her sister's hair. "You really do look strange, you know, floating there like that. How did you make it work?"

"I just looked into the mirror and thought of you," said Fliss. There was a sense of jubilation about her, the same way Betty had felt when she had used the nesting dolls. "And there you were, reflected back at me."

"Is this the first time you've used it?"

Fliss looked slightly guilty. "It's the first time I've used it to speak to anyone, but I've . . . I've watched people a few times, without them knowing."

"Felicity Widdershins!" Betty exclaimed, pretending to be shocked. "Like who? Let me guess . . . Jack Humble?"

"No!" Fliss blustered. "Well, once." Annoyance crossed her face. "He was sweet-talking that awful Fay, you know the one who works in the fishmonger's?" She pursed her lips. "So that's the end of that." She paused. "I thought about using it to see Father, but I've never quite managed to go through with it."

"Not even now that you know he's not in Crowstone?"

"Especially now." Fliss bit her lip. "If he's somewhere worse, I wouldn't want to see."

Betty thought of the leech emblem on Father's letters. It was hard to imagine prisons worse than Crowstone. Her thoughts returned to Colton. "As soon as Granny's busy with the Crosswicks, we get that bag."

In the pause that followed she realized she could no longer hear Bunny's voice. "Darn it, I think Granny's finished with Charlie. You'd better put that mirror down in case she comes in here and sees what we're up to."

"To be continued," said Fliss in a spooky voice, then, "Oh, bother. I've been in here so long I'm wrinkling up like a raisin."

The apparition-like image of Fliss's face vanished, and

Betty was left with the far less exciting sight of the blackened tin she was still scrubbing.

After Betty had bathed and washed her hair, which dried to a spectacular frizz, Granny settled Charlie to sleep and returned downstairs. At once, Betty and Fliss sprang into action.

"My room, quickly," said Fliss.

Fliss's room was smaller than the one Betty and Charlie shared, and far tidier, which was just as well, due to the fussy trinkets, homemade rose-water scent, and love notes everywhere.

"Got the bag yet?" Betty asked.

Fliss shook her head. "Still need to find it. But I thought it'd be sensible to look in on Colton before . . . before we do this."

Betty nodded. "You're right. There's no point in us arriving in his cell if the warders are patrolling; we need to know our timing's right."

Fliss took the mermaid mirror from her dressing table.

Leaning over it, she whispered, "Let me see Colton."

At once a hazy mist clouded the mirror's surface. Betty leaned closer, wide-eyed and feeling slightly guilty, like she was listening at a door. The glass cleared, revealing a tiny, darkened cell with an iron-barred door. A hunched figure lay shivering on a thin mattress. His teeth were chattering and his eyes were closed, lips moving in what Betty could only guess was a silent prayer. Thin lines had been scratched into the wall next to him: all the days he had spent there. Betty looked away. It was easy to see why Colton was desperate to get out.

So desperate he'd say anything to escape? Uncomfortable, Betty kept the doubt unspoken. She was desperate, too, she reminded herself. The stakes for her and her family were just the same: freedom, and a new life without this curse they didn't deserve.

Silently, Fliss turned the mirror face-down, breaking the vision. "I can't help feeling sorry for him."

"Me either," Betty admitted. She let out a slow breath. "He's alone. Let's go now."

"Keep a lookout," said Fliss. "I'll search Granny's things."

They left Fliss's room. Betty stood in her own doorway, shifting from one foot to the other in a nervous dance. Her eyes were on Charlie curled up asleep, her ears concentrating on the stairs and any sign of Granny. By now the Crosswick gathering was in full swing. Someone had struck up a fiddle, and a drunken chorus was being brayed. The building rattled and thrummed, as though humming along.

Earlier, after Charlie had gone to sleep, Betty had stuffed rolled-up blankets under Fliss's bedcovers and her own to make shapes like two sleeping figures. At a quick glance they were convincing enough, and Granny's eyesight was poor anyway. Tucked under Betty's blankets was a note for the morning, when it would become evident that the two girls were gone, though Betty planned to be back way before then.

Granny, it said, *we're sorry. We've taken your bag and gone to break the curse. We'll be back as soon as we can. Please don't come looking for us, and please don't be too angry. Betty & Fliss.*

Would Charlie be the one to find it, or would it be Granny, wondering why her two eldest granddaughters couldn't be roused the following morning? Betty hugged herself guiltily and gazed past Charlie to the window. Through the gappy curtains the sky was navy blue, dotted with bright stars. There would likely be a frost later; already the air was chilly. She thought of the prison, and of Colton in darkness and silence. It was probably best that he didn't know when to expect them.

A muffled squeal sent her abandoning her post and skidding into Granny's room.

"What's the matter?"

"Found it." Fliss was on her hands and knees, scuttling backwards. "It's under the bed, but there's a huge . . ." She trailed off, and gazed past Betty with a shocked, sheepish look on her face.

Betty whirled around. Charlie blinked at them sleepily, barefoot and rubbing her eyes.

"What you doing?"

"N-nothing," Fliss stammered. "Just putting some things of Granny's away. Come on now, poppet. Back to bed."

"You're not putting nothing away," Charlie said stubbornly. She regarded each of them with suspicion, wide awake now. "You're looking for the bag."

Betty and Fliss exchanged glances, unsure what to say.

"I could've told you where it was." Charlie kneeled and crawled under the bed, then emerged with the bag and a thick cobweb stuck to her arm. "This what you were scared of?" she asked, flicking the web away scornfully.

Fliss pursed her lips. "Give it here."

Charlie shrugged and tossed it at her feet. "What do you want it for?"

Betty sighed. "Look, we need to go somewhere. There's something important we have to do, and—"

"Are you going to the prison again?"

Betty and Fliss shared stricken glances. Charlie might only be six, but she was sharp.

"I'm coming, too," Charlie announced. "I can keep a secret."

Betty shook her head. The memory of being trapped on the ferry in swirling mist, and how foolish she'd been to put Charlie in that situation, was all too fresh. "Oh, no, you're not. It's dangerous."

"Then you need me!" Charlie said fiercely. "I can help! I'm not scared of anything." She made a face at Fliss. "Even spiders!"

There was a long silence; then finally Betty nodded. "Go and get dressed."

Fliss stared at her incredulously as Charlie skipped past her in a tangle of hair and bare limbs.

"You can't be serious!"

Betty shook her head, picking up the bag. "I'm not," she whispered as the wardrobe in the next room creaked. "Quick, grab our coats."

Fliss vanished, returning seconds later with thick overcoats. They shrugged into them, breathing fast. Fliss wound a thin scarf around the mermaid mirror and tucked it in her coat pocket. "Got everything? The nesting dolls? Keys?"

Betty nodded, linking arms with Fliss at the exact

moment Charlie came hurtling down the hall. She stopped in the doorway, open-mouthed.

Betty's skin crawled with shame. "I'm sorry, Charlie."

"No!" Charlie roared. "You can't!"

Betty flipped the bag inside out. "Prisoner five-one-three!"

She closed her eyes, bracing herself for the sickening whoosh . . . but it never came.

"Er, Betty?" Fliss said doubtfully.

Betty opened her eyes. Charlie was staring at them with an injured expression. She stomped up to Betty.

"You said I could come. If you don't let me, I'll shout for Granny!"

"You won't!" Betty retorted. She was cross now, both at being discovered and at the bag's failure to work. "I'll lock you in the creepy cupboard if I have to!"

"Beast!" Charlie's mouth dropped open in horror. "You always leave me out!"

Betty sighed, regretting her threat already. "Charlie, we just can't take you." She stared at the bag, its musty old lining hanging inside out. "Anyway, I don't think we can even use it without Granny— Hey!"

Charlie had snatched the bag and, quick as a fox, plunged the lining back in, then out again. "My room!" she shouted.

Air sucked past Betty's ankles. In the next eye blink, Charlie vanished and a gleeful giggle rang out from the girls' bedroom. Betty stepped toward the door, but there was another whoosh and Charlie reappeared, grinning.

"See? I can do it!"

"And we can't," Betty said slowly as Granny's explanation came back to her. An item couldn't be swapped, because it simply wouldn't work unless it was the one you owned.

Charlie danced a jubilant jig. "Ain't your bag, so it won't work for you."

"Ain't yours, either!" Betty snapped. "I mean, isn't!"

"Yet," Charlie said smugly.

Betty glanced at Fliss. Her older sister stared back helplessly.

"What'll we do? We can't take her with us!"

"Can, can, can!" sang Charlie, twirling around with the bag.

"Our whole plan depends on that bag," Betty said desperately. "Besides Granny, Charlie's the only one who can work it." She took a deep breath, thinking. "We have to take her."

"No!" Fliss whispered. "We really, really can't . . ."

"Looks like you really, really have to," said Charlie.

"Only until we get Colton out," Betty said. "The bag is fast. We'll get him to Lament, find out what he knows, then come back here in the shake of a feather. After that he's on his own."

Charlie stopped twirling. "Who's Colton?"

"Someone who can help us break the curse," Betty told her.

"Let's wait," Fliss begged. "Think of another plan, the dolls—"

"No," Betty argued. "Not now that Charlie knows. She could blab to Granny."

"Yep," Charlie agreed. "Sometimes things just pop out!" Downstairs, there was a surge of voices.

"Let's go while it's rowdy. If it goes to plan, we could be back before closing time."

"And if it doesn't?" Fliss snapped. "What then?"

Betty didn't know what then, but she tried to sound brave by saying, "We've got the bag, the dolls, and the mirror. We'd have to be pretty unlucky for things to go wrong."

"Because the Widdershinses are known for our luck," Fliss muttered.

Betty bundled Charlie's coat on. "Charlie, listen. This is going to be a real adventure. Not one of our silly pretending games. So I need you to do as we say. And if

162

we tell you to come back, you must come straight back. Promise?"

Charlie nodded vigorously, ready to agree to just about anything.

Betty swallowed down a hard lump in her throat. Everything would be all right. They would be the ones to break the wretched Widdershins curse. This would be worth it; it had to be. "Victory favors the valiant," she whispered, trying to draw strength from another of her invented mottos. Hopefully this one would stick.

"Ready?" she asked, more nervous than she had ever been. Another enthusiastic nod came from Charlie. Fliss twitched like a hunted bunny. Betty stood in the middle, one arm through Fliss's and the other firmly linked with Charlie's. "Take us to Crowstone Prison, Prisoner five-one-three," she instructed, as another swell of noise rose from downstairs.

Charlie nodded, eager to please. She cleared her throat and spoke in a firm voice: "Crowstone Prison, prisoner five-three-one!"

In the time it took for Betty to shout "No!" Charlie had whipped the bag inside out. All Betty could feel was her hair flying past her ears and her insides churning as she realized that before they had even arrived, their plan had already gone terribly wrong.

Chapter Thirteen

Jarrod

*P*RISONER *FIVE-THREE-ONE COULD EASILY be asleep,* Betty thought, in the fractured moments when the wind was whizzing past her ears. Perhaps he would be old, frail, and posing no threat to them. Or they could get incredibly unlucky . . . again.

It was a bad landing. Without Granny to steady them they were flimsy as rose petals, each of them going a different way. Despite Betty's hopes for a quiet entrance, Charlie squealed, Fliss yelped, and even she gave an *oof!* as she landed on her bottom on a freezing stone floor.

The room was dim, lit only by the glow of some outside beacon filtering in from a high, barred window. Right away Betty was uneasy. This was not like the other cells.

Though it shared the same freezing stone walls, it was half the size of Colton's. Unlike the glimpse they'd had of Colton's door, the one to this cell was of solid wood, with an eye-level hatch that could only be opened from the other side. This, Betty thought, was not a good sign. The next thing she noticed, as the three of them clambered to their feet, was the stench. It was like being walloped in the nose with a sack of stewed cabbages, though strangely, there was no sign of a prisoner.

There was no bed, just a heap of old sacks thrown in a corner. In the other corner was a bucket, which Fliss had landed next to. As she stood up, she peered into it and made a retching sound. It was then, too late, that Betty saw the figure rising from the sacking just beyond Charlie: a hulking giant of a man.

"Charlie!" She made a grab for her sister, who was still clutching the traveling bag and oblivious to the movement behind her.

The prisoner was surprisingly quick for someone so large. He lunged at Charlie, seizing her arm. His meaty fist was almost the size of his head, which was bald as a beetle. Charlie mewled like a captured kitten.

"What have we got here, then?" His voice was menacing. "Wasn't expecting company in solitary!"

Solitary confinement! Betty's worry was crystallizing

into dread. The last thing they needed. They were dealing with not just a criminal, but an incredibly dangerous one.

"Ouch, you're hurting me!" Charlie complained. She gave Betty a wounded look. "Why'd you tell me to bring us here?"

"I didn't," Betty said tightly. She was so horrified she could barely get the words out. "I said five-one-three, not five-three-one! You muddled it up."

"Lucky me," the prisoner said. "That still doesn't explain how you got in here." He gave Charlie a jerk. "Talk!"

"We're ghosts," Charlie said, recovering from her shock a little. "And now that you've seen us, we'll haunt you . . . forever!"

The prisoner guffawed. "Nice try, but I've never heard of ghosts tripping over themselves and making such a racket."

"That's because we're new at it," Charlie persisted. "We died . . . um . . . recently. We're still learning."

The prisoner leered down at her, grinning. The inside of his mouth was like a chessboard, with black gaps where half his teeth were missing.

"A ghost could get through a locked door," he said. "But you're as real as I am, pumpkin." He tightened his hold on Charlie's arm.

"Let her go," Betty said, screwing up her courage. She stepped toward Charlie, holding out her hand. Perhaps if she could grab Charlie and Fliss at once, Charlie might be able to use the bag to get them out of here. "Please. This is just a silly mistake and we shouldn't be here."

Her pleas went ignored.

"Prisoner five-one-three, you say?" His eyes lit up with recognition. "What would three young ladies want with him? Three young ladies who can appear from out of nowhere? See, I'm getting a whiff of witchcraft, or magic, or sorcery . . . whatever you call it."

No one answered. Betty was frozen, Charlie was squirming in the man's grip, and Fliss had backed up against the wall. To Betty's relief, the prisoner released Charlie. The relief didn't last, however, for his next move was to snatch the traveling bag from Charlie's hand.

"Oi!" Charlie grabbed at the bag, but he held it out of her reach.

"What's in here, then? Something you're bringing to Colton?" He pawed inside it with his beefy hand.

"Give it! S'mine!" Charlie raged, and she aimed a swift kick at the man's shins. He swatted her as if she were a gnat, and she toppled backwards, plopping onto the lumpy sacking.

"Nothing in it," he said in disgust, after rummaging

through and even checking the small pocket sewn in the lining. Betty saw his suspicion deepening, and the knot of dread inside her tightened. She couldn't bear to consider what this man would be prepared to do to escape, but one thing was certain: if he figured out the bag's secret, the girls would be in grave danger.

"Why would you be carrying an empty bag, eh?" His eyes narrowed. "This how you got in here? Is it a portal or summat?" He held the bag out in front of him, fitting it over his huge foot like an ugly, misshapen slipper. He looked ridiculous, almost funny, but Betty wasn't fooled. Everything about him oozed menace.

"It's . . . it's just a bag," she muttered. She gave Charlie a warning look to keep quiet as he continued to puzzle over the bag, and allowed herself to relax slightly. Only they knew its secret, and Charlie was the only one who could make the bag work. If they could convince the prisoner that it was worthless, then all they needed was a moment's distraction and they could escape.

He shook it again, losing interest, but Betty sensed he wasn't ready to give it back to them just yet.

"If you must know, we needed it to take something out of the prison," she said.

"What?" he asked, glowering at her.

"I . . . I don't know. We're doing a favor for someone. They said it was best we didn't know about the, um, item, beforehand."

"Mmm."

She waited, unsure what the noise meant.

"You still haven't explained how you got in here," he said. "I know I'm not dreaming. And I reckon if you got in, you know how to get out."

"All right." Betty opened her eyes wide and made her bottom lip tremble. It wasn't hard. She was already trembling a bit under the man's scrutiny; he really did look mean. "Give me the bag, and I'll tell you. But you must promise to let us go, unharmed."

The prisoner grinned his broken grin at her. "Oh, I promise," he said, in a sugary voice that managed to sound sinister. He tossed the bag, which Betty missed. It landed with a soft *whump* at her feet. She picked it up, glancing at Fliss. Her elder sister was nibbling her lip, but she caught Betty's look and crept away from the wall, toward her.

"Charlie, come here, poppet," Betty said, trying to sound casual. Charlie got up from the sacking, but as she went to pass the prisoner, he clamped his hand roughly on her shoulder.

"How about the little one stays here," he said, in the same honeyed tone, "just till you've told me?"

"Fine," said Betty, in a choked voice that made it clear it was not at all fine, but before she could say anything else, Charlie turned her head and sank her teeth into the meaty hand.

"Now!" Betty yelled as the prisoner bellowed in pain. He shook Charlie off and she shot across to Betty, seizing the bag.

"Not so fast!" he yelled, nursing his bitten fingers.

For a moment, Betty thought they had gotten away with it. But as Charlie flipped the bag inside out, shouting "Prisoner FIVE-ONE-THREE!" prisoner five-three-one lunged at them, his eyes bulging with rage. Charlie began to yell.

The whooshing this time made Betty feel twice as giddy, her tummy turning somersaults as the stale prison air blasted past her nose. She squeezed her eyes shut, feeling the ground fall away from her, knowing she would never, ever get used to this feeling. She was aware of Charlie still shrieking, and all the while the same thought echoed in her head: *I wish we'd never left the Poacher's Pocket, I wish we'd NEVER left the Poacher's Pocket . . .*

They landed in Colton's cell in a scatter of bumps. Betty barely hit the ground before she was scrambling over to Charlie to clap her hand over her sister's mouth. It was too late, however, for their noise had already disrupted the peace. In the corridors came sounds of beds creaking and muttering, and finally someone bellowed, "Who was that? Screaming like a little girl! Keep your nightmares to yerself!"

Colton shot up in bed like the sheets were on fire. He shook himself from sleep, gaping as he stared past Fliss to the corner where Betty's own gaze was fixed. She'd known what she would see before they even arrived.

There, motionless on the floor, lay prisoner five-three-one. Colton's expression wavered between relief and fear. "Why don't you make a bit more noise?" he said sarcastically. "And I hope you've got a really, really good reason for bringing Jarrod along!"

"It was an accident!" Betty hissed as the murmuring in the corridor grew quiet. The other prisoners were beginning to settle. "We ended up in the wrong cell and he grabbed Charlie as we escaped!" She could barely believe the disaster unfolding around them, and fear was making it hard to think clearly. They had to get Colton out before Jarrod came around, but once he did, he wasn't likely to sit quietly in Colton's cell until morning. The alarm would be raised, and all of Crowstone would be swarming with warders. Looking for Colton, looking for them, unless Betty could think of a solution.

Fliss poked the unmoving prisoner with her toe. He didn't budge.

"He's knocked out," she said, pointing to an egg-sized bump on his shiny forehead. "He must have hit his head."

"Finally, some luck," Betty muttered.

"Luck?" Colton was incredulous. "Luck? One of Crowstone's most feared prisoners is here, in my cell! How is that lucky?" It was the first time Betty had seen him rattled, and the feeling was infectious, sending her own nerves skittering into the dark corners of the cell. Being here, surrounded by dangerous criminals, was nothing like talking about it. It was terrifying, and she was beginning to wish she had listened to Fliss and thought of another plan.

"I didn't mean that he's here. That's rotten luck. I meant that he's out cold."

"We're the Widdershinses," said Fliss. "We know enough about bad luck to recognize good luck. Trust me."

Betty glanced around. Even though she and Fliss had viewed the cell through the mirror, being in it felt far worse than she had expected. It was so cold and lacking in comfort that she wondered how Colton hadn't gone mad. Living in these conditions—especially if he was innocent—must have been horrifying.

"What are we waiting for?" Colton snapped. "Let's go!"

"Wait," said Betty. "How often do the warders look in?"

"Every couple of hours. Why?"

Betty stared at the growing bump on Jarrod's head. They had gotten this far; now she needed to make sure Jarrod couldn't mess things up further. Getting him back to his own cell wasn't something she was prepared to risk, but perhaps there was something they could do. A plan was forming in her mind, inspired by what Fingerty had told her . . .

"Betty?" Fliss said, uneasy. "You've got that look on your face. The one that usually means you're thinking up trouble."

"Distraction," Betty whispered.

Colton huffed out an impatient breath. "Eh?"

Charlie fidgeted, a hand darting under her coat like she had an itch. Something about the movement registered in Betty's mind, but she was too busy thinking.

"If the warders come around on a check and see your

cell empty, they'll send out search parties. But if we leave Jarrod here, the warders might think it's you. It'll buy us more time until morning."

"Won't work," Colton said, his voice flat. "He'll start hollering the moment he comes around. The warders will hear and come immediately."

"Not if we tie him up," said Betty.

Chapter Fourteen

Escape

"TIE HIM UP?" Colton gave a hollow chuckle. "You're just like your granny, you know that?"

"Betty's right," said Fliss, finally recovering her wits. "Your chances are better if we can delay the warders' realizing you're gone."

"And if they notice Jarrod's missing, at least they'll be searching for him and not you."

"Then let's hurry. We don't know how long we've got before he comes around," said Colton. He stepped around the unconscious Jarrod, watching him as if he were a coiled snake ready to bite.

"We should lift him onto the bed, like he's sleeping," said Betty. Her knees were shaking. There was nothing she wanted to do less than approach the meaty figure, let alone touch it. However, the idea of him grabbing any of them the way he'd grabbed Charlie was driving her forward, forcing her to act. They'd caught Jarrod off-guard once. She doubted they'd get the same chance twice.

"After he's tied up," Colton replied.

Someone in another cell along the corridor coughed; then a voice grumbled: "Who's whispering to themselves? Pack it in!"

Someone else laughed, low and mean. "Maybe it's five-one-three, crying in his sleep again."

Crying in his sleep? Betty glanced at Colton, but he avoided her eyes, a muscle in his jaw twitching. When she'd first met him, cocky and uncooperative in the visiting room, she couldn't have imagined him crying into his pillow. Seeing him here, afraid, changed things. For the first time, she cared that Colton was getting out. She darted over to the bed, grabbing the sheets. She handed the corner of one to Colton and another to Fliss.

"Quickly, tear these into strips." She took a corner and began to pull at the worn edges. With Fliss tugging one side of the sheet and Betty gripping the other, they tore a long strip as thick as Jarrod's arm, wincing as the fabric cut into their palms.

Colton tore two more, grimacing. "We need to bind

his hands, knees, and ankles as well as gagging him," he said. He worked quickly, his eyes never leaving Jarrod. Next to the older, powerfully built man, he looked very young.

Betty raised an eyebrow. "That's . . . thorough."

"Hey, this was your bright idea," Colton snapped. He kneeled at Jarrod's side, his nostrils flaring with heavy breaths. He touched Jarrod's chest softly, then prodded harder when there was no response.

"Is he really dangerous?" Charlie asked, backing away a little.

Colton nodded grimly.

Betty looked up. Dare she ask exactly what Jarrod was capable of? No, she decided. There was no point in scaring them all further, although her imagination was unhelpfully making terrible suggestions—and not just about the prisoner who was unconscious. "More danger-ous than you?"

Colton glared at her. "Yes."

Suddenly Charlie swooped on something glinting on the stone floor.

"My tooth!"

"You knock a tooth out when you landed?" Colton asked, surprisingly concerned.

Charlie shook her head, pocketing it. "No, I just carry

it with me. It must've fallen out of my pocket when I landed. I call it Peg."

"Right." Colton looked slightly mystified, then shook himself. "Let's do his legs first." He took a strip of the sheet and wound it around Jarrod's ankles before tying a firm knot at the back.

"Is that too tight?" Fliss asked.

"Nope. He'll be furious about this." Colton gave a mirthless chuckle. "You don't want to see him mad. You really don't."

"Hopefully we won't have to," said Betty, but the sheen of perspiration on Colton's forehead was making her twitchy. How had he coped in here all this time? Already, she felt as though the tiny space were closing in, becoming airless. She couldn't wait to get out. "Roll him onto his front. It's best his hands are tied behind him."

In the corridor, the muttering had become a drone of voices that Betty had been able to tune out until now. But it was getting louder, more insistent. The prisoners knew there was something going on. Doors began to rattle.

"Hurry," said Colton. "Their noise will bring the warders!"

They crouched beside the unmoving Jarrod, grabbing handfuls of clothing. They heaved, grunting with the effort.

"It's like trying to shift a fallen tree," Fliss gasped. Eventually they maneuvered him onto his side.

"Now set him down gently on his front," Colton warned. They began to turn him, but before Betty knew it, Jarrod's weight pulled them forward and he landed heavily, like a slab of meat.

Colton rolled his eyes. "If that's your idea of gentle, I'd hate to see rough."

Fliss gagged, covering her nose as a smell of stale sweat wafted up from Jarrod.

Colton smirked. "That's prison for you, princess. It ain't pretty."

Fliss glared at him. "I can see that for myself." To Betty's surprise, she grabbed Jarrod's hands and held them together as Colton twisted another piece of the sheet tightly around Jarrod's wrists.

All three of them jumped as his thick, sausagelike fingers twitched, then curled. Colton reared back, dropping the sheet. The hand slowly moved, forming a fist, before relaxing and becoming limp again.

Colton crawled forward warily. "We don't have much time. He'll come around soon."

"Want me to bash him over the head?" Charlie asked. She looked around, searching for a suitable weapon.

"No!" Fliss said, shocked.

Charlie shrugged, looking suspiciously like she was enjoying the drama. Betty, on the other hand, was not. She was starting to wonder whether adventures agreed with her at all. She felt neither bold nor brave.

Colton looped the sheet around Jarrod's wrists again, knotting it tight. Betty slid a length of sheet just above Jarrod's knees.

He let out a low moan.

"Forget his knees," Colton said shakily. "Let's get him on the bed before he wakes."

Betty held up the final rag. "Mustn't forget the most important one." She jammed it between Jarrod's teeth and tied it behind his head.

With that, the three of them heaved Jarrod onto his back again, then got into position around him.

"Lift!" Colton said through gritted teeth.

The murmuring of the other prisoners swelled around them, becoming a low chant. "Col-ton . . . Col-ton . . . Colton . . ."

"Lift!" Colton repeated, and somehow, with the chanting in their ears, their rising panic lent them strength, and they threw Jarrod on the narrow bed. His eyes flew open as he landed. Fliss picked up the rest of the sheet from the floor and tossed it over him. He writhed underneath it, but the bindings held firm.

The clang of a door echoed through the corridors. The warders were coming.

Colton turned to Betty, wide-eyed. "Now can we go?"

"Gladly," Betty answered, trying to organize her thoughts over the din of prisoners' voices. The last thing she wanted was Colton and Charlie—and the bag—getting separated from her and Fliss. "Colton, you hold on to Fliss. Then I'll link arms with Fliss, and Charlie can go on the end, so she has an arm free to work the bag."

"You're letting the kid use the bag?" Colton asked in astonishment.

"It has to be her."

"So that's why you don't want me holding on to Charlie," said Colton slowly. "In case I let go of Fliss."

"Right," Betty answered bluntly. "You haven't earned our trust yet. Maybe that's about to change, but for now I'll stick with being careful." Privately, she wondered whether they should have insisted Colton be tied up, too, but they hadn't the time now that the warders were coming. And though she was unsure of Colton, she didn't feel the same threat from him that she did oozing from Jarrod. She hoped she wasn't wrong.

The other prisoners' voices were belting out Colton's name now, as loud as they could and so fast there was barely a breath between the words. "Colton! Colton!

Colton!" Then it broke, giving way to loud jeers. Sharp, authoritative voices rang out across the prisoners' burble.

"The warders," Colton whispered. "They're here!"

"Betty?" Charlie's voice was panicked.

"Get in line!" Betty instructed.

"But, Betty, I've lost Hoppit!"

"Then he'll have to stay lost," said Betty in exasperation, bundling Charlie into place. Her little sister's fidgeting made sense now. "I can't believe you brought that rat with you. I told you to get rid of it!"

"I didn't mean to! He was in my pocket," Charlie protested. "He can't sleep otherwise!"

They couldn't dash their escape for a silly rat! "Everyone ready?" Betty said abruptly. "Charlie, take us to Lament."

Charlie's bottom lip wobbled. "Not without Hoppit. We can't leave him in this awful place!"

"I'm sure he'll be right at home," said Colton drily.

"Quickly, Charlie," Fliss urged. "The bag!"

Charlie's lip stopped quivering and began to jut obstinately. "I said no! We have to look for him!" She began to bend down, but Betty took her arm firmly.

"No, Charlie. We leave, now! We can't let the warders find us!"

"Look!" Fliss gasped, nodding to the bed.

There on the sheet covering Jarrod, a small dark shape was scuttling along, sniffing interestedly at the sweaty bulk underneath.

"Hoppit!" Charlie exclaimed. She tried to squirm away, but Betty held her fast. Something was happening: Jarrod shifted under the sheet, groaning like an angry bull. Through the cell-door bars came the glow of an approaching lantern.

"We have to go!" Betty whispered desperately.

"No!" Charlie thrashed, but there was no way Betty was letting her near Jarrod, who was now grunting and writhing.

"For crow's sake!" Colton broke away from Fliss and lunged for the rat, just as the creature vanished into a dip in the sheet between Jarrod's knees.

"Got it!" He grimaced in disgust—but with those words, Jarrod's thighs snapped shut, trapping Colton's hand.

Colton's eyes widened with shock as he tried to pull himself free, but he was no match for Jarrod. He was stuck like a fox in a trap.

Footsteps scuffed the stone corridor, closer still, lamplight glowing brighter.

Colton wrenched at his hand again, but Betty knew from his expression there was no way Jarrod was letting go—at least, not in time.

"Grab him!" she yelled to Fliss. Then to Charlie, "GO! For crow's sake, go!"

And as Fliss lunged for Colton, Charlie plunged her hand into the traveling bag. "Lament!"

They landed on soft, damp grass that smelled of sea salt and earth. Betty's legs crumpled beneath her, and her arms were yanked in both directions, forcing her to release Fliss and Charlie. She sank to her knees, feeling wetness seep through to her skin. Her relief at escaping was crushed by dread. The warders would know now that Colton was gone. They should have just left immediately; a bellowing Jarrod signaling the escape from the confines of a cell was much better than a broken-out Jarrod— even if he was tied up. Betty dragged herself up, her eyes everywhere, anxious for her sisters. A small copse of trees surrounded them.

Charlie had landed neatly as a cat, and was staring around, wide-eyed, and her hair more like a bramble-bush than ever. Betty's eyes rested on Jarrod, who was lying face-down, squirming. Angry grunts came from behind the gag as he struggled against his constraints. Fear prickled her skin like icy raindrops. They had tied him tightly enough . . . hadn't they?

A short distance away, Fliss had landed on top of Colton in a tangled heap.

"And there I was thinking you didn't like me," said Colton.

"You wish," Fliss growled, but the color in her cheeks deepened. She rolled off him, flicking her hair in his face.

Colton grunted as he clambered to his feet. He cast a wary glance at Jarrod, then stared up at the star-sprinkled sky, his eyes dancing in the moonlight. Faint squeaks came from his outstretched hand, but Colton was too entranced with his new freedom to notice he was still holding Charlie's squirming rat.

"It's so big," he murmured at last. "So vast . . . I'd forgotten how huge the world is outside of the prison walls."

"Better make sure you don't end up back on the wrong side of them, then," Betty retorted. Her eyes darted across the wide, flat expanse of Lament. All she could see of mainland Crowstone were gossamer threads of light in the distance. She had only been to Lament twice before, to lay flowers and feathers on her grandfather's and mother's graves. It was the farthest she had ever been from home.

If the escape had gone smoothly, Betty would have been thrilled by this, but now the thought of home appealed more than she wanted to admit. The only excitement she felt was for what Colton was about to reveal.

A blast of freezing wind blew in her face. She remembered now how open and flat the land on Lament was, how little shelter there was. It was so empty and mournful here. When they were younger, Fliss had wanted to continue bringing flowers to Mother's grave, but Granny had discouraged them. "Better to remember her as she was, in here," she'd said, tapping her head, "rather than remind yourselves of where she is now."

"Fliss?" Charlie whined, pressing into her. "I know this is an adventure, but does it have to be so c-cold?"

Fliss pulled her younger sister closer, though she was shivering herself.

Betty stepped in front of them. "We won't be out here much longer, Charlie," she said, looking at Colton pointedly. "Well? We got you out. Now it's your turn. Tell us how to break the curse."

Colton turned to look at her and his expression changed, becoming uncomfortable. He lowered his gaze, shifting from one foot to the other. Already, Betty knew with a sinking feeling that she was not going to like whatever she was about to hear.

"Soon. I still need your help."

Betty's eyes narrowed to slits the size of rice grains. Why was he stalling, after all they'd just been through? She stalked over to him, temper flaring. "You said once we got you out of the prison you could do the rest. That was the deal!"

"There's a boat hidden in one of the caves," Colton said. He looked up at the glittering stars, then across the marshes to the lights on the mainland. "I thought I'd be able to get my bearings, but . . ."

He's struggling with the directions, Betty thought. It wasn't surprising. She had heard that long spells in small places could do strange things to the mind. Even Betty, who'd spent hours studying all her maps, was finding it more difficult to navigate than expected, now that she was here. If she hadn't been so annoyed, she might have felt a pang of pity for him. But the thought of the curse pushed her sympathy aside as her earlier doubts niggled. How much did Colton really know?

"Can you tell us how to break this curse or not?" Fliss asked stonily, evidently thinking the same. "Or are you just stringing us along?"

Colton met her eyes for a second, then broke away. "Get me to the caves," he muttered. "Then I'll tell you everything I know."

"You were supposed to tell us now," Betty said. "You're breaking your word!"

"Why should we do anything else for you?" Fliss added.

"Because if we don't, we'll have wasted our time," Betty said in a hard voice. It was an unbearable thought, to have risked so much for nothing. If Colton didn't give them the answers they needed, it was back to groveling to Fingerty . . . which held no guarantees, either.

Charlie marched up to Colton, glaring with as much disdain as she could muster. She held out her hand. "My rat," she said icily.

"Oh." Colton was shamefaced as he handed back the wriggling brown creature. "Here. I wasn't planning on keeping it."

"Huh!" said Charlie, pocketing Hoppit. "So you ain't a thief, then. Just a liar." She turned on her heel and rejoined her sisters.

"We'll get you to the caves," said Betty. "Then you tell us. No more stalling."

"What do we do about Jarrod, though?" Fliss asked, jerking her head over her shoulder. "Leave him there for the warders to find?"

Betty glanced back at the copse of trees where they had landed. She stiffened, scouring the ground.

"We might not have to worry about that," she whispered. A short way in front of them, squelched into the mud, was a torn piece of rag, its loose end fluttering as if waving cheerily.

Jarrod was gone.

Chapter Fifteen

The Island of the Dead

BETTY'S STOMACH FELT LIKE A PANCAKE being flipped. "Is that . . . one of his bindings?"

Colton gulped. "Sheets must have been weaker than we thought."

Betty's eyes darted between the trees, but the branches created shadows that the moonlight couldn't reach. With Jarrod missing she suddenly felt like an insect being watched by a hungry spider, a spider in a dark corner hidden from sight. *He knows about the bag,* she thought. Would he try to get it? The fact that he'd vanished reassured her slightly, but she was still jittery. Jarrod could be too busy taking his chance to escape to worry about them, but who knew the dark workings of his mind?

"We need to move," she managed to say. "Find this cave so we can do what we need to and get off this awful island."

"Can we use the bag?" Fliss asked quietly.

"Best not," Colton said gruffly. "If the tide is in, half the cave will be underwater. It's better we go on foot, quietly and carefully. Especially with Jarrod on the loose." His forehead creased. "For all we know, he could try to make it to the caves himself."

"Which ones?" Betty asked urgently. She glanced back at Crowstone, then across at Repent, trying to picture her maps in her head. "There are caves all over these islands."

"The Three Widows," said Colton. "Some of the prisoners used to talk about a boat and supplies being hidden and joke about using it as a getaway. The trouble for them was they had no way of getting out of the prison and across to Lament."

She nodded. "I've seen them on maps. Let's go."

They began walking, Betty in the lead with her too-large boots rubbing her heels. Colton followed with Fliss and Charlie.

"Where do you think Jarrod went?" Betty asked. Her breath misted in front of her. "Could he have rolled out of the way and hidden somewhere?"

"Probably." Colton's mouth pressed into a grim line.

"With one of his ties broken, it's only a matter of time until he snaps the rest."

Dread curdled in Betty's stomach. Again she wondered what he was capable of, and only Charlie's presence stopped her from asking.

"Let's just hope it's the warders who find him first." Colton glanced about nervously. "Aside from us, would there be anyone else on Lament now?"

Betty shook her head. "Not even the gravediggers would be here in the middle of the night. We're the only people here." She glanced at Charlie, lowering her voice. "The only living ones, anyway."

They walked faster, spurred on by urgency. Every so often Betty turned to check that Fliss and Charlie were near. She had half expected one or both of them to be in tears by now, but Fliss's face was steely and alert, and Charlie seemed more concerned with making sure Hoppit was still in her pocket. She felt a rush of affection for them both. In all her dreams of adventure, she'd imagined herself alone and independent, needing no one. Now that it was happening, she couldn't help feeling glad they were in it together.

Underfoot, the waterlogged grass gave way to freshly turned soil, with smaller, narrow paths of grass between them. In some places the mounds had flattened and become grassy. On each of them was a small pile of stones. Some had toppled over with time.

"Graves," said Colton, stooping to pick up a fallen stone. He placed it back on the nearest grave, then began to pick his way through them.

Betty followed, her skin prickling. She couldn't help being reminded of the stones falling from the prison tower. Her eyes skimmed over the rocky heaps uneasily. She had always known about the piles of stones—or cairns, as they were called—on the graves after a burial, but this was the first time she had made the connection to the Widdershins curse. In both cases the stones were a marker of death.

"I don't like this," said Fliss from behind. She made the sign of the crow hurriedly. "It feels wrong to be walking over the graves."

"We're not," Colton replied. "We're walking between them. They're not going to hurt you."

"I know that. I just . . . I don't like the idea of it."

"You mean you've never walked through a graveyard in the dead—sorry, bad choice of word—of night before?" He smirked. "Where's your sense of adventure?"

"Not here, clearly."

"Don't worry, princess. You'll soon be back in your palace and all this will seem like a bad dream."

"You've obviously never been to the Poacher's Pocket," said Betty, torn between sticking up for her sister and being mildly fascinated at Colton poking fun at her. Fliss's prettiness didn't seem to affect him as it did other young men, who simpered when she looked their way. But then, Betty supposed Colton had bigger concerns. "It's no palace, that's for sure."

"Depends on your idea of riches," said Colton, the humor leaving his voice. "A home and a family to go back to . . . that's enough for some folk."

Betty didn't answer. She didn't want to know about Colton's life or family, not if it meant feeling sorry for him. All she wanted was to find out what he knew and never set eyes on him again. So when Fliss predictably began to ask personal questions, she cut across her.

"Wouldn't it be better to keep to the edges of the graveyard? There's more shelter, trees and bushes we could hide behind if Jarrod shows up. Out here he'd see us right away."

"And we'd see him right away if he came at us," Colton replied. "Besides, all those hiding places, they could just as easily be hiding him."

It was an eerie thought. They hurried on silently, past graves and an endless landscape of stones. Betty glanced at the low wall dividing the graveyard. She had never before walked on this side, where people from Torment were buried. Those from mainland Crowstone were allowed proper headstones and decorations, but the graves on this side were only marked by cairns. After all her years of wanting to tread new ground, now that she was on it, she felt out of her depth. Imagining adventures was nothing like living them, especially with villains like Jarrod in the shadows—and this was only the start. What dangers would they need to face to actually break the curse?

After a while she stopped looking directly at the stones, concentrating instead on the grass under her feet. That way it was easier to imagine the cairns as other, less threatening things, such as piles of balled-up socks or clusters of mushrooms.

"I'm hungry," Charlie said suddenly. "And cold. I want my bed. And I want Granny!" She sniffed loudly, tugging at Fliss's arm. "This isn't how an adventure should feel!"

Privately, Betty agreed. But they were so close now! Once Colton got to his stupid boat and they got their answer, this awful part would end, and they could concentrate on changing their futures. "It's nearly over now," she murmured. "You've been so brave, Charlie!"

"That's right," Fliss soothed, glancing warily about. "We can go home soon."

Colton turned back to Charlie, touching her shoulder. "There should be food in the caves."

Charlie looked instantly more cheerful. "I want toast," she declared. "Hot, thick toast all dripping with butter."

Colton chuckled, shaking his head. "It'll be stuff that keeps. Salted fish or meat."

Charlie was thoughtful for a moment. "Do rats eat fish?"

He pretended to look surprised. "Are you a rat, then?"

Charlie giggled, before remembering she was supposed to be cross. Betty repositioned herself between them, frowning. She was unable to tell whether his kindness toward the little girl was genuine or he had his eye on the traveling bag. Either way, it was safer to put some distance between them.

They were past the graveyard now, only spongy grass beneath their boots. Ahead, Colton slowed. A chilly breeze hit Betty in the face, and then she saw that the land ahead dropped away. Beyond that, she spied a tiny lone light out on the water, perhaps a wisp, perhaps a hopeful fisherman.

"We've reached the edge of the island," said Colton. "How far are the caves now?"

Betty checked the position of Crowstone Tower again.

"According to the maps I've seen, the Three Widows are north. So they should be more or less below us on the cliff face; we just need to find the steps down."

Shivering, they scouted the overlook. After a couple of minutes Betty began doubting herself and wondering about rock falls that might have left the steps ruined.

She neared the land's edge, Fliss holding tightly to Charlie behind. She could just make out a set of crude, chunky steps carved into the rocky surface.

"Here!"

"Are we supposed to get down those in one piece?" Fliss asked. "There's nothing to hold on to!"

Betty stepped down, one hand on the crumbling edge. "There are roots and rocks we can grab. We should hold on to each other, too."

Once they were on the steps, it wasn't as bad as Betty had feared. Colton went first, with Betty next. Charlie went after, one hand in Betty's and the other held by Fliss.

The steps were steep but wide. Soon they got into a steady rhythm, going down, down, down, and Betty welcomed each step closer to the bottom away from the harsh wind.

They were about halfway down when the ground crumbled under her feet. Charlie squealed, her fingers gripping Betty's hand as Betty skidded. A vision of the cliffs rushing past her nose flashed through her mind as she imagined the three of them being pulled over.

Colton flung his hand out, grabbing her wrist. He hauled her back in with a grunt, tight against the cliff face. No one spoke, only waited for her to catch her breath before moving on in silence. Down, down, down, like it would never end, like a clock that just went on ticking.

And then, finally, they were there. Crunching shingle at their feet, water lapping over rock pools ahead . . . and a series of black shapes yawning like mouths before them.

"There they are," Betty murmured. "The Three Widows."

Fliss stared into the black caverns doubtfully. "Could they sound any more ominous?"

Charlie tugged at Betty's sleeve. "What's 'oni-muss'?"

"It means a bit gloomy," said Betty. The caverns were certainly that, but a thrill went through her at the sight of them.

Colton began picking his way over the shingle. Wordlessly, the girls followed, briny wind whipping through their hair. The beach became coarser, and in places there were chunks of broken wood and smashed china. It made Betty think of shipwrecks, an idea that had always excited her before. That seemed foolish now. The scattered debris was real, maybe all that survived of someone else's adventure that had gone terribly wrong.

They crunched past the first two caves. A glimpse into their dark insides gave nothing away. Colton continued to the final cave, vanishing inside. The sisters ducked in after him, out of the brittle wind. They heard scrabbling in the darkness. Then came the sound of a match being struck. A golden glow followed as a candle was lit.

Colton loomed before them. Beyond him, the cave stretched back. Betty squinted into the gloom, finding a jumble of shapes: wooden crates, bottles, heaps of sacking, and crucially, a small rowboat with two jutting oars. Colton went to it, picking off strings of seaweed. He circled it, running his hands over the wood, lifting the candle to inspect it.

"It's actually here." He rubbed a hand over his chin, his voice light with relief. "And in working order. Good."

"You weren't certain it would be?" Betty asked, unsettled. It seemed too huge a thing to risk after all they'd been through to get here.

A shadow flickered across Colton's face. He didn't answer, instead rummaging through the crates. He threw a bundle of paper to Charlie. "Here."

Charlie unfolded it, sniffing like a puppy before popping something dried into her mouth. She chewed uncertainly, then nodded and tucked the rest in her pocket.

Betty glanced at the cave's entrance. How far behind them were the warders? And where was Jarrod? "Enough with the picnic," she said. "We got you to the boat. So, out with it—how do we break the curse?"

Colton stiffened, his back to them. Slowly he straightened from the crates and turned to them with a shaky breath.

And in that one breath, Betty knew.

"I'm sorry," he said quietly. "I—I lied to you. I don't know how to break it."

Betty felt herself sway and reached out to grab a rocky ledge for support. Waves crashed in the distance, and it was the sound of all her hopes being dashed against the rocks. The cave closed in, tightening the world around her. All she had hoped for . . . gone. Her dreams shattered for the second time in as many days. She had put her sisters' lives in danger and broken two prisoners out of a high-security jail, and for what? Nothing, except to be used and become a criminal herself.

"You . . . you don't know anything?" she asked. She felt hollow, dizzy. Like a low wave could wash her off her feet. She'd had her doubts about Colton, but she had wanted so badly to believe him. There was nowhere to go from here except back to the start, to try to find another way. Already, she didn't know if she had the strength or whether she could harness the swirling rage within her. She released the ledge and stepped toward Colton unsteadily, her hands tightening into fists. No wonder Granny had never taken the risk to get him out. She must have been tempted but never quite convinced. She'd been wiser than Betty, much wiser.

"I'm sorry," he said again, holding up his hands in what was meant to be a calming gesture. It enraged Betty all the more.

"Don't you dare apologize!" she cried. "Don't you know what we've just done for you? What we risked?" A sob of anger and frustration forced its way into her voice, choking her. "And for what? We're still stuck in Crowstone as much as we ever were! We helped you for NOTHING!"

Fliss appeared at her side, ashen-faced. "All of it . . . lies?" Her voice was cold, un-Fliss-like. Under the bubbling anger, Betty could hear hurt and disappointment. "Shame on you! You haven't a shred of honor!"

Colton hung his head, his lips moving soundlessly.

"What did you say?" Betty demanded.

"I said it wasn't for nothing." Colton finally met her gaze. "I know what you risked to get me out, and I wish I could repay you. I honestly do."

"Honest?" Betty scoffed. "You wouldn't know honesty if it bit you on the nose! You're a lying, cheating—"

"Lying cheat!" Charlie put in.

"You saw what it was like in there!" Colton cried. His eyes were wild, haunted. "You think it's tough being stuck in Crowstone? Try being locked in a tiny, stinking cell day in, day out! Bitten by fleas, existing on scraps! Then you'd know what it's really like to be trapped." He shook his head bitterly. "Two years of my life wasted in that . . . that sewer. And the worst thing? I shouldn't have been in there in the first place."

"How can you expect us to believe you're innocent now?" Fliss asked, aghast. "You've lied about everything else!"

"One lie doesn't mean everything else was." Colton stepped toward Fliss. "What, you've never told a lie?" He threw up his hands, as if trying to rid himself of frustration. "What I did wasn't right, and I do wish I could help you, whatever you might think of me—"

"Not a lot," Betty interrupted, the familiar feeling of betrayal hooking its claws in. *How could I have trusted him?* she berated herself.

"—but I lied because I had to. I saw a chance, and I took it. I reckon any of you would've done the same." He gave a thin, tired smile. "You say I've no honor, but I'm honoring my vow to get far, far away from this place and never set eyes on Crowstone again. We all do what we need to do, princess. There's no room for honor in this world, not when it comes to looking after yourself."

"Perhaps not for you," Fliss said softly. "But that's not what I believe. I won't."

Colton's eyes glinted in the darkness. "Maybe one day you'll change your mind."

"Or maybe you will," Fliss replied. A chill wind blew into the cave, creeping into sleeves and around ankles, nipping like a ferret.

"You know, there was something else about the tower," Colton added, looking wretched. "The only other thing I know—"

"Oh, save it," Betty retorted. "Like Fliss said, why would we trust another word from you?"

"Fine. It was just that . . . No. You're right, fine." He let out a weary sigh. "I hope you break the curse. And for what it's worth, I wish you luck."

"Yes, well," Fliss muttered. "If we had any luck, which we don't, we wouldn't wish it back." She rubbed her nose angrily, her eyes shimmering with unshed tears.

Betty unclenched her teeth. "So, what now? You just sail away to a new life?" Her voice was bitter. She couldn't quite believe that this was it: the end of the dreams and hopes she'd built up in such a short time. This liar got to leave because of them. Why should he win his freedom when they couldn't? In that moment she hated him enough to consider anonymously tipping off the warders once they returned.

"I'm surprised you care enough to ask," he said.

"We don't." Betty glared at him. "I just want an idea of when the warders are likely to catch up with you. That's if you even get past the rocks."

She was pleased to see the worry lines on Colton's face deepen.

"Rocks?"

"Surely you know?" She watched as he hurriedly began loading the boat with sacking and food provisions. His movements were jerky and rushed.

"I'll take my chances," he muttered, more to himself than to any of the sisters. His face was tight; a muscle in his neck twitched. "This whole night . . . this hasn't gone to plan."

"How dare you complain?" Betty seethed. "Because of us, everything has gone to plan—for you!"

"It was meant to be easy!" Colton shot back. His

bravado had deserted him, leaving only a scared boy. "I had it all figured out until you brought Charlie along!"

"Brought Charlie?" Betty snapped. "We didn't want to, believe me! But like I said, she's the only one who can work the bag."

"We'd never have gotten you out otherwise!" Fliss added.

Colton whipped to face her, his voice hoarse. "I wasn't to know that, was I?"

Understanding crashed over Betty like a wave. "You . . . you were planning to steal the bag, weren't you?"

He hesitated, unable to look at either of them. "Yes. But that was before. Until tonight, I thought anyone could use it. I didn't know Charlie was the only one of you who could. It's the truth, I swear."

"Oh!" Fliss sniffed, looking outraged.

Betty's skin prickled. She wanted to scream at him, to thump him, but her body remained rigid. What a fool she'd been to let herself be taken in, when she had seen how badly he wanted to escape. Her own desperation had blinded her to his. "Don't pretend you actually care what happens to us. For all we know, you might have thought of making Charlie take you somewhere to save your own skin!"

He gave a short, choked laugh. "I may be a thief and a

liar, but I'm not a murderer! I wouldn't make Charlie take me away from Crowstone, or any of you. I couldn't. I'll have to take my chances out on the water."

"Sounds like my kind of plan," a voice growled behind them. Betty spun on her heels, her breath caught in dread.

Jarrod stood a little way into the cave's entrance, one hand clamped over a squirming Charlie's mouth.

"No!" Fliss gasped.

He grinned, displaying his checkerboard teeth.

Colton stepped forward. "Y-you can come with me," he said hoarsely. "We'll leave in the boat together . . . Just let the girls go."

"I wasn't talking about the boat," Jarrod scoffed. "I was talking about the bag."

Chapter Sixteen

Gone

"NO!" BETTY CRIED, HORRIFIED. "You can't take the bag!" After what they had lost, she wasn't about to lose this, too. She darted forward and snatched it from a crate where Charlie had left it. Curiously, Jarrod didn't seem bothered.

"Of course I can." Jarrod cast a wolfish look at Fliss. "I can do anything I want now." He gave Charlie a little shake, like there might be money rattling inside her. "Pumpkin here can take me anywhere."

"She can't." Fliss's voice was low, terrified. "We can't leave Crowstone. If we do . . ."

"It's true," Betty added, struggling to speak above a

whisper as the danger of Jarrod's intentions set in. She had thought things couldn't get any worse—another mistake. "If we leave, we die. We're—"

"Cursed," Jarrod cut in, his voice dripping with sarcasm. "I heard." He smirked. "It's amazing, the things you can learn just by keeping quiet."

Jarrod had been busy, thought Betty. Not just wriggling free of his bonds, but listening, too.

"If it even exists, did you really believe this fool could help you break it? He lured you here with lies," Jarrod said cruelly. "And you fell for them. Luckily for me, he's too much of a coward to use the bag—but I'm not."

"You're not having it," Betty said in as fierce a voice as she could manage. But instead of sounding like a tiger, she sounded like a feeble kitten. "Take the boat and take your chances on the water."

Jarrod grinned down at Charlie. "I'd say my chances are very, very good."

He's got no intention of letting us go, Betty thought. Hopelessness seeped through her. Jarrod knew his freedom would cost lives, and it was a price he was happy to pay.

"Did you hear anything we just said?" Colton's voice rose. "She'll die!"

Jarrod tilted his head to one side, considering. "How soon would she die?"

"By sunset," Fliss said hoarsely.

He nodded. "Good. That gives me a whole day to get as far away as possible. Plenty of snappy little journeys, so I'll get my use out of you."

"But she's just a child!" Fliss gasped. "How could you?"

Charlie stopped struggling and glanced at Betty, then Fliss. "Will it . . . will it hurt?" she asked, trembling.

This can't be happening, Betty screamed silently. *It can't . . . but it is. And all because of me.*

Tears streamed down Fliss's face. She reached out to comfort Charlie, but Jarrod snatched her away.

"You're despicable." Colton took a step toward Jarrod, his eyes blazing. "And you're not leaving this island with her. I won't let you."

"Nor will I." Betty stepped closer to Colton, feeling something that was almost gratitude. He might be a lying swine, but she could see from his own horror that he wasn't evil. Jarrod towered over them both, but perhaps if they fought hard enough, together, Charlie might be able to scramble free.

"Brave talk." Jarrod's voice hardened. "But in the time it'd take for you to reach me, an arm can easily be snapped." The words stopped Betty and Colton in their tracks.

"Won't do it!" Charlie snarled tearfully. Jarrod grabbed her collar and shook her as she went to bite him again.

Fury, red and blazing, seared through Betty's fear at the sight of her little sister being handled like a rat and on hearing the threats being made. "Don't you dare hurt her!"

Jarrod looked bored. "No one needs to get hurt as long as they do as I say."

"I won't take you anywhere!" Charlie cussed, using words she could only have heard from Granny. "And if you break my arm, I can't work the bag, can I, stupid?"

"True," Jarrod agreed. He glowered down at Charlie, who glowered back up at him equally fiercely. "But I never said it would be *your* arm." His free hand shot out and seized Fliss, twisting her arm behind her back. She cried out, knees buckling.

Charlie stopped squirming and held still. "Let her go. Please!"

"That's better." Jarrod relaxed his hold on Fliss a little. "So, now that I know how to get this little savage to do as she's told, we'll have some extra company. Sweet cheeks here can keep the brat under control." He paused, chuckling. "Although she's mighty nice to look at, too."

"Then take me as well!" Betty cried, for the thought of her two sisters being whisked away to their fate and leaving her alone was too terrible to take.

"I don't think so." Jarrod eyed Colton. "You keep the one with the smart mouth. If she's as clever as she thinks she is, she'll break the curse before sunset, won't she?"

"No!" Charlie yelled, reaching for Betty. "No, no, no!"

"Now. Let's try this the nice way, shall we?" Jarrod ruffled Charlie's hair in an almost fatherly gesture. "When you're ready, pumpkin. Take us to Windy Bottom." He held out a hand to Betty, motioning for the bag.

Gritting her teeth, Betty handed it over.

His voice changed, becoming harsher. "Any mischief, taking us back to the prison, or somewhere else you've dreamed up . . . anywhere but where I've said, and it won't be your pretty sister's arm I snap. It'll be her neck."

Charlie's bottom lip trembled. Strands of tangled hair stuck to the tears on her face. "Betty?"

Die now, or die later. Betty stared back at her sisters helplessly. *We can't win*, she realized. *If we leave Crowstone, we die. If we don't obey Jarrod . . .*

"Just . . . just do it." Her voice broke. "Just . . . take him wherever he wants to go."

"B-but . . . the curse," Fliss began.

"Do as he says," Betty whispered. "It will be all right."

As she said it, she felt hopeless, as though something inside her had broken beyond repair. Nothing was all right. If only she had never listened to Colton. Her sisters were going to die because of her. And . . . Granny. Her heart ached. How would she ever tell Granny what she had caused?

"It's not all right." Fliss was fighting tears, holding them back—just—for Charlie's sake, Betty was sure.

"I'll figure it out." Betty was babbling now, grasping at the thinnest of hopes. "I'll put all this right. I swear it." She gave Fliss a meaningful look. If Fliss could keep her wits about her, then there was a chance she could use the mirror to tell Betty where they were. And then, somehow, Betty would have to find them, though she hadn't the first clue how. All she knew was that she didn't want Fliss and Charlie to give up, which meant she couldn't, either. Betty took a deep breath and addressed Jarrod. "As for you, when I catch up with you—and don't think I won't—you'll pay for this."

Jarrod smiled, not threatened in the least. "Promises, promises." He bent down to Charlie, who glared at him hatefully. "Now, listen, pumpkin," he said softly. "When I hand you this bag, you're going to take us to the place I just told you about. Do you remember what it's called?"

"Windy Bottom," Charlie growled.

"Very good." He straightened up with a warning look at Betty. "Stand back."

She refused to look at him, instead focusing on what might be her last look at her two sisters. Too late, she realized she had spent her life wishing for bigger things, for what could be bigger than family? Than love, and being loved? What use was adventure with no one to share in it? Along with Granny, her sisters were all she had. Her whole world, which was about to be torn away . . . and opened up to the curse, the very thing they'd been trying to undo. Now, with one command, Jarrod was about to set the terrible event into motion.

"I'll find you," she promised, stumbling back. Though she meant it with every fiber of her being, she knew — everyone knew — that finding them would not be enough. Even if she could save them from Jarrod, the curse would still kill them. "Wherever you go, I'll find you."

In a voice that suddenly sounded weary and much older than that of a six-year-old, Charlie spoke quietly: "Windy Bottom."

In an eye blink the three figures were gone. The only proof that they had ever been there was their footprints in the sand.

Betty's vision blurred. And no matter how hard she tried to stop crying, or to tell herself that tears wouldn't bring her sisters back, she was helpless to do anything but sob. Her sisters were gone, and the curse had been triggered. Unless Betty found a way to break it, Charlie and Fliss would be dead by sunset.

Chapter Seventeen

The Devil's Teeth

A MINUTE PASSED, OR PERHAPS TWO. She couldn't tell. And yet time was more important now than ever before. Time was her sisters' lives, and it was ticking away. Bringing them back before sunset wouldn't save them . . . unless Betty found a way to undo the curse. But at least she'd get to see them again. Perhaps that was the best she could hope for.

She was crying so hard that she never saw Colton moving closer to her. The touch of his hand on her arm came as a surprise. She blinked away her tears, sniffing. He patted her awkwardly, the actions of someone who had forgotten how to be near people, but the fact that he was trying brought her some small comfort.

"I'm sorry," he whispered. "I'm so, so sorry. This is all my fault. I should never have brought you here. I lied, but I never wanted any of you to get hurt. You have to believe me."

"I do," she managed, between sobs. Colton had acted despicably, but she knew he had done so out of desperation, and despite the fact that he had tricked them, she had seen his disgust when Jarrod had announced his plan. More than that, he had tried to stop it. For that, she couldn't hate him, even if she didn't forgive him. It was Jarrod who had triggered the curse, not Colton.

It's not over yet, she thought. *There's still time before sunset . . . time to at least get my sisters out of Jarrod's clutches and stop him from getting away with this.* And sniveling in a cave wasn't going to save any of them.

She stopped crying and steeled her voice. "I need that boat."

Colton gaped. "The boat? Surely you're not—?"

"I'm going after them."

"But you can't leave Crowstone! You know what that would mean. You could go back to your granny, try to get help from the warders, tip them off somehow—"

"There's no time," Betty snapped. "It's hours before the first ferry! I have to help my sisters and break the curse before it's too late. If it even can be broken."

"My father once told me that everything that's made can be broken," Colton said softly. "And most things that are broken can be mended. There has to be a way."

Betty nodded wretchedly. *Why couldn't I have just lived with staying in Crowstone?* she asked herself. Charlie and Fliss could have. But because she hadn't accepted it, they might not live at all. Deep down, she couldn't let go of the hope that the Widdershins curse could be undone. "The question is, can I do it in time?"

"We." Colton exhaled shakily. "Can *we* do it in time."

"We?" she croaked.

"I'm coming with you."

"But . . . why?"

"You know why. I'm responsible for this. If your sisters died, I wouldn't be able to live with myself." He shrugged helplessly. "Besides, there's only one boat."

Betty bit back a sarcastic remark. She didn't doubt Colton's guilt, but saving his own neck was still his driving force, though she couldn't really blame him. Crowstone punishments were always harsh. The penalty for escaping was death. Helping someone escape meant prison time, usually followed by banishment to Torment.

"All right." In her mind's eye she pictured the maps she had spent so many hours poring over. Finally, the hours had paid off. "Windy Bottom is north, not too far from Marshfoot on the other side of the water. Once we're across we'll need a faster way to travel, but I'd say we can make it by late morning." *If we make it across the water alive*, she thought grimly. "The question is, will Jarrod still be there? With the bag and Charlie he could be anywhere in an instant."

"If that was the first place he thought of, then he must have links to it," Colton said thoughtfully. "Perhaps he grew up there, or had family. My guess is he'll hide out for a while."

"What makes you think so?"

Colton chewed his lip, considering. "Jarrod never planned any of this. Everything that happened to him tonight happened by chance—he's thinking as he goes along, which means he's more likely to stick with what he already knows."

Betty nodded, reassured a little . . . and surprised to be taking comfort from Colton. "And if he's gone when we arrive?"

"Let's worry about that when we get there. If they're gone, someone might have seen them or might know something that could help us."

"Then let's go," said Betty.

Colton heaped more sacking into the bottom of the

boat. "The prison patrol will already be on the water looking for Jarrod and me."

Betty gazed out to the water, a ribbon of moonlight shimmering on the choppy surface. The shingle between the cave and the water had narrowed, the waves creeping closer. They seemed to be beckoning, urging her toward her sisters . . . but they could have just as easily been luring her in, waiting to swallow her.

Her pulse quickened. "Look. The tide is rising."

Colton glanced around in alarm, then began loading things into the boat more quickly.

"Let it come. We need the tide." She watched the flow of the water rising, then curling back. Daring them to take the gamble. "It's our only chance of clearing the Devil's Teeth."

Some of Colton's confidence trickled away. "The Devil's Teeth?"

"I told you there were rocks!" Worry began to build in the pit of Betty's stomach. "Deadly rocks. There's a reason these caves are called the Three Widows—because of all the shipwrecks. Smugglers used to hide here at low tide and shine lights to guide the boats in. They'd hit the rocks and sink, and their cargo would wash ashore." She paused, watching the choppy water rushing up the shingle. "You can't see the rocks too well at night, just the water breaking over them. But they're there, under the surface." She swept her arm in a wide arc. "Formed in a crescent shape, like a moon, or . . ."

"Jaws with teeth," Colton finished. "As cheerful as the rest of Lament, then."

"Have you ever rowed a boat?"

Colton threw the oars in the boat. "Not for years."

Betty's chest tightened. She knew from stories of sinking ferries that crossing the water could be dangerous with an experienced boatman. Crossing the water with a novice was madness, but what choice did she have? Abandoning Fliss and Charlie wasn't an option. Together they heaved the boat down to the shingle and got in. Colton handed Betty a wad of sacking to wrap around her shoulders as she sat on the narrow bench.

Betty stared at the shingle and the slimy mud oozing beneath the side of the boat. How many lives had the rocks claimed over the years? Too many to count, that was for sure. And now she and Colton were about to grapple with them, too. As she watched, murky water trickled over the pebbles, slicking them with moisture. The tide was coming in, faster now.

She swallowed but stayed silent. Would she ever see the Poacher's Pocket again? Or would her final moments be spent with a stranger, fighting for their lives on the Devil's Teeth? She wondered if Granny had discovered that the girls were gone, or if she'd only find out in the morning. Granny. Betty tried to remember the last time she had hugged her. If only she had known things would come to this, she would have made the hug a little longer, a little tighter.

The water was lapping around the boat now. It lurched suddenly. Betty gripped the side, steadying herself as Colton dug an oar into the shingle, pinning the boat where it was.

"Not yet," he muttered, squinting across the water to where several jagged rocks were breaking the water's surface. "Not until those final Devil's Teeth have been swallowed." He handed Betty the other oar. "Here."

She took it, thrusting it into the sludgy water below them, holding it tight. The boat bobbed, eager to take to the waves, but she angled the oar, resisting its pull until her arms throbbed. *Not yet, not yet, not yet . . .*

And just when she thought she would have to let go, Colton said, "Now!" He took the oar from her, and she heard a gulping glug as he pulled it from the sludge and began rowing. Betty glanced back as the cliff face moved away from them. The Three Widows watched them, the yawning blackness of the caves like faces covered with mourning veils. Her stomach lurched, not from the water but from the fear of what lay under it: those treacherous, jagged rocks that were just waiting to tear into the boat's wooden flesh.

"Let me help you!" she cried. "I can row!"

"No. I need your eyes on the water," Colton grunted. "Look for the Teeth breaking the surface. If you can see any, then we need to hold back. There's a current pulling us toward the rocks."

Betty rushed to the front of the boat. She trained her eyes on the inky water, familiarizing herself with the push and pull, until she was able to see the little spots where the water ebbed differently.

"There!" She pointed, panic rising in her throat. "There's one just ahead, breaking the surface!"

"How far?" Colton asked urgently.

"Not very — a stone's throw." She waited as the retreating tide swept back over the glistening shard of rock, hiding it. For as far back as she could remember, there had always been drownings and accidents in this cove. Lungs filled with water, heads bashed on rocks. She sensed the Three Widows watching, ready to mourn.

"Will the water rise higher if we can hold off?" Colton asked. He strained against the oars, rowing backwards now to keep them on the spot. Sweat shimmered above his eyebrows.

Betty glanced back to the shore, her gaze locking on a layer of crusted seaweed partway up the cliff face. The water had almost reached its full height here.

"Maybe a little, but not enough to get us over the rock. Our only chance is to use the waves. You'll need my help."

"Rowing is hard," Colton said. "I need to know you're up to it."

"I'm up to anything if it stops us from getting smashed to smithereens," she said indignantly. "Give me an oar."

Colton passed one to her. "Face the caves. It'll be easier to row, and one of us needs to be looking that way for this to work."

Betty took the oar, less confident now she was no longer holding the edge of the boat. She shifted her weight, trying to get her balance. The oar was heavy, and with the waves growing ever choppier, it felt as though the water was sucking on it, trying to draw her into its murky depths. The boat began to drift.

"Row, then!" Colton snapped.

"All right!" she retorted hotly, dragging the oar through the water in the same direction as Colton. Immediately she realized it was harder than it looked, but she gritted her teeth and found the rhythm.

Colton nodded approvingly. "Good. Now, I'll watch the front of the boat. You watch the waves breaking by the caves, and count how long it takes for them to wash back and clear the rocks."

Betty nodded. With a bit of luck and a lot of work, they could ride the waves, the swell giving them the lift they needed over the rocks. She tried not to think of the Widdershinses' track record when it came to luck. She fixed her stare on a large wave as it broke, crashing against the cliff before rolling back toward the boat and then out to sea.

"One, two, three . . ."

The boat lifted considerably on "three," rising on the wave before dipping. The wave carried past them and over the rocks, clearing them easily.

"We have to catch one of those waves," said Colton. "The next big one. You ready?"

Betty gulped. "As I'll ever be."

The boat bobbed like a cork, dancing on smaller waves as if it were teasing them, testing them.

"Not yet," Colton murmured. "Hold fast . . ."

Betty clenched her jaw, working the oar. She felt

the pull of muscles rarely used, between her shoulder blades, in her arms and stomach. It was an effort keeping the boat steady, and her swings of the oar in time with Colton's. She felt the next wave rise up from under them, lifting and then lowering the boat as it coursed toward the caves.

"Now!" Betty yelled as it crashed, and with that they changed direction, pulling backwards for all they were worth. She was unable to look away from the wave as it swept into the cave, before rushing back toward them and out to sea. Would it be enough?

Please let it be enough . . .

Already the boat was moving with surprising speed. She heard Colton's breathing, rasping and ragged, and realized that she, too, was gasping with the effort. Glancing over her shoulder, she searched for those treacherous teeth, waiting to gnash the boat to pieces. And when she saw four of them jutting from the water, she wished she hadn't looked. They were so close, greedy for blood and bone. They surely wouldn't make it over them . . .

"Give it all you've got!" Colton roared.

The boat surged upward, carried on the wave. Betty rowed, with every breath and every screaming muscle. And then they were rushing out of the cove, riding the water like a great fluid dragon, and still Betty pulled the oar for all she was worth. Blisters rose on her palms, but she wouldn't let herself stop.

As the wave got away from them, the boat jerked as something caught its belly from below, like a fingernail scraping a scab. Colton gasped, reaching out to grab her. Together they froze as the water's surface calmed. For a moment neither of them moved; then, slowly, Betty turned to face him.

"We made it." Colton's voice was incredulous. "I can't believe we made it."

Betty peered back through the darkness, searching the water. The pointed tip of a rock jutted from the surface, like a skittle that refused to fall. Colton crouched down, running his hand along the bottom of the boat.

"Can't feel any leaks," he said hesitantly. "But that was close."

"Too close," Betty whispered. Her hands were still clamped around the oar. She realized she was shaking. How narrowly they had escaped! The Devil's Teeth had had a taste of the boat but had not quite managed to swallow it. She stared at Colton, seeing her own relief mirrored back at her.

It remained unsaid, but Betty was certain he knew as well as she did that strangely, the experience had bound them, somehow—for neither of them would have made it without the other.

Silently, Colton took the oar from her and began to row farther out, the job easier now that they were away from the pull of the cove's currents.

Betty stayed frozen where she was, teeth chattering. Ahead, she saw only a vast expanse of water. Behind, Lament was blocking any signs of life from mainland Crowstone. She stared, waiting and hoping to see the lights in the distance, and the irony was not lost on her that she now longed for a last glimpse of home, of the place she'd waited so long to escape from. She had always thought this moment would be a victory. Instead, she was with a stranger, and stood to lose everything she cared about. She had never felt more lost.

She blew into her numb fingers, trying to coax warmth back into them.

"How long before we reach land on the other side?" Colton asked.

Betty squeezed her eyes shut, recalling past trips to Repent on the ferry, and the timetable for Marshfoot. "Hard to say. A couple of hours, probably, if we're going farther inland." What time was it now? Midnight? Later? She had no idea. The night had stretched for what felt like forever. How many hours until sunrise, when they would no longer have the cover of night to hide them? Each hour that passed was an hour closer to her sisters' deaths . . . and her own, now that she was leaving Crowstone, too. She had thought she would feel different, more afraid, yet all she could think of was Charlie's and Fliss's faces, painted with horror . . . and Jarrod's cunning, broken smile. If they were going to die, it couldn't be afraid and alone with him.

"Are you going to tell me what he did?"

"Huh?"

"Jarrod. You said he's dangerous." Her voice quavered. "And now that he has my sisters, I need to know what we're up against."

Colton hesitated, deepening Betty's fears.

"Tell me!"

"All right! He . . . he kills people. I mean, killed people. He was a lifer in that place. He would never have been released, so the warders say."

"Kills people?" Betty asked faintly.

"For money." Colton's disgust was plain. "There were no limits to what he'd do . . . or who he'd do it to. Revenge, money owed . . . whatever the reason, he'd do it." His voice hardened. "He's a monster. Last year there was a riot. Jarrod broke one warder's legs and almost killed another. They say his youngest victim—"

"Stop!" Betty cried. The memory of her sisters' terrified faces swam before her, their panic becoming hers. How ready Jarrod had been to hurt Fliss to get what he wanted. He could make them do anything, Betty realized. His greatest weapon was their love for each other. "I can't bear to hear any more!"

"Hey." Colton stopped rowing and touched her arm. "I'm sorry. I didn't mean to frighten you. But you asked. For what it's worth, I don't think he'll hurt them as long as they're useful. And that bag makes them very, very useful."

This was the only grain of comfort Betty had to cling to.

"What if we don't find them? Saving them from Jarrod is just the start!" Her throat closed as tears swam in her eyes. She had wanted so badly to change things. Though Fliss had always been content at home, breaking the curse could have meant more for Charlie: happier memories of growing up and visiting new places. Tonight could mean no more memories made for any of them. Betty had changed things, all right. At least if she failed, she wouldn't have to live with the guilt over her sisters' deaths . . . because she would die with them.

"You need to get that bag," Colton said thoughtfully.

"Once you have it, Charlie can get you anywhere, and fast. Then you can search for answers."

"We could if we knew where to look," Betty croaked. "All I can think is that the answer to breaking the curse must be in Crowstone, if that's where it all began."

Colton stayed silent for a moment. Then he nodded to the bundle of rags in the bottom of the boat. "You should lie down and rest. You're going to need your strength."

Betty shook her head. "I couldn't possibly sleep. My tummy is all tied up in knots, for one thing. And for another, it's too bleedin' cold."

"Lie down anyway," Colton said gruffly. "At least it'll be warmer in the blankets."

Reluctantly, Betty lowered herself into the jumble of sacking. It smelled fishy and stale, but at least it was dry. Her mind churned over the events of the night, chopping and changing with the waves. Unexpectedly, something came back to her.

"Earlier, just before Jarrod turned up, you said you knew something else about the tower. What was it?"

"When we first met in the prison, I told you the curse began in the tower," he continued. "I—I told your granny the same thing. Whether it's true or not, I don't know—"

"So another lie."

"Wait. Just hear me out." Colton paused to wrap

230

scraps of rag around his palms, then took the oars again. "During the summer, a handful of us were chosen to clear the tower out, make repairs, that sort of thing."

"Wasn't anyone being kept in there?" Betty asked.

"Not anymore. Rumor has it that no one's been held in there since that girl flung herself from the window. The one they called a witch."

"Sorsha Spellthorn," Betty whispered.

"As soon as you go in there, you can . . . feel it's not right. On the surface it's like any other cell: cold, cobwebbed. A threadbare bed. But in that place, it's the walls that really tell a story . . ."

"What . . . what was on the walls?" Betty asked.

"Words." There was a sheen of sweat on Colton's face now. "They made us paint them. Covered in words, they were. She'd started marking the days she'd been locked in there, along with these four words: 'malice,' 'injustice,' 'betrayal,' 'escape.' Just those same words, over and over, scrawled until they were barely readable. Until, right by the window, there was only . . ."

"Only what?"

"One word." He hesitated. "'Widdershins.'"

"Widdershins?" Betty sat up, tense. "Are you sure?"

He nodded. "I know what I saw."

Anticipation flared like a beacon within her. If this

was true, Sorsha Spellthorn had been linked to the Widdershinses. "This had better not be another one of your lies, Colton."

"It's not, I swear!" He stopped rowing and stared at her in earnest. "What reason would I have to lie to you now?"

Betty found she was gripping the edge of the sacking. She could think of no motive for Colton to lie—he'd gotten what he wanted from them. More importantly, what he'd said fit like a puzzle piece into the rest of the information she had about Sorsha. Someone who could work magic, and who had scratched her family's name into the walls of Crowstone Tower as the result of some deep-rooted grudge. She felt certain this was it: the beginning of the curse.

"By the end of that first day, the place looked completely different," Colton continued. "Cobwebs gone, the bed cleared out, and the walls freshly painted. But the next day we were hauled back again, and from the way the warders were whispering, we knew something was wrong. And when we entered that tower room the second day, we knew."

"Knew what?"

"Knew the place was cursed. We thought it was a trick at first. Some of the warders would take any chance to scare us or to make our time there as unpleasant as they could. But we could see they were as shocked as we were. Because the entire room was exactly as it had been the morning before. Every word on the walls, every last cobweb. Like we'd never lifted a finger."

Two days before, Betty would have scoffed at this. Now the words easily conjured up an icy foreboding.

"So we did it again. Only, that second day we worked twice as fast and twice as hard. My knuckles bled from scrubbing those walls. I wanted to get out of there as much as everyone else did. But the next day, just like before, it was all back. And that time, they didn't make us try again."

"So it's just left, the way it was when Sorsha Spellthorn was there?" Betty asked. "That's more than a century!"

Colton nodded. "They can do nothing with it. Can't empty the place, can't knock it down. It's like her death left a stain on it."

Betty's dread deepened. A stain . . . or a curse? Sorsha Spellthorn wasn't just some story. She'd been a real person: desperate and angry enough to fling herself from the tower. Whatever her powers, they hadn't saved her. "There's something I don't understand. If Sorsha was a sorceress, why didn't she use magic to escape?"

"That's one of the mysteries of the place," Colton said.

"There had to be something about that tower that rendered her powerless."

"Did you tell my father?" Betty asked. "About the name being carved into the wall?"

"No. It all happened after he'd been moved. But by then, I knew about the traveling bag and what it could do, so—"

Betty pounced. "How? How did you know about the bag? You never did explain that."

"The first time I saw it, it was being used by your granny to hit your father on the head," he admitted.

"Nothing strange about that," Betty replied. She'd seen Granny do that more than once.

"She was in his cell at the time."

"But visitors aren't allowed . . ." Betty stopped. Of course. The only way Granny could have visited their father's cell was in the same way she and her sisters had reached Colton's. "She was using the bag to visit him in secret?"

"Only once, that I knew of," said Colton. "In the middle of the night. And she made it pretty clear it wouldn't be happening again."

"Why would she risk that?"

"It was just after he found out he was getting moved. They were whispering, arguing."

Betty nodded. Granny and Father always bickered, about everything. She felt a tiny thrill laced with longing at the thought of Granny visiting in secret. How daring she was, how like Betty in more than their bluntness!

"He was asking her to get him out," said Colton. "To visit his girls one last time before he moved. At first I didn't pay much attention. I thought he was being dramatic, that he could just as easily be visited wherever he was getting moved to. I was more interested in how an old woman had got into the cells in the middle of the night, so I crept out of bed and watched through the bars. That's when she walloped him with the bag and told him he couldn't risk coming home.

"They quieted down after that, and I struggled to hear, but two words that kept rising up were 'bag' and 'curse.' They argued some more, getting louder. Other prisoners started to wake. And that's when I saw her put her hand in the bag. The next moment, she'd gone. Disappeared completely.

"I couldn't sleep after that, not till sunrise. After waking, I almost convinced myself it was a dream, but something in me knew what I'd seen was real. A week later your father was transferred out. And so . . ."

"So from that, you plotted the whole thing," Betty finished. There was something sickening about knowing he had used her family's misfortune for his own gain. But then, she reminded herself, she had done shameful things to get what she wanted, too. She had lied and stolen, not from strangers but her own family. Perhaps that made her a bigger wretch than he was.

He nodded. "I wrote to your granny at the Poacher's Pocket and said I had information for her. It was enough to bring her to the prison."

"For you to start weaving your lies."

"Yes." Colton spoke quietly, his words threaded with shame. "I knew it was wrong. But I told myself I was surviving." Abruptly he stopped rowing and sat up straighter. The boat continued to slide through the water in silence.

"What is it?" asked Betty.

Colton stared past her, his eyes narrowed. "I thought I saw something."

Betty turned to look over her shoulder. She met with a chilling sight: thick, gray fog was slowly creeping toward them over the water.

"Jumping jackdaws," she breathed in horror. "We'll never find our way out of that!"

"We may not have to," Colton said grimly.

Betty frowned. "What?"

Then she saw it: a light straining through the hazy,

foggy darkness. Growing bigger, getting closer. "Is that . . . ?"

"A boat," Colton finished. He drew in the oars and stowed them, then crouched next to her. "It must be the warders. Quickly, get down!"

Chapter Eighteen

Hostage

BETTY DUCKED INTO THE BELLY of the boat. Her nostrils filled with the smell of stale fish and old nets. "You really think it's the warders?" she whispered. "Could it be someone else? A fishing boat, perhaps?"

"We'd have to be lucky. Very lucky. The warders are probably checking every boat in case Jarrod or me are on it." Colton's words were rushed, tumbling over each other. "Perhaps we could capsize the boat and hide under it . . . but even then, the water would only finish us off. Unless . . ." His dark brows furrowed in concentration. "They're only looking for me, not you. If you were caught, you wouldn't be in any trouble—"

"Except the Widdershinses' name is linked to yours in the visiting book, and has been for months," Betty said at once. "And I'm thirteen years old! They'd take me straight home." She rolled onto her knees, keeping her head low. "We've come too far now. I'm not giving up and going back to Crowstone. I'm finding my sisters, with or without you." She reached into her pockets and took out the nesting dolls. Up till now there had been no need for Colton to know about them—but now she had no choice. They needed to hide. Using her fingernails, she pried the first one apart, then removed the next.

Colton's eyes widened. "What are those?"

"Something that's going to save our skin."

"How?"

"We're going to vanish."

"Vanish? You mean, disappear?"

"Exactly."

Colton's eyes raked over the dolls. "They're magical, just like the bag, aren't they?"

Betty nodded. "And they're our only chance now. If the warders can't see us, then they can't catch us, right?" She looked at him desperately, willing him to agree. "If they think it's just a drifting boat, they might pass us by."

Colton's face was layered with doubt. "They could just as easily tow the boat back to shore."

"Maybe," Betty admitted. "But it would still buy us some time, to figure out another idea. We've a better chance this way, surely?"

"Better chance of what?" Colton hissed. "Ending up back where we started?" He glanced back, shaking his head violently, and Betty glimpsed the resolve in his face. Colton had as much to lose as she did, and he wasn't quitting. It lent her strength. He peered over the side of the boat, eyes glinting with reflective light, before dropping back down, breathing hard. "They're close now. Two of them rowing, I think."

"Did they see you?" Betty asked. She fumbled with the smaller dolls, panic making her clumsy.

"Don't think so." He nodded at the dolls. "Just do it. Make us disappear."

Betty finally managed to open the second and third dolls, her frozen fingers trembling. "I need something of yours, quickly. A strand of hair, piece of jewelry . . . something like that."

"I don't have anything like that!" Colton gave her a fierce look. Her eyes swept over him: his closely shorn hair, the rags he wore that barely classed as clothing. No jewelry, of course. She glanced at his hands, seeing only fingernails so chewed they were bleeding in places.

"For crow's sake," she muttered, then spied a corner of

his tunic collar that was coming unstitched. With no time to think about it, she rolled closer and tore at it with her teeth. The taste of old sweat filled her mouth.

"Ugh." She spat the scrap into the lower half of the third doll, then clamped the top half of the doll in place, carefully lining up the intricate painted patterns on the outside.

"You're all crazy, you Widdershins girls," Colton muttered in bemusement.

"Don't let Fliss hear you say that. Anyway, we got all our bad habits from Granny." She placed the doll inside the second one, biting off her thumbnail and flicking that in, too, once again taking care to line up the two halves exactly. Finally, she placed them into the largest one.

He waited. "Now what?"

Betty held the nesting dolls tightly to her chest, wishing she could hide the thundering of her heartbeat. "Now nothing," she whispered. "We can't be seen."

"You sure?" Already Colton was leaning over the side of the boat. "Hey . . . my reflection is gone!" He turned to her in confusion. "But I can still see you . . . ?"

She nodded. "And we can still be heard . . . and felt—"

She stopped speaking at the sound of oars splashing

through the water. Lifting a warning finger to her lips, she curled herself into the boat's seat. Colton was too tall for that, so instead lay back silently along the opposite side of the boat, mirroring the curve of the wood. They waited.

It was the fog that found them first, thick and fish-belly gray, reaching over their heads like a shroud. The slap of oars on water grew louder, then stopped as the approaching boat cut through the water. It bumped into them without warning, causing Betty to bite her tongue. Something cold rattled under her elbow. Lifting her arm, she found a fish hook, pointed and sharp. If they were caught, perhaps it could act as a weapon. She tucked it into her sleeve, alarmed at her own ferocity. She had never hurt anyone before . . . but no one was going to prevent her from reaching her sisters. She would do whatever it took.

Light flooded from above as a lantern was held aloft, blurring everything beyond it into gray. A man's voice cut through the mist.

"Empty, save for a load of old rags."

Betty tensed. She knew that voice; she was sure of it! But from where? Before she could place it, a second man spoke. "The oars are still in it. I could've sworn I saw movement . . . a figure."

This voice was younger, sharper, and not one Betty recognized. There was something confident about the way he spoke. This was someone who didn't scare easily.

"The boat's solid. No signs of a struggle or an accident. Looks like it's been abandoned."

Without warning, a hand reached past Betty's face to rummage through the supplies Colton had thrown in. Carefully, she lifted her shawl to cover her mouth, afraid the warmth of her breath might be detected in the cold air.

The lantern shifted, and light played over two faces. The younger fellow had a hard, waxy face. He was dressed in a warder's uniform, and beneath a sparse mustache was an equally thin mouth that was spiteful in appearance.

The other man, to Betty's great astonishment, was Fingerty. What was he doing out here?

"Well?" The warder's voice was impatient. "Could the felons have been using this boat?"

Fingerty frowned at the oars and scratched his chin with long, thick fingernails. "Yerp. I mean, it's possible. But . . ." He hesitated, glancing through the mist as though trying to decipher something. "From the path we've jest taken, I'd say this boat's come from Lament."

The warder spat. Betty heard it hit the water. *Phlat.* Her lip curled in revulsion.

"How could they have got to Lament? Makes no sense! No boats were seen, none were taken from Repent!"

At this Betty grinned to herself, both with glee and relief. The only people being searched for appeared to be Colton and Jarrod. There was no mention of the girls, and the bag's magic had created a baffling mystery that had thrown the warders off the scent. Her smile vanished at the thought of the bag, now in Jarrod's possession. It was the most valuable item they'd had, and now it was out of reach, in the grasp of someone infinitely dangerous, along with something even more precious: her sisters.

"Well, they got off the island somehow," Fingerty remarked drily. "Either that or they're still there, which means the warders are crooked or useless."

"And you'd know all about that, wouldn't you?" the warder growled. "You were the most crooked one of them all."

"Heh." Fingerty snickered. "Lucky for you I was."

"You're the lucky one." The warder's voice dripped with contempt. "As lucky as a weasel like you can be, anyway. You could be slammed away again like that"—he snapped his fingers—"if we thought you were up to your old tricks, or if anyone on the mainland finds out you're our eyes and ears there." He chuckled unpleasantly. "And you're never too old for a beating. We own you, Fingerty, and that's the way it'll stay . . . unless you get yourself a good catch. A very good catch."

All traces of humor left Fingerty then. His face creased back into its usual scowl like a chicken settling to roost.

"Bring the boat back with us," the warder ordered. "Can't have it floating around by itself; never know who might come across it."

Betty silently bit into her shawl. This was all going so very wrong. Being taken back to any of the islands was going to cost precious time—time they didn't have, and wherever they ended up, Colton would be in danger of being discovered.

Fingerty leaned over the boat. "Can't see no towing rope."

"Then get in and row," the warder snapped. "And the lantern stays with me, so you'd better keep up."

Fingerty stepped into the boat. It rocked a little under his weight, but he stayed steady, surefooted as if he were on dry land. He remained standing, scanning the boat with a perplexed expression.

"Boat don't feel right," he muttered, more to himself than to the warder. Using his toe, he nudged aside the blankets, as though searching for something.

"What are you bleating about now?"

"This boat," Fingerty repeated. "S'not sitting quite right. Feels heavier than it should."

Betty glanced at Colton in alarm. Fingerty was an experienced boat man; he'd know exactly how an empty boat should feel when he stepped into it. Only, this boat now carried the weight of three people. She wanted to scream. Why, why, why, did it have to be Fingerty? If he discovered her, took her back, there would be questions, delays, and absolutely no chance of finding Charlie and Fliss before sunset. The hook trembled in her fingers. She couldn't hurt someone she knew, who had helped her, could she?

"Probably just the timber." The warder yawned, setting the lantern down. Betty heard the scrape of wood as he picked up the oars.

"Nah." Fingerty stood rigid, like a dog whose hackles were up. "Nowt to do with the timber. I'm telling yer, somethin' ain't right." He shifted his weight from side to side, and Betty clutched the nesting dolls even tighter to her, afraid they would roll away or rattle.

The warder gave a low, mocking chuckle. "I suppose the next thing you're going to say is that it could be the weight of dead souls aboard it. That we've come across a ghost vessel, drifting out and looking for fresh souls to claim."

"Shouldn't make jokes like that," Fingerty snapped. "Strange things have happened out on this water. Terrible things."

"Just row." The warder sounded bored now. "It'll take more than your stories to scare me. And keep your eyes peeled. Those two cretins are out here somewhere, and I want to be the one to return them."

The sound of rippling water reached Betty's ears: the warder had begun to row.

Fingerty sat down finally, breathing heavily. He grabbed the oars, then peered into the mist up ahead. As quickly as she dared, Betty slid out from under the seat behind Fingerty, taking care not to sway the boat. She raised herself up onto her knees. Already, the warder's boat had vanished from sight, swallowed by the soupy fog.

"Slow down!" Fingerty called. Then, "Is there a spare lantern?"

"No," came the abrupt reply. "So keep up!"

Fingerty began to row, cursing under his breath. Betty's hand skimmed his grizzled hair as the action propelled him back, and he gave a slight shudder. With each drag of the oars, desperation surged within her. She glanced at Colton, willing him to act, to push Fingerty overboard, to do anything that would change their course away from Crowstone, but he had folded himself up so impossibly near to Fingerty's foot that he couldn't move without being discovered. All Betty could think of was her sisters getting farther and farther away from her. The only way she could change things and give them a chance was to take a risk.

Shoving fear aside, she leaned close to Fingerty's ear and spoke in a low, cold voice: "Listen up, Fingerty, and don't make a sound—"

Fingerty let out a loud yelp and turned, dropping an oar. The boat lurched as he lashed out with his hand. Betty tried to move backwards but wasn't fast enough, and his fist caught her in the chest. She lost her balance and toppled, landing on the fishing nets with a heavy bump.

"Who's there?" Fingerty yelled. His head whipped from side to side, terror in his eyes as he searched for this unseen enemy.

"Fingerty?" the warder called. His voice was irritable, but faint, indicating that he had put some distance between himself and them. "What's rattled you? Keep up, you old goat!"

Betty rolled onto her side, a groan escaping her.

Fingerty flinched at the sound, his breath quickening in quick puffs on the misty air, and she realized how eerie her groan must have sounded to someone spooked, who couldn't see her. And then, she saw, as Fingerty raised the oar he still held, how fear could make someone dangerous. He swung the oar blindly, and Betty trembled as it cut through the air above her head.

"Fingerty!" the warder bellowed. "What're you doing back there?"

"Here!" he yelled. "Get me off this boat . . . There's something on it!"

Betty cowered below the oar. She had hoped that Fingerty might freeze with fear when she had spoken to him, but he had reacted far more quickly — and differently — than she had expected.

With a gasp, Fingerty was pulled backwards as strong arms wrapped around him and pulled . . . hard. His legs went from under him as he tripped over the bench. He landed in the bottom of the boat. By the time Betty had hauled herself up, Fingerty was on his back like a beetle and Colton had the old man's arms pinned beneath his knees, with one hand holding the oar and the other clamped over Fingerty's mouth. Fingerty, of course, saw nothing except the oar hovering above his nose. Over the sound of his panicked breathing the only thing that could be heard was the warder's oars cutting through the water, drawing ever nearer.

Betty darted across and kneeled by Fingerty, scarcely believing her own actions. She pressed the fish hook to his neck.

"As I was saying," she whispered fiercely, "don't make a sound. Do everything we say, and you won't get hurt. Understand?"

Wide-eyed with fright, Fingerty nodded vigorously. Warily, Colton took his hand away from the man's mouth.

"We?" Fingerty managed. "Are you sp-spirits of the marshes? What magic is this?"

"Not spirits. And all you need to know is this is powerful magic." Betty leaned close to Fingerty's face, so close she could smell the greasiness of his hair. "Magic that could make you disappear for good."

She felt mildly ashamed as Fingerty gulped, but she squashed it down. She had to get him onside in any way she could. By hook or by crook, she thought grimly, removing the sharp crescent from his neck. In a single motion, she sliced a brass button from Fingerty's overcoat. "Now, here's what's going to happen, so listen carefully." She thrust the hook at Colton, then pulled out the nesting dolls and wrested them apart. "In a moment, you're going to vanish from sight, just like us. When the warder gets here, you say and do nothing to draw his attention, do you hear?"

Again, Fingerty nodded. He licked his lips, and croaked, "Who . . . who are you? I'm sure . . . your voice seems familiar . . ."

"You're about to find out," Betty said grimly. "What's that warder's name?"

"Pike," Fingerty replied. "Tobias Pike."

"Good. Now, quiet, not one word." She searched through the mist. The sound of Pike's boat was louder, but thanks to the thickening mist, there was no sight of it yet. They still had time, just.

Betty opened the nesting dolls, and Fingerty jumped with surprise as she and Colton reappeared.

"You!" he whispered, his face contorting with shock and rage. "But yer jest a child—! And you . . . yer one of the ones we're looking for! Jest what is going on here?"

"Shut up," Colton hissed. He brandished the fish hook above Fingerty's nose. "You'll give us away!"

Fingerty clamped his lips together, watching as Betty added the severed button from his coat to the hollow space inside the dolls.

"That's it?" Fingerty whispered.

Betty nodded. "None of us can be seen. Now, quiet."

Colton lowered the oar next to the one Fingerty had

dropped, before crouching next to the old man, keeping the hook by his throat as a dangerous reminder. Betty positioned herself at the rear of the boat. Her heartbeat quickened as a dark shape loomed through the fog, and a pale orb of light floated nearer as the lantern was lifted.

"Fingerty!" Pike growled. "Where are you, you sniveling coward? I thought you knew these marshes! That you didn't scare easily!" He leaned over the boat. His face creased into confusion as his eyes swept over the oars, then blindly over Fingerty and Colton, and vaguely in Betty's direction.

"Fingerty?" he yelled, wide-eyed. "Fingerty!"

Betty's insides churned. The temptation to call out was etched on Fingerty's face, but with Colton glowering over him, his fear was stronger.

Pike's own eyes narrowed. "Where is the old fool?" he muttered. "Can't have vanished into thin air . . ." He swung the lantern about him, then back to the seemingly empty boat, making no effort to leave.

Betty hesitated, then drew in a breath. When she released it, it was to speak in a hissing, high-pitched whisper. "Tobiasssss Pike!"

The warder jerked back at the sound of his name.

"Wh-who's there?" he asked in a voice that was suddenly shaky. He clutched the oar like it was a sword, but it shook like a reed in the wind.

"Leave thissss place, Tobiassss Pike!" Betty whispered. "Leave and never return . . . or elsssse you will ssssuffer a terrible fate!"

Pike's face drained, becoming haggard. "Fingerty . . . ?" he croaked, all pretense at bravery forgotten. "Is this a trick?"

"Gone . . . gone . . . gone . . ." Betty chanted. She was almost beginning to enjoy herself now. Pike was a bully who deserved a taste of what he dished up to others. "Claimed by the sssspirit of the marshes . . ." She paused dramatically. "Yet sssstill, I hunger for another sssssoul . . ."

Pike let out a strangled half sob. He fell back and began dragging the oars through the water as though he were pulling himself out of his own grave. Within seconds he was surrounded by the fog once more, and all that could be heard was the frantic splashing of the oars as he made his getaway. And Betty couldn't help it; she began to laugh in relief, which only made Pike row faster. She cackled until her sides ached, an eerie, echoing noise that sounded strange even to her. She only stopped when Pike's thrashing oars could no longer be heard.

When it was clear they were alone on the water, Fingerty spoke. "Yer going to t-tell me what yer want from me now?"

"Yes," Betty replied. "It's simple. You know these marshes better than us—you're more useful than any map. So we want you to get us through this fog and take us to Windy Bottom."

Fingerty looked aghast. "Yer know what happens to people who help prisoners escape? Prison! Banishment! And if they've done it before, like me, their necks get stretched!"

"Only if they're caught," said Betty. She almost laughed bitterly, for what did prison or banishment matter to her? She wouldn't be alive long enough to suffer.

"No one ever plans on getting caught," Fingerty muttered. "That's usually when they become unstuck."

"All you have to do is get us there," said Betty. "After that you can forget you ever saw us, unless . . ." She paused, thinking. Perhaps there were other ways Fingerty could be useful, if he could be persuaded. "Unless you want to go back a hero." What was it Pike had said? "With a good catch."

There was a moment of silence. Then Fingerty asked, "How?"

"By bringing Jarrod back with you."

Fingerty laughed a long, wheezing laugh. "Yer think that's possible? The man's an ogre, from what I've heard!"

"Just as possible as being invisible."

Fingerty watched her, his expression a mix of curiosity and wariness. His eyes shifted to the dolls. "Yer granny'll have summat to say about all this."

"Yes," Betty agreed. "I expect she will."

She glanced at Colton, who had remained silent since the warder's departure. She wondered if he was angry, or worried, or both. "Let's get moving."

Colton handed Fingerty an oar. "Don't try anything, old man," he warned.

Fingerty took the oar, scowling. "So not only are yer kidnapping me, yer expect me to do the donkey work?"

"Think of it as a favor," said Betty. "Like the ones you used to do for people on Torment."

"Favors? Weren't favors! Got paid for those, and handsomely, too! Gah!" He struck the oar into the water bad-temperedly.

The boat moved off and Betty settled on the rags. At least they were heading toward her sisters now, tackling part of her problem. The other part reared in her mind again. *Widdershins* . . . etched into the tower wall. Had someone wronged Sorsha? Could the curse have stemmed from jealousy, or even lies?

"What happened next?" she asked, shivering. The tips of her ears and nose stung from the freezing fog. "To Sorsha Spellthorn?"

Fingerty's eyes narrowed to slits. "And now she wants a history lesson!" he said shrilly. "You've got a cheek, girl. Yer know that? Shouldn't even say that name out here on the marshes!"

"I need to know." Betty's voice was firm.

"That what all this is about?" Fingerty said hoarsely. "Seems like you know plenty about Sorsha Spellthorn already, without my help!"

"What do you mean? I wouldn't be asking if I did!"

"Hah!" Fingerty lowered his oar, jabbing at Betty with a crooked finger. "Yer don't fool me, girly. Seen it with me own eyes, so I have."

"What is he babbling about?" Colton asked.

"The dolls!" Fingerty spluttered. "What else? Yer must know they were hers!"

Betty stared back at him, then down at the nesting dolls cradled in her hand. Finally, she understood what the old man meant, and the significance of the tale he had told her in the Poacher's Pocket.

A tale in which smugglers and a spy had sacrificed their lives for a newborn child. And in which Sorsha had used mysterious powers to observe people in an impossible way . . . and hide herself and her sister from danger. Spying . . . hiding. Whipping from one place to another in seconds.

"They belonged to her," Betty whispered, stunned. The Widdershins heirlooms—as well as their terrible legacy . . . they had all come from her. "All these years, passed down through my family . . . Sorsha's powers survived."

She grabbed Fingerty's bony knee and shook it urgently. "Please, Fingerty. You have to tell me, now, everything you know about Sorsha Spellthorn. My life and my sisters' lives depend on it. How did Sorsha end up in Crowstone Tower?"

Fingerty yanked on his oar, propelling the boat through the water.

"She trusted the wrong person."

Chapter Nineteen

Sorsha's Tale

THE PRISON BELL ECHOED in Sorsha's head from across the marshes. It had been going all morning, and the island was rife with gossip. Within hours, warders had arrived, scanning the beaches, knocking on doors. The prisoner—a con man—was young, they said. Strong, but not strong enough to swim the currents and survive. Yet no body had been found.

After they'd left, Sorsha had gone down to one of Torment's sandy coves. There were often cockles and mussels to be found in the rock pools, along with other treasures from the deep. Once, she had found a pearl, which she had given to Prue on her sixteenth birthday a few weeks ago.

She heard him before she saw him. The long, pained groan rolled out over the mudflats. Sorsha shielded her eyes from the sun, expecting to see a sea lion. When the groan came again, it was followed by movement, and Sorsha discovered that what she had taken for a mud-covered rock up ahead was a near-lifeless body.

Checking that she was alone, she picked her way across the shingle and kneeled by him. To her surprise, he was not much older than her, and she wondered how he could have done the things they said in such a short life. Any concerns for her safety were dismissed; the young man was weak as a kitten. He gazed up at her with sand-crusted but beautiful gray eyes. The dried mud around his mouth cracked as he spoke.

"Help me . . . please . . ."

She could have left him or called for the warders, but pity tugged at her heart. Any life left in him would surely be snuffed out if he was thrown into a damp cell. Gently, she used her skirt hem to wipe the mud from his face. It was the way he looked at her then, with such gratitude and trust, that won her over. No one here had ever looked at her that way. She'd known then that she would help him, hiding him away in a secluded cave.

His name was Winter Bates. He grew stronger with each passing day and every meal she smuggled to him, sharing with her his past as well as his hopes for the future. Sorsha had never known anyone who made her laugh the way he did, for Ma and Prue never joked, and smiles were wry or did not reach the eyes. And though she told herself not to, she couldn't help being drawn to him and imagining a future where they would not have to say goodbye.

As Winter gained strength, so did Sorsha's feelings.

So, too, did the danger.

There had been whispers on Torment all week, but Sorsha was used to that. At first she'd dismissed the stares, and the conversations that stopped as soon as she entered a shop, or the chapel, or passed an open door on the street. During her eighteen years on the island, there had always been some fly in the ointment, some gossip or rumor involving her doing the rounds. It always blew over eventually, if she ignored it long enough.

This time, though . . . something felt off. Different. But then, she reminded herself, things *were* different. She had taken a huge chance. One that put her life, and the lives of her family, at risk. Her underarms prickled with sweat in the muggy early evening. She swiped her fingers across her upper lip, blotting the moisture there. It was nearing the end of August, and the long, dry summer showed no signs of letting up.

She hurried down the lane to the ramshackle cottage that she, her mother, and Prue called home. Dozy bees bumbled around the lavender, exhausted by the heat. When she reached the cottage, she saw that every window was thrown wide open, along with the door.

Her mother was outside, peeling potatoes over a basin of muddy water.

"Late this evening," she remarked. "Again."

"It's this heat," Sorsha said, barely pausing as she passed her mother and went into the dark, stuffy cottage. Inside, a wall of hot air hit her. She placed her basket of reeds on the table and returned outside, wiping a fresh layer of sweat from her forehead.

"T'ain't the heat." The warning in her mother's voice cooled the air a little. She spoke quietly. "I know where you've been, my girl."

Silently, Sorsha sat on the ground by the door. A plume of dust rose as she flopped down. Next to her, a young ginger cat snoozed in the grass. Her mother had given up her efforts to shoo it away after it had appeared a week ago, flea-bitten and yowling an announcement that this was its new home. Sorsha extended a fingertip to stroke the tip of its tail.

"Shouldn't welcome things in when you don't know where they've come from." A potato plopped into the water, sending brown droplets onto the cat's coat. It didn't flinch.

"Could say the same for us," Sorsha said. The resentment in her voice failed to reach its usual level, smothered by the heat. "Although no one ever really welcomed us here, did they?"

"They tolerate us. We should be grateful enough for that."

"Why?" It was a question Sorsha had asked many times. "Why should we be grateful? Why can't we just leave and go somewhere where no one knows us, and no one blames us?"

"And how would that look?" her mother snapped. "Leaving the community that took us in?"

"Barely," Sorsha muttered.

"The community that sacrificed three of its own for strangers? For us?"

"And don't we know it!" Sorsha slapped the dirt, sending another dust cloud up in the air. The cat sneezed. "Aren't you tired of feeling guilty, Ma? Of never being allowed to forget?" There was a whole world out there. Why did Ma insist on keeping theirs so sheltered?

"You get used to it." Her mother's voice was brisk. "It's a small price to pay in return for our lives. They can't forget, so neither should we."

"But that's just it, Ma," Sorsha said sadly. "Our being here on Torment keeps all that bad feeling fresh. We may as well be locked up on Repent!"

"Like I say. Small price to pay." Her mother scraped at another potato. "Besides, I don't know if we're even allowed to leave. No one else can; that's the whole point of this place."

"They're here because they were banished," Sorsha protested. "We aren't!"

"Doesn't matter. We live like everyone else here, not picking and choosing the parts that suit us." Her mother's hair gleamed copper in the sunlight, glowing around her head like a sunflower. Though Sorsha's was the same shade, she'd inherited none of its frizziness. Her own hair hung like fine silk, the type of hair that would never take on a curl.

"People are talking," Ma added.

"Don't they always?"

Her mother looked at her sharply, lowering her voice. "You give them good reason!" Her fingernails were brown with grit as she scrape-scrape-scraped, and with each scrape of the knife, Sorsha felt as though she herself were under its blade; being stripped back and exposed. "Some things aren't so easy to hide, or to blame on lies or superstition. Hiding a person isn't the same as—"

"I didn't choose to be able to do these things."

"No. But you choose to do them. Just because you can doesn't mean you should."

"I'm not hurting anyone," Sorsha whispered. Her eyes filled with tears. She wiped at them stubbornly. "I just wanted to help."

"I know that." Her mother dropped the knife and turned to her, cupping her chin with damp, earth-scented fingers. "But that's not how others will see it. They know the man survived the escape. The marshes would have given him up by now. They know he's being hidden. There's been warders on the island again today. Searching. If you're caught, they'll take you to Repent and you'll be locked up in that cursed place, and . . . and . . ." She trailed off, releasing Sorsha's face to dab at her own. Nearby a bird chirruped in the hazy silence as she composed herself.

"They couldn't lock me up in there," Sorsha said. "They could try, but I'd get out, somehow . . . hide until their backs were turned . . ."

"Not if they locked you in the tower," her mother whispered. "That's where they'd put you. It's where they always put anyone suspected of sorcery."

Something in her mother's voice turned Sorsha's stomach. "Why?"

"Because it can't be done in the tower. You remember, don't you, the stories of how it was built? What it was made from?"

Sorsha frowned. "The cairns?"

Her mother nodded. "Resting places should never be disturbed, but that's what they did to those poor souls. Robbed their graves of the stones—the only markers they had. That tower is steeped in death. It's why magic can't be done there. You know the penalty for treason, don't you?"

Sorsha nodded; everybody knew it. The penalty was death.

"You think we have it so bad here," her mother said in a hushed tone. "Because you've never known any different, or any worse. Let me tell you, there is."

"Where had you escaped from, Ma? When they rescued you on the marshes? You've never told anyone, not even me."

"Somewhere I never want to go to again. A place where womenfolk and girls have no voice, no power, no names, even. So that place no longer has a name to me."

"But most people here don't have names, either," Sorsha said, puzzled. This was one of the things about Torment that bothered her most: many of the islanders were known only by family names. Aside from children born there, Sorsha and her family were the only people with first names.

"True. But the difference here is that it's punishment for past wrongs," said her mother. "And for everyone, menfolk and womenfolk."

"I know you're grateful we were taken in, but we could go anywhere!" Sorsha paused, searching her mother's face, but the closed expression she knew so well was already forming. Unless . . .

"It's because you think no one would look for you here, isn't it?" she said, finally understanding. "It's the perfect place to hide. An island for sinners and banished folk. No one chooses this!"

Her mother stabbed at a potato with a knife, not meeting Sorsha's eyes. "There are worse places to be."

"Maybe," Sorsha said sadly. Yet she knew there were better, too. Places where their past could not haunt them and where folk would treat them as if they were ordinary. Like how Winter treated her. "I wouldn't know, though."

Somewhere in the hedgerow nearby, a dry twig cracked under the weight of a foot. Sorsha snapped to attention, her brown eyes searching the thicket for rabbits or a fox. Instead, her gaze met with the palest of eyes, rimmed with sparse, fair eyelashes. There was a faint rustle; then the eyes vanished from view. Crackles of brittle grass under retreating feet followed.

Sorsha was about to call out but stopped as she heard her mother make a sound of exasperation.

"That was your sister, wasn't it?" Her voice was cool in the warm evening. "Prudence? Come out, there's work to be done!"

"Don't be too hard on her, Ma." Sorsha's eyes darted over the hedgerow, but her sister showed no signs of emerging. The tone of her mother's voice was unmistakable whenever she addressed Prue. It was frequently clipped and always sharper than it was when she was speaking to Sorsha. Though Sorsha always tried to pretend for Prue's sake, it was clear which daughter was favored.

"I sent her to check the snares over an hour ago." Her mother lifted the basin and carried it inside the cottage. Sorsha followed her in, her skin immediately clammy in the airless space. "We'll have no supper if she doesn't hurry. Only the crows know how she wastes so much time slithering around in the hedgerows doing nothing."

"Ma!" Sorsha scolded. "She'll hear you! Please be kinder."

Her mother shrugged, tipping the potatoes into a pot of fresh water. "She's difficult. Always has been."

"No more than me, surely?"

Her mother paused. Sorsha waited for a denial, or cross words, but none came.

"She's jealous," her mother said at last. "She wants what you have. Sometimes she has a certain look in her eyes . . . A mother always knows."

"That's not fair, Ma." Sorsha sighed. It was no secret that Prue wished she could do the things Sorsha could —she had said so to Sorsha many times—but was that wrong? She stared out the window. A trapped fly bobbed against the inside pane. Her mother's comments were nothing she hadn't heard before. Prue was more awkward than Sorsha; larger, clumsier, slower. It was always Prue who'd fall into nettles, or have a coughing fit during Mass, or break dishes when washing them. She ate twice as much as Sorsha, and needed things explained more when their mother was short on time and of temper.

Despite all this, Prue always tried hard, always wanting to please. How could Sorsha feel bad toward her, when her sister was her only friend?

"Call her in." Her mother clapped the heavy iron lid on the pot. "Else she'll be lurking out there all evening."

Sorsha ducked outside, grateful to escape the stifling heat. A thorn snagged at her hair from the roses climbing over the doorway. Later, she would think about this and wonder if it had been a warning, some tiny earth spirit trying to prevent her from going out.

She had not gone far down the lane when she heard light footsteps echoing her own. She spun around and found herself almost nose to nose with Prue, her pale eyes exactly level with her own.

"Jumping jackdaws!" she hissed, her heart racing. "Must you sneak up on me like that?"

Prue grinned, displaying gappy teeth that had a grayish tinge to them. Sorsha's neck itched with nervous sweat as her sister fell into step beside her. How near had she been to the cottage . . . and the conversation between Sorsha and her mother? Again she wished Ma would be more forgiving of Prue. It couldn't be easy living in Sorsha's shadow, of both her abilities and her place as Ma's favorite. And though there might be a resentful glance every now and then, who could blame her?

"You checked the snares yet?"

"Nothing in them." Prue stuck her hands in the pocket of her pinny, whistling through her teeth. "Didn't want to go back empty-handed, so thought I'd wait and check again. Doesn't take much to make Ma cross."

"It's the heat," Sorsha muttered. She was always making some excuse for Ma's sharp tongue. Too hot, too cold, too tired, too hungry.

Prue stared at her for a moment too long. "Of course," she said at last. "Poor Ma."

"I'll come with you," Sorsha suggested. "There might be a breeze by the overlook."

They covered the short distance in a few minutes, making small talk about the heat, but a sense of unease was growing, hanging over Sorsha like a storm cloud. When they reached the cliff's edge, the sensation left her momentarily as a gust of wind swept up off the marshes, cooling the sweat on her forehead. She stared into the distance at the hazy smudge of mainland Crowstone. In the daylight there was nothing much to see, for it was too far away. At night, however, the lights were beautiful.

As always, her gaze was drawn closer, to Lament. It was also too far to see much in detail, the chapel or cairns, but she could make out the caves in the cliff face. The Three Widows were set back past the crescent of deadly rocks jutting from the mud.

"Devil's Teeth look hungry," Prue commented.

Sorsha nodded. The rocks were more pronounced today; the tide was out, exposing the Teeth in all their horror. No water to blur their edges or dull their sharpness. It was impossible for Sorsha to look at them without imagining a night, nearly two decades earlier, when it had been her mother on the water, moments away from being dashed to sea foam on the rocks. Saved at the cost of three strangers' lives. Strangers who lived on within her.

"They're saying things, you know. People don't see me in the long grass . . . I've heard whispers."

The hairs on Sorsha's arms lifted, despite the warmth of the evening. She hadn't admitted her secret about Winter to Prue, or to Ma . . . although Ma had guessed. *A mother always knows . . .*

"Tell me, then," she said, distracted. "What's being said?" All she wanted was to take a long, cool swim and think about Winter, and later slip into the dark caves to be with him.

Prue flicked a pebble off the edge of the cliff with her toe. "They're saying they think the escaped prisoner is still here, on Torment. That the water's been too low for him to have got away. So he must be hiding somewhere."

"I'm sure they'd have found him by now if that were true." There was an edge of irritation to Sorsha's voice. Curse this heat! And those gossips! She'd already had this from Ma. "They must have searched every corner of the island, surely?" Despite her calm words, Sorsha was unable to control the fluttering within her chest. It was true that no one (apart from her mother, and not for some time now) had ever managed to find something Sorsha had hidden, yet despite her confidence in her ability, she was not arrogant enough to feel completely safe.

"Not if someone was helping him." Prue kneeled and plucked a dry blade of grass. "Oh, they've searched. But there are always hidey holes, aren't there? And everyone knows you're good at hiding things." She stuck the grass between her teeth, chewing. "All those times we played as children you never gave up your secret places." She elbowed her playfully. "Not even to me."

Sorsha smiled uncomfortably. Why did Prue always have to push and wheedle? To invade every corner of her mind? Even before Winter, there had been things Sorsha had never wanted to share, but Prue didn't seem to understand that.

"And, you know," her sister continued, "if there are places that only you know of, you really should tell the warders."

"If the warders are too stupid to be able to find hiding places used by children, then they don't deserve any help." Sorsha kept her eyes on the low, swampy water, afraid that the truth might be seen in them, but already she knew it was being unpicked like a piece of stitching.

"We both know there's more to it than that."

The fluttering in Sorsha's chest became bigger, harder.

Like a moth changing into a bird. "Yes, but no one else aside from you and Ma knows for sure. They might suspect, but they've never had proof of the things I can do."

The pale eyes looked troubled. "You still need to be careful." She paused, looking over her shoulder around them. "It's true, isn't it? You're hiding the prisoner?"

"Of course not." The lie stuck in Sorsha's throat like dry dust.

"Only, I overheard two warders talking up by the well about an hour ago. I'd sneaked there to get some water to drink. I stayed hidden in the hedge—I wasn't paying much attention till I heard your name. Someone saw you with a stranger by the caves yesterday evening."

Sorsha closed her eyes. So she had been seen. Ma's warnings of the tower loomed frighteningly close, but the pull of Winter was stronger, like a tide she couldn't control. "Stop asking questions, Prue," she said in a tight voice. "It's best you don't know the answers. If there's trouble ahead, then I want you and Ma having no part of it."

"Oh, Sorsha!" Prue whispered. "What have you got mixed up in?" She placed a clammy hand on Sorsha's arm, but instinctively Sorsha moved away. She was too worried and irritable to be touched or coddled . . . or to notice the hurt on Prue's face.

"Wait—you said I was seen by the caves?"

Prue blinked, her expression blank.

"No one would have seen me by the caves." Sorsha watched her sister carefully. "I was . . . hidden then."

"Cove, not caves," Prue said quickly. She moved off, away from the cliff's edge.

Sorsha followed as Prue wound through the scrubby grass toward the snares. The feeling of unease was back again.

"Prue," she said sharply as her sister halted before a snare. "Have you been watching me?"

Prue hunched over the trap. "Don't be angry," she whispered. "I—I was watching you. And the boy, and then I saw you both vanish . . . so I kept watching. And then I saw the footprints appearing in the sand, by the caves, and I guessed where you were taking him."

Sorsha's stomach roiled. "Did anyone else see?"

"N-no."

"Good." Sorsha's heart was racing now. She watched as her sister's small, pale hands released the snare and removed a dead rabbit. Its eyes were dull, its limbs stiff. She frowned, unsettled further. "I thought you said the snares were empty when you checked them? That rabbit's been dead longer than an hour."

"Oh," said Prue. "I must have forgotten this one."

Sorsha averted her eyes. It was disturbing how at ease her sister always was when it came to handling dead things. "Let's get back. Ma's waiting."

"I didn't mean to pry," Prue said in a small voice. "I just saw you with someone and wondered who it was, that's all."

"It's all right." Sorsha took a long, deep breath, trying to gather her wits. "I need to be careful." Yet someone had seen her, someone other than Prue. What if they'd noticed two sets of footprints from unseen people appearing by the caves? Could she continue to risk her own life for Winter's? If what Ma said was true, her powers wouldn't save her if she was thrown in the tower. And everyone knew that once in there, madness or execution were the only ways out. Sorsha turned away from the cliff's edge. "Let's go," she repeated.

When she arrived, her mother yanked her through the door, almost slamming it on Prue. "Warders have been here!" she hissed. "Asking where you were yesterday evening! I lied, told them you were here, but if they find out—"

"They won't." Sorsha's legs buckled under her and she sat weakly in a chair at the table. "I'll be more careful."

"You'll stop, now," said Ma, as sharply as if she were addressing Prue. "Let him fend for himself. Because if you're caught helping him, all three of us are doomed!"

Sorsha said nothing as Prue began skinning the rabbit. Already, she knew she wouldn't manage a bite. The rabbit's lifeless eyes seemed fixed on her. She looked away.

"I'll go to him, one last time—"

"Sorsha!" her mother gasped.

"To tell him I can't help anymore," Sorsha finished. "I have to do that, at least. You can't start a thing and not finish it." She glanced at her mother desperately. "Unless . . . we help him, and leave, too . . ."

It was the wrong suggestion. Her mother's eyes flared. "You'll be no help to anyone if they throw you in that tower. If they have their eyes on you already, they're probably setting a trap as we speak! Not only are you hiding an escaped convict, but you're using magic to aid you!"

They stared at each other, breaths coming in shaky bursts. This was the first time either of them had used the word *magic* for Sorsha's abilities. How strange it was to name it after all this time: this thing that had always been a part of her. Like teeth, or breathing.

"You'll be helpless in the tower," her mother hissed. "Your powers won't work within those walls of death."

"Perhaps . . . perhaps they wouldn't need to," Sorsha

said slowly. The word *magic* shuffled around her head, made bolder, stronger by its new name. She could hide things, couldn't she . . . ? "If I'm not the one who's using them. Perhaps I could buy some time, to save myself even if they throw me in the tower."

Prue paused in her grim task, open-mouthed. Something stringy dangled from her hand.

Her mother stared at her. "What do you mean?"

"I mean . . . what if my powers could be . . . transferred? Hidden?" Sorsha scanned the cottage shelves. "Hiding things is what I do . . . What if my powers were hidden, within ordinary objects, so they could be used by someone else to help me?" Her eyes came to rest on a set of nesting dolls, one of the only things her mother had brought with her from her mysterious life before Torment. As a child Sorsha had always been fascinated by the dolls hidden within a doll, like secret little doorways into another world. "I wonder . . ."

"It's perfect," Prue breathed. She tucked a strand of hair behind her ear, smearing her cheek with rabbit blood. "No one would think—"

"It's just an idea," Sorsha said. "In case the worst should happen. They wouldn't have to be used unless they were really needed. It's the best way to protect myself."

"The best way would be to stop dabbling with danger,"

said her mother. "If you walk away now, no trouble will find you."

"What if people had walked away from us, Ma?" Sorsha asked. "That night on the marshes eighteen years ago? We deserved a chance, didn't we?"

"Do you really think you could transfer your powers?" Prue interrupted, still staring at Sorsha. Her eyes were pale orbs, caught by a ray of the setting sun. It fired them up like cats' eyes in the dark. "How sure are you?"

Sorsha hesitated. She had never questioned whether she was able to do any of the things she could, only known that she was able to, somehow. It was like trying to remember a time before she knew she could walk. She had to have learned it, and yet she couldn't imagine not knowing how to do it.

"I can do it," she said. "So if anything does go wrong, I need to know one of you will get me out."

"I will," said Prue at once. "No one's ever accused me of working magic. No one will suspect."

Was she too bright, too eager? Sorsha wondered, then scolded herself. It wouldn't do to think like Ma. Prue had always longed to experience Sorsha's powers for herself. It was nothing to feel uneasy about . . .

The rabbit dripped softly in Prue's hand. Drip, drip, onto the table. Ma's words floated back.

Jealous . . . wants what you have . . . a mother always knows. She pushed the words away, hid them in a little corner of her mind. She could count on Prue; she was sure of it. In any case, she didn't have much choice.

Besides, a little envy between sisters didn't mean anything . . . did it?

Chapter Twenty

The Crow's Chorus

"PST! BETTY!"

Fingerty gurgled with fright as a voice cut across his own, interrupting his tale. Betty, who had huddled down in the sacking to listen to him, sat up, dazed at the sound of it. She had been so wrapped up in the story that the cold, damp fog in the present almost came as a surprise after the long, hot summer of Sorsha and Prue's.

There, between the marsh mists, Fliss's face hovered like an apparition above the boat. Joy and relief coursed through Betty like a wave. How wonderful—and weird —it was to see her sister's face in this way again!

"Fliss!" She reached out to the image of her sister's

face, not quite touching it—but Fliss's eyes were searching the boat in earnest.

"Betty, where are you?" she whispered.

"I'm here!" Betty said, then realized Fliss was unable to see her. "Oh, wait—the dolls!"

Fingerty clutched his oar to him like a shield. Blinking, he recovered himself and peered closer at Fliss.

Colton had stopped rowing and was gazing at the hovering, ghostlike face with curiosity and possibly a degree of fear. During Fingerty's tale he had listened, as enraptured as Betty. "Does Fliss have something, too? Like the bag and the dolls?"

Betty nodded. "A mirror." Hastily, she twisted the outermost doll so that the two halves of painted key no longer met. Instantly Fliss focused on her, and Betty knew they had reappeared.

"Fingerty?" Fliss gasped. "What's he doing with you?"

"He was with the warders looking for the prisoners. Colton and I . . . Oh, I don't have time to explain now, but we had to kidnap him." Betty gripped the edge of the boat, hope and fear soaring in her heart as questions tumbled out of her. "Where's Charlie? Are you safe? Did you escape Jarrod?"

Fliss shook her head. "Charlie's safe. We haven't escaped. Jarrod's asleep with the bag, and he's brought us to this creepy old mill. It's deserted, all boarded up. The only way out is the door and he's blocked it, so we're trapped. Wait—Charlie's here . . ." Fliss's face vanished momentarily and was replaced by Charlie's.

"Charlie!" A lump lodged in Betty's throat at the sight of her little sister. She so badly wanted to hold her, to feel her sister's hot, sticky little hand in her own again. There was no way to tell if that could happen now. The curse had begun to bring them closer than they'd ever been —before ripping them apart. "Are you all right?"

Charlie nodded, a tangle of hair bobbing over her forehead. Her cheeks were grubby and tearstained. "I'm awful hungry now. And there's birds squawking in my head. I want it to stop!"

"Oh, Charlie," Betty said again. Her eyes filled with desperate tears. It had begun: the crows' caws counting down the hours until sunset.

"I can hear them, too," Fliss said quietly, reappearing in Charlie's place. "The crows. It's awful. I can barely hear myself think."

"Hearing crows?" Colton asked, perturbed. "That's part of the curse?"

Fliss nodded, her eyes brimming with tears.

"Are you in Windy Bottom?" Betty asked urgently. "Is that where this mill is?"

"I think so. I—I don't know how long he's planning on staying, but he's mentioned getting supplies and working out a plan before we move on. Perhaps once you've made it back to Granny you can send help, but even if we escape Jarrod, we're no closer to breaking the curse . . ." Fliss paused, frowning. "Wait, why is Colton in the boat with you if you're heading back to Crowstone . . . ?"

Betty gulped. "About that, I . . ."

"Betty?" Fliss repeated sharply. "Answer me! Why is Colton . . . ?" She emitted a sudden gasp as Betty shook her head guiltily.

"I never said I was going back, Fliss. Not without you and Charlie."

"But the curse!" Fliss croaked. "You can't do this! You mustn't!"

"I'm not going back alone," Betty repeated.

"Don't be a fool!" Fliss begged. "Turn around! You must still be within Crowstone's borders . . . Save yourself before it's too late!"

"I'm coming to find you whether you like it or not."

Tears dripped down Fliss's cheeks. Betty glanced at the water, half expecting them to land there, but they vanished the moment they left her sister's skin. "I could shake you, Betty Widdershins!"

"Let's hope you get the chance," Betty whispered, but at that moment Fliss's eyes took on a panicked look.

"I have to go—Jarrod's stirring. I think he's waking up!"

"Fliss!" Betty reached out just as her sister's face vanished. "Charlie?" Her fingers found only swirling curls of mist, like her sisters were already phantoms.

No! She couldn't think like that! They were alive, unharmed. For now.

She felt Colton's and Fingerty's eyes on her and buried her face in her hands.

"It's not too late for you," Colton said. His eyes were haunted. "I could take you back . . . search for Charlie and Fliss myself. You're not out of Crowstone yet—"

"No." Her voice was muffled. Less than an hour ago Colton had been her sworn enemy. Now, even with their fragile truce, she didn't want him—or Fingerty—feeling sorry for her. For them to help her they had to believe she was strong.

"Yer want to listen, girl," Fingerty said. His gravelly voice was softer than usual, like some of his hardness had chipped away from seeing Charlie and Fliss. "Won't do yer sisters no good chasing after them, not if it means getting yerself killed." He blinked suddenly, eyes reddening. "An' poor old Bunny . . . she can't lose you all . . ."

"I said no. I'm going." Her sisters weren't lost! She couldn't let herself think that, not yet. She held out her hand to Colton. "Give me the oar. I need to do something, I can't just sit here!"

Colton shook his head. "You should rest."

"Row faster, then," Betty snapped. She turned to Fingerty, who was squinting into the mist looking troubled. "And I need to hear the rest of Sorsha's story—"

But Fingerty lifted a gnarled finger to point silently into the fog. Betty and Colton stared.

A tiny flickering light was hovering above the water close to the boat, glowing like a ghostly orb. Betty had never seen a wisp so closely before. It had a mesmerizing quality, and she could suddenly believe all the stories about them as wraiths luring travelers to danger. Spooked, she blinked, remembering Fingerty's superstitious talk to the warder.

Strange things have happened on this water . . . Terrible things. He glanced at her and made the sign of the crow. "I'll not say another word about all that until we're on dry land." With that his lips clamped shut like a mussel and he grabbed an oar from Colton. Together, they rowed in silence, each as eager as the other to get away from the mysterious wisp.

Betty settled into the pit of the boat, dragging her

gaze from the wisp. After fumbling with the dolls to hide the three of them from sight once more, she turned her face into the musty sacking and wept silently, trying to make sense of all she knew about Sorsha and the curse. Thoughts and images muddled in her head: fishy eyes, magical dolls, and musty carpetbags . . . *Widdershins* scratched into stone. She felt strongly that Prue was the person Sorsha shouldn't have trusted, but without the rest of the tale she couldn't be sure. Answers were there, somewhere . . . she just couldn't make them fit. Though she wouldn't have thought it possible, exhaustion and the lull of the waves tugged her into sleep.

She dreamed of her sisters and picking merrypennies in the meadows beyond Nestynook Green. She woke with damp eyes to the shriek of birds and bleak dawn light, and jolted up from the bottom of the boat. Ahead lay a bay of golden sand shaped in a perfect crescent. Beyond it, the land was lush and green, and despite the sky being overcast, Betty was surprised to see that the water was blue and clear; so clear she could see tiny fish swimming alongside them. Somewhere near, too near, a crow rasped, soon joined by a second. The last traces of sleep left her as she scanned the skies. No crows, only scavenging gulls. It was happening, just like Granny had said.

It starts with birdsong. The crows' chorus. No matter

how hard you look, you'll never see them. The sound exists only in your head . . .

Panic rose in her throat, and she clapped her hands over her ears. The crows in her head croaked louder. The sound itself was horrible, like the inside of her skull was being scratched and pecked at . . . but what it meant set her limbs shaking with terror.

"Stop," she whispered. "Please stop . . ."

But there was no stopping it, no going back; the curse had been set in motion. Even if a tiny, deep part of her had clung to the possibility that it couldn't be real, there was no denying it now. And as surely as the sun would set, it would also mark the last day of the Widdershins sisters unless they uncovered the secret to breaking the curse.

Colton touched her arm lightly. She looked up, her eyes wild. Fingerty hung back, squinting and twitching as if he had gas.

"It's started," she whispered. "I can hear the crows." She pulled herself onto the seat. Every bone in her ached. "Where are we?" she croaked.

"Horseshoe Bay," Fingerty answered. He was huddled at the other end of the seat, like a gnarled old tree stump. "Had to come farther around the mainland, as Marshfoot'll be swarming with warders."

Betty's gaze swept over the beach. Here the sand was like coarse golden sugar, not the dull, ugly shingle she was used to. She had always thought she'd be happy for such a sight, but instead, she felt cheated. Without her sisters and Granny to share it, the bay's beauty was bittersweet. She had risked everything to be here, and yet now that she was about to step onto dry land that wasn't Crowstone for the first time in her life, her hopes were smaller than they'd ever been. She tried to tell herself that it was still possible, that they had come this far, but the crows in her head were doing their best to drown out the practical little voice she always tried to listen to.

Colton leaped out as the boat ran ashore. Betty wavered, momentarily queasy. Colton offered his hand to her, not quite meeting her eye. She hesitated, then took it, allowing him to help her out. They might not be friends, but there was no point in her being proud. After, he went to help Fingerty, but the old man slapped his hand away, still sore from having a fish hook held to his throat.

"I can manage."

"Suit yourself," Colton replied.

"Need no help from a pecking crook," Fingerty continued as he climbed awkwardly over the side of the boat.

"Takes one to know one," Colton muttered.

Fingerty's fleshy nose reddened, but he said nothing. Together, they hauled the boat up over the sand.

"Over there." Colton pointed. "We can leave the boat behind those rocks. There's plenty of seaweed to cover her up with."

"You could make a wish here, for yer sisters," Fingerty said unexpectedly. "Folk say wishes made in this bay be sure to come true." He frowned, the roughness leaving his voice as he watched Betty. "You look like yer could use a bit of luck."

Betty looked back over the shimmering water and remembered Father's cousin, Clarissa. She had traveled here all those years ago, wishing for the curse to be broken . . . but it hadn't worked. Perhaps the curse was too powerful. Or perhaps, with the crows overpowering Clarissa's thoughts, she hadn't wished for the right thing . . .

Betty closed her eyes, trying to blot out the sound of the birds and focus. The logical side of her knew that wishing alone couldn't give her what she wanted, but right now she'd take all the help she could get. If she was going to die, she would at least try everything in her power to change things first.

"I wish for the knowledge that I need to break the curse," Betty whispered. Her words were whipped away on the wind before they had barely left her mouth. She blinked, shaking a frizzle of hair out of her eyes, and searched for a path away from the cove. They trudged up it in silence, the sound of their invisible footsteps on gravel and sand confusing the gulls that were circling and pecking. Betty welcomed the noise, though it was still not enough to mask the crows' rasping.

"If I live past today, I never want to hear another crow again," she muttered.

Fingerty's eyes darted from side to side. "Crows . . . curses . . . cuckoo, all this," he said, shuffling farther into his coat.

It was then Betty stopped abruptly. Something heavy in her skirt was bumping against her knee as she walked. From her pocket she withdrew a flat, rough gray stone . . . like those Crowstone Tower was built from. Her fingers trembled. She flung it away into the scrub, but not before Colton saw.

"What was that?"

"A stone from the tower," she said quietly. "Whenever the curse is triggered, one falls from the walls."

Colton gave a low whistle, shaking his head. "This is some curse."

Betty nodded wordlessly and set off again. She had

only taken a few paces when the weight in her pocket returned, along with the dull thud against her leg. The stone was back. She continued, not bothering to remove it again. It echoed the heaviness of her heart.

Did you really think you'd be any different? it gloated. She curled her fingers around it, its weight a cruel reminder of all the other Widdershins girls before her.

Let it be, she thought. It stood for all she was fighting for, too.

The sandy path gave way to cobbles. They found themselves on the outskirts of a town that was just rousing itself from sleep as the sun rose, starting to break through the cloud.

From a baker's cart Colton stole three buns and an urn of milk. Too hungry to feel guilty, Betty wolfed down the still-warm bread. Even Fingerty ate gratefully, without a single snippy comment about crooks, and was far better tempered for it.

Betty tapped her foot impatiently. The sun had risen, but instead of being warmed, she felt chilled. She wondered if she would see it mark this point in the sky again after today. "Can you hurry? We need to keep moving."

"Give us a chance!" Fingerty spluttered, wiping milk from his chin.

"I need you to make some inquiries. Find out how far away Windy Bottom is. It's too risky for Colton or me to ask."

Fingerty hiccupped. "Best undo this spell, then, unless yer want folk scared, thinking they're talking to spirits."

Betty rolled her eyes. She hadn't foreseen that she would be quite such a bossy leader, but in her imagined escapades the stakes had been about adventure. This was about survival. "Obviously. But Colton goes with you, unseen, and so does the fish hook."

Fingerty scowled. "Hmm."

They found a narrow stone bridge and ducked into the shadows underneath. It was deserted but for a beggar woman selling matches, intent on counting her meager takings.

"Here," said Betty. She took the nesting dolls out from the folds of her clothes. After twisting the top of the outer doll counter-clockwise, she removed it, taking care not to dislodge Colton's scrap of cloth or her own piece of bitten thumbnail that kept them invisible. She took out Fingerty's button, then sealed the dolls carefully once more, lining up the keys.

Fingerty blinked as he became visible, looking this way and that now that he was no longer able to see Betty or Colton. Then he tensed as Colton leaned over to say something in his ear.

"Still here, old man." He nudged Fingerty in the ribs. They began to walk, passing the beggar. She called out to Fingerty, but he did not answer, and her face fell. Betty watched her pityingly. Some people did not need magic to be invisible.

She was pacing impatiently, kicking up a small tornado of dried leaves at her feet (much to the confusion of the match seller), when Colton and Fingerty returned.

"Any luck?" she asked.

"Yerp." Fingerty cuffed his nose, speaking quickly. "Windy Bottom is a couple o' miles west. There's a coal wagon over yonder that'll be going through it—if we hurry we can catch it."

"Good," said Betty. Finally, it seemed, her luck might just be changing. A few minutes later, having sneaked onto the coal wagon, she didn't feel quite so lucky. The three of them were perched uncomfortably upon mounds of coal that shifted every time the wagon went over a bump. Soon they were covered in coal dust, and it was an effort not to sneeze or cough too loudly as the horrid stuff got into their noses and throats.

Betty lay back, closing her eyes, which had started to

stream. If she concentrated hard, the wagon's rumbling almost drowned out the incessant cawing of the crows in her head.

She lay there, willing Fliss's face to appear before her with the news that she and Charlie had somehow escaped, or were at least still safe, but there was nothing. Betty wondered if the wish she had made in Horseshoe Bay had been as wasted as Father's cousin Clarissa's.

She glanced at Colton, her thoughts souring further. He hadn't needed a magical bay to make his wish come true. The Widdershinses had done that. Whatever he might desire now could only pale in comparison. Her curiosity deepened. "What did you wish for?"

"No point, so I din't bother," Fingerty grunted, unaware that the question hadn't been directed at him.

Betty raised an eyebrow. "You're the one who said it'd come true."

He scowled. "Yerp. Well, too late by then. Else I'd have wished never to have clapped eyes on either of you."

"Maybe you should've wished for some manners," Betty said under her breath.

Fingerty eyed her suspiciously. "Eh?"

"Nothing." She turned to Colton. "And you? What was your wish?"

"To escape," he said, without hesitation.

"What do you mean? You already have escaped."

"No. I just got out of the prison. That's not the same as being truly free. I've escaped Crowstone, but I can't stop looking over my shoulder, not yet. Maybe not ever." He chuckled softly. "You wouldn't understand."

"I think I do," said Betty, softening toward him a little more. Colton was as haunted by Crowstone as she was. Perhaps neither of them would ever completely shake it off. "I know better than anyone that some prisons don't need any walls."

"And you're still not free, even now." He chuckled sourly. "Just like me. Some things . . . I know I won't ever forget them. The stench, the cold . . . the cruelty. A place like that . . . it gets its claws into you and won't let go."

"Ain't a good place," Fingerty murmured in agreement. Their eyes met, something passing between them. Not quite a truce, but the start of an understanding.

"You said you were innocent," Betty blurted out. "Is that true?" Suddenly she found herself hoping that it was. That breaking him out had served some noble cause if her own failed.

A sullen note crept into Colton's voice. "Absolutely."

Betty stayed quiet, waiting for him to continue.

"After my father died, my mother became a servant," he said eventually. "For a wealthy household. She worked hard for poor pay, though we were at least fed and clothed. But she wanted more for me, and saved as much money as she could so that one day I might have enough to start a new life for myself. We were treated like nothings by those we worked for. Oh, they didn't hate us, but it was like . . . like we weren't really people, with hopes and feelings.

"The only one who was different was the youngest of the house, a little girl. Her name was Mina, and she was seven years old. Perhaps it was because as the youngest, she knew what it felt like to be ignored. She'd often come to us for a kind word or a bit of comfort, always happy to listen to my mother's stories or sneak off to climb trees with me. She taught me how to read. She was a wild little thing—a bit like your Charlie." He smiled faintly at the memory, and Betty was reminded of Colton's concern for her younger sister in the cell when he thought her tooth had been knocked out, and later, his distress when Jarrod had taken Charlie hostage.

Colton rubbed his nose. "Mina was the only one who cared when my mother became ill and died." He blinked, but Betty could see the glassy sheen his eyes had taken on. "It was then I knew I had to leave. I couldn't live that life anymore, not when my mother had worked so hard to change things for me.

"So I took out the money she had saved and packed up what little I had. But when I told them I was leaving, they laughed at me." His lips pursed angrily. "Laughed! They told me not to be so stupid, that no one would take me as an apprentice or a scholar and that I'd end up begging on the streets. So I showed them the money." He grimaced.

"That was a mistake. They wouldn't believe my mother could have saved so much. They never noticed, you see. Never paid attention to what she went without, just to put by that little bit of her wages every week. Over a while, the money wasn't such a little amount anymore. They accused me of stealing it and locked me in the cellar." He leaned his head back on the rattling wagon, closing his eyes. "It was thanks to Mina stealing the key that I escaped. She was the only one who believed me, but of course, no one listened to her. When I got out, it was with nothing but the clothes on my back. All my mother's money had been taken from me."

"But . . . but that's not fair!" Betty said fiercely. Poor Colton. No wonder he'd been so desperate to escape! He had already been through so much before he'd ever set foot in prison. He knew loss, just as she did.

"Needless to say, I didn't get far," Colton continued. "I tried, but having no money meant I couldn't. I was hiding in a cow shed when they caught up with me, and of course by then I had no chance of making anyone listen. Running had only made me look guiltier." He opened his eyes and met Betty's. "And so I was thrown in Crowstone prison, where no one believed me, either."

"I believe you." Betty reached out and touched Colton's hand. "And I understand why you lied to us to get out."

"Doesn't change anything, though, does it? I've escaped, but you three girls are paying the price." His voice cracked with remorse.

The ache of wanting to cry filled Betty's throat. Colton had a conscience; he wasn't a monster. She couldn't say she forgave him completely, but she was now certain that he had never meant the girls harm and would never have forced them to leave Crowstone. That had been Jarrod's doing. But the person Betty blamed most of all was herself. "I'm glad you're out," she said at last. "You didn't deserve to be in there."

"It's a bad enough place for those who are guilty," Fingerty added gruffly. "An' for some, the nightmare ain't over even when they're let out."

"The ones sent to Torment?" Betty asked.

"Yerp."

"Is that why you helped people escape? You felt sorry for them? Or was it only for money?"

For a moment it seemed Fingerty was struggling

to answer. "Both," he admitted finally. "I saw the way people are treated in there. Life on Torment ain't much better."

"People say you were nearly sent there," Betty said. She winced as the wagon went over a bump.

"Wish I had been," Fingerty growled. "Better that than to be a spy for the warders fer the rest of me life. No one likes a crooked warder less than another warder, that's a fact! Some of them . . . there's no sense of justice or fairness. They're there to be cruel, because that's what they enjoy. But not all of them. Some care . . . especially for the prisoners who really could be innocent."

"Is that why you know so much about Sorsha Spell-thorn?" Betty asked. "Because you thought she was innocent?"

Fingerty nodded. "Her tale fascinated many of the warders. My father, his father. Stories got passed down. Mostly of her being a witch, because those tales justified locking her up. The story I'm telling is the one they tried to stamp out. The one that's frowned upon. Added to the strangeness of the tower—how it still survives—and of course her leaping to her death, no wonder it's still going strong after all these years." He paused, swaying with the cart. "And now that you've heard most of it, there's not much else to tell except the final part."

Chapter Twenty-One

Sorsha's Tale

IN THE END, SORSHA CHOSE the set of wooden nesting dolls that her mother had owned as a child, an old gilt-edged mirror that they had dug up while planting the herb garden, and the traveling bag that had carried her mother's few possessions to Torment on the night Sorsha had come into the world.

She'd selected the items carefully, both for their qualities and because to anyone else, they would appear to hold little value. If the worst should happen and Sorsha was taken, it wouldn't do to have the items stolen, which was why she'd stuck to the humblest things they owned. Not that this was difficult; they possessed nothing that could be considered valuable. Of the three of them, Prue would be the least likely to be accused of anything, for she had been born on Torment. The islanders might not be warm toward her, but she was considered more one of their own than Sorsha and her mother, the water witches from the unknown.

Later that evening in the still-muggy cottage, she poured all her concentration and skill into hiding her three abilities in those objects: the hiding into the strange little wooden dolls that concealed each other; the spying into the looking glass; the transporting into the bag. She told herself it would work, willing it, imagining the abilities ebbing out of her while simultaneously using them for the very task at hand.

When it was done, she felt empty, vulnerable, ordinary.

Ordinary. It was something she'd wanted her entire life, just to fit in and not draw unwanted attention. Now she didn't even feel like herself anymore.

But it needn't be forever, she told herself. Just until it was safe.

When will that be? a little voice chimed in her head. She pushed it away. When she returned the items to their places, they no longer felt like the same objects. They felt fragile, breakable. Like treasure. But no one knew, she reminded herself, except her and Ma, and Prue.

Her mother finished stacking the dirty dishes and

wiped her hands. "Perhaps . . ." She hesitated. "Perhaps you're right."

"About what?" Sorsha asked.

"Leaving." Her mother's voice was low, hesitant.

"But, Ma," said Prue, looking up from her sewing. "You said disappearing would only make the islanders think they were right about us all along!"

"Let them." Ma's voice trembled. "We've never set a foot wrong in the eighteen years since we arrived, yet nothing's changed. And it never will, not now. There will always be some finger pointing. We'll never be truly safe."

"Are you sure?" Sorsha stared around the cottage, the only home she had known. She had always longed to leave, but she hadn't wanted it like this. She had wanted it to be an adventure, not an escape.

"We'll gather our things," her mother said. "We should leave as soon as possible."

"This evening?" Sorsha asked. "After sunset?"

Her mother shook her head. "Before. It'll be more suspicious if we're seen moving around in darkness."

"I can move us quickly," Sorsha said. "No one will see a thing. We just need to decide where to go." She paused guiltily, staring around their home. "And we'll only be able to take whatever we can carry. The rest will have to be left behind."

Prue set down her sewing. "But where will we go? We don't know anywhere, haven't been anywhere . . ."

Sorsha walked to the door. "Then decide by the time I'm back. I won't be long."

Her mother stared at her, exasperated. "You can't be serious? You need to save yourself, not take further risks!"

"I can't just leave him," said Sorsha. "Now that my powers are in those objects, he's not hidden anymore! I need to warn him—that's the least I can do."

"Sorsha, please . . ." her mother began. "Don't be a fool for someone who will probably get caught anyway!"

"That may be so." Sorsha bowed her head. "But if he's caught, I don't want it to be because of me." She glanced at the traveling bag, hesitating.

"Don't." Her mother's voice was firm. "It will only take the wrong person to see something . . ."

So Sorsha snatched the water pail and hurried out into the balmy evening before her mother could protest further. It was still light, just, and the drone of bees had given way to the hum of gnats. Later, she would remember the scent of wildflowers and sounds of wild creatures rustling in the hedges, and she would wish she had taken time to look around the cottage and kiss her mother. She headed for the well, drawing water from it, then went to the cliff's edge.

Before starting down the rocky cliff path she checked in every direction, but saw no one. She descended the steps, welcoming the light breeze off the water. About halfway down, she stopped by an area of rock covered in moss. The little beach below could be seen from here, brown sludgy mud and boulders that had broken off from the cliffs. It was deserted. She glanced back the way she had come. The path was clear.

She turned to the mossy rock. Part of it jutted out, and in between was a narrow space that wasn't first noticeable from above. It was an easily overlooked spot Sorsha had discovered when she was small. She had been following a lame gull, trying to scoop it up to bring it back to the cottage, but the creature had led her a dance on the cliff's edge, before vanishing into the gap. Only when Sorsha had followed had she discovered what lay beyond it: a crawl space that burrowed into the cliff like a vole.

It was a good hiding place—especially when combined with her power to render someone invisible. If the warders came searching, the echoes of them entering the caves would be heard in plenty of time . . . enough time to cover tracks and press into some nook of the wall so that grasping hands couldn't discover them, for as she had explained, what couldn't be seen could still be heard—and touched.

She crawled into the dank space. It smelled fishy and salty, a smell that took her back to her first discovery of this place, and a smell she associated with adventure and secrets. Soon, the light filtering through from the entrance vanished, and she was blind, using only her hands to explore familiar bumps and twists to the tunnel. Moss caught under her fingernails and scraped her knees.

She remembered the first time she had ventured into the crawl space all those years ago. Back then it had felt like the tunnel went on forever, but in reality it was short, and already she could see a yellow glow ahead, where the tunnel opened out into a cavern. She shuffled closer, trying not to breathe the musty air, then paused as she heard a low voice. Sorsha gave a three-note whistle, then waited.

There was silence, broken by a scrambling sort of sound . . . and then the yellow glow vanished, leaving the tunnel pitch black. Though she was in the dark, Sorsha instinctively willed herself to be hidden . . . then remembered that she was unable to. Her powers were no longer with her, instead hidden within trinkets half a mile away at the cottage. For the first time in as long as she could remember, she was afraid. Something wasn't right. Slowly, she backed away, trying not to make a sound.

Then came a whistle being returned; the signal that all was well.

She hesitated. A voice whispered out of the depths of the cavern.

"Sorsha? Is that you?"

Her fear and suspicion lessened. "Winter?"

"Of course. Who else?"

She stayed where she was. "I just thought . . . when you didn't answer right away, and then the lantern went out . . . Who were you talking to?"

"Myself! I stubbed my toe." He gave a nervous laugh. "I worried for a moment that it might not be you, so I shut the lantern out. Is all well?"

"Yes," Sorsha replied. "Well, no . . ." She nudged toward the wider part of the cavern. It smelled of smoke and burning oil. She edged farther in, blindly feeling for the drop she knew was ahead. There. Her legs dangled over the precipice, feeling air. She wrinkled her nose, sniffing in the blackness. There was something different about the cave tonight, something she couldn't place . . .

"Did you bring food?" he asked. His voice was flat, not hopeful, as it usually was at the thought of getting fed. Perhaps he knew as well as she did that this was the end. Why had she ever let herself hope they had a future?

After tonight she'd be left with nothing of him except memories of dark caves and devastation.

"No, sorry. It was too risky. I came to tell you that I can't help you anymore, it's too dangerous. And I can't . . . hide you anymore." She broke off, distracted. Uneasiness thickened. "It sounds different in here," she blurted out as the thought came into her head. "Less echoing."

"Does it?"

This time, she recognized the difference in his voice. So small that perhaps it was only noticeable in the dark, because her hearing was the only sense she could rely on.

"Winter," she croaked. "Why haven't you lit the lantern again?"

"Oh . . . I was just about to . . ."

She wasn't imagining it, his strained, strange voice. Something was wrong. Suddenly, Sorsha realized that the darkness wasn't her enemy here; it was her friend. She also knew that it was probably too late, but she had to try. She'd said too much, but there was still a chance. They hadn't seen her face.

With a cry she turned, treading air, her fingers scrabbling for the tunnel as the hiss of a match flared behind her. An unfamiliar voice roared, "Seize her!"

Hot fingers wrapped around her ankle. Sorsha gasped, kicking free. There was a thud as her boot struck flesh, and a roar erupted below her, filling the cave. From some air pocket, nesting crows shrieked and flapped at the noise. Sorsha had one moment of hope before her other ankle was grabbed, and this time she was pulled back, grazing her palms. She landed awkwardly, twisting her leg under her, skirt tangling.

She blinked away tears of pain and terror as the cave swam into focus. No wonder their voices hadn't echoed: the cavern was much fuller tonight. Full with eight people crammed in, six of them warders. Someone had seen her, given her away . . . Prue? Could they have made her talk, somehow? The thought stung like a slap, and she hated herself for it. Moments ago she had been sure her heart was breaking, but now it was crashing in her chest like the waves against rocks. Clinging to survival.

She looked at the warders. Fat, thin, old, young, stern, mean. Their differences meant nothing. They were all in the same uniform, all here for the same reason: her. And him.

Winter stood motionless, shackled between two warders. There were no signs he had put up a fight. His eyes met hers, and they were dull and blank. Empty of hope.

"That's her," he said tonelessly. "The one who brought me here and hid me."

"We know that," a warder sneered. "We all heard what she said." He leaned into Sorsha's face, so close she could see the pores in his skin. "Her guilt is clear . . . and we have six witnesses to testify what they heard." He shook his head, tut-tutting in mock sympathy. "Such a shame. One so young with her life ahead of her."

"Careful," another warder interrupted. The flickering lamplight picked out a squashed nose and oily skin. It was then Sorsha recognized him: pig-boy. The bully from her childhood. "Don't provoke her. She has . . . powers."

She held back a sob, desperation and fear threatening to overwhelm her. Any hopes of mercy faded. Pig-boy had waited a long time for this. He would do his best to seal her fate.

The first warder looked unconcerned. "She just looks like a scared girl to me. Besides, wouldn't she be working her spells on us right now?"

"She might be thinking of it," said a third. "And you know what they say: there's no smoke without fire. From everything we've heard, this girl has roused suspicions for years. Perhaps she's just biding her time, or . . ." He studied Sorsha curiously, like she was an object in a museum.

"Or perhaps she's realizing that right at this moment, her home is surrounded . . . and that any mischief she makes for us won't end well for her mother—"

Sorsha's head snapped up. "You leave my ma and sister alone!"

A couple of the warders flinched at her outburst, but quickly recovered themselves when nothing more followed. Whatever they believed about her, Sorsha was aware that they knew exactly what she did: she was helpless, and at their mercy.

"That true?" The warder shook Winter. "Did anyone else help you? Her family?"

"No." Winter stared at his feet. "Just her."

Sorsha held in a scream. Why had Winter allowed this to happen? Why hadn't he warned her, or at least tried to? Even if he was afraid, or if the warders had a dagger to his throat, he could have done something. Whistled the wrong whistle, just to give her a chance. The betrayal crippled her, hurting more than a thousand nasty looks ever could.

"Get her up," someone said. "The sooner she's locked in the tower, the better. She won't be able to work her sorcery in there."

Sorsha winced as rough hands hauled her to her feet. "Shackle her."

It was pointless to resist. Heavy iron manacles were snapped onto her wrists, tethered by a thick chain. Dimly, as she was shunted up and into the narrow tunnel, she became aware that Winter was speaking.

"And you'll keep your word?" His voice was earnest. "You'll look out for me, and I'll get a better cell, more food?"

"Yes, Winter," the warder drawled. "Your helpfulness will be rewarded, by the warders, at least. As for the prisoners, I can't promise anything."

"What?"

"No one likes a snitch. And that's just what you are, Winter. A snitch."

And with that, Sorsha understood why Winter hadn't warned her, or tried to. Because he had been part of the trap they had set for her, and he had bargained for his own good. She felt his treachery as fiercely as if it were an open, bleeding wound. She felt weak, a fool. How could he betray her after all she had risked for him? She thought this was as bad as it got.

She was wrong.

No one saw them leave. Four warders marched Sorsha down to the cove, jeering as she stumbled. There were two boats in the cove, each with their own boatman: one for her, and the other, presumably, for Winter, although she never saw him board it. For most of the journey the warders divided their time between watching her in pairs or playing cards. None of them spoke to her, and she remained quiet, watching the hulking mass of Repent approaching. Several times she thought about jumping overboard, and would have . . . if she had ever learned to swim.

When the boat ran ashore, she was forced to jump out into the shallow water, soaking her boots and skirt hem. Then she was taken up the incline toward the prison, its high walls blocking out the light. Slimy green moss reached up its stones, like the water was trying to pull it down and swallow it.

The tower was different. Nothing grew on its walls, and there were no signs anything ever had. It was as if the building itself was dead, dead as the cairns it was made from, and nothing living belonged there or dared to touch it. Inside, the high ceiling had been engraved with strange markings and symbols, which the warders gloatingly told her were to prevent dark magic being worked. She could have told them it was needless, for inside, the tower felt as lifeless as it looked from the outside. As lifeless as she felt.

Magic was a living entity, like hope. Neither had a place in this stony tomb.

The room was sparse, with only a horsehair mattress,

a wash basin, and a chamber pot. They left her with stale bread and water before the door was bolted behind her.

"When will I see my ma?" she shouted to the retreating footsteps. "Please?"

She received no reply. Nor did they ever answer, when the door was opened to toss her food and water, and empty the chamber pot. She whiled away hours at the windows. She could just make out mainland Crowstone: the rooftops, church spire, and high up for all to see, the gallows. All of it so close, and Sorsha had never even been there.

She wondered what had happened to Ma and Prue. Were they safe, or being held in the prison, too? Tortured to extract confessions about her? Or bribed, as Winter had been? No matter how much she begged, the warders would tell her nothing. Day by day, the not knowing ate away at her. She grew thinner, dirtier, and finally resigned herself to never seeing either of them again.

And then, after three long months, she had a visitor. It was not her mother.

Sorsha had been standing by the window overlooking Crowstone, though she hadn't been looking at the mainland. Today it was only a gray smudge through rain and clouds, so Sorsha had been looking straight down at the ground. It was severe, dizzying. Still she leaned out, wondering how long it would take her to hit the ground if she fell. Or leaped.

Lost in terrible thoughts, she jumped as the door was pounded three times. "Stand back," a warder ordered.

The lock clicked, and bolts were unlatched. The door opened, and two warders entered. One stayed by the door. The other motioned for her to move to the wall, where an iron cuff was shackled to the stone. He clamped it onto her wrist without a word, then stood aside.

The warder by the door jerked his head. Someone entered the room — and Sorsha almost wept.

"Prue!" she cried. She tried to run to her sister, forgetting the restraints until they jerked her backwards.

Prudence took tiny steps into the tower room, stopping close to the door. Her hands were clasped demurely in front of her, resting on her neat white apron. Sorsha looked down at her own clothes for the first time in weeks. They were filthy, torn. Her hair was wild and unwashed, her nails black and ragged. She looked every bit the witch she was rumored to be. But none of that mattered, for Prue was here, after all this time. She hadn't been forgotten.

"How are you, sister?" Prue asked. Her voice was calm, unreadable.

"Wretched," said Sorsha. "And hungry. But it's so good to see you!" Her eyes filled with tears, which she blinked angrily away. So far, she had managed not to cry in front of the warders, but seeing her sister was wearing away her resolve. She cast a wary look at the warders, wondering if they were going to allow the two girls some privacy, but soon saw that it was a ridiculous thought. They were going nowhere. "How is Ma?" she asked at last.

"She has been ill." Prudence gave a little cough. "They say it's her nerves and the shock. The doctor has given her a tonic to help her sleep. I've been taking care of everything."

Sorsha closed her eyes. Poor, poor Ma. This was all Sorsha's fault. She should have listened. Ma had always warned her not to use her powers. If she had the chance again, could she have discarded them into the objects years ago, and cast them into the sea? It would have meant a safer life, but at a cost of losing part of herself. Without it, she no longer knew who she was. Sorsha's eyes snapped open. "You appear well, Prue," she said slowly. "Have they . . . treated you well? Is everything at home as it . . . as it should be?"

She gave Prue a meaningful look, trying to will her unspoken message into her sister's consciousness: Were the objects safe?

Prudence nodded. "Yes. All is as it should be."

Sorsha's flesh prickled uneasily. There was something odd about her sister— She corrected herself. Odder than usual. Her voice, even the way she held herself . . . It was smug, almost. A coil of worry shifted somewhere deep within. All this time Sorsha had been imagining terrible things, worrying, starving. And here was Prue: clean, well fed, more rosy-cheeked than she had ever been.

"When will Ma be well enough to visit?" she demanded. "And why has it taken you so long to come?"

"There will be no more visits," Prue answered. "From either of us."

The tower room swayed like it had been caught in a gust of wind . . . but no one else felt it but Sorsha. "What? Why?" Her voice was high and faint.

"They're not permitted. I was only granted this visit in return for my cooperation."

Cooperation? Like Winter had cooperated?

"What do you mean?" Sorsha croaked.

"I have been helping the warders," Prue said. Her pale eyes glittered. So eel-like, so different from the earthy warmth of their mother's eyes. "And now they are preparing for your trial."

"Helping them how?" Sorsha asked. Her insides churned with fear, this new emotion she was growing so used to. Just what had Prue been saying?

"If you are found guilty, I will pray for you," said Prue, in a grave voice.

Sorsha narrowed her eyes. "Guilty of what, exactly?"

The warder next to Prue spoke up. "You know why you're here. You're under suspicion of sorcery. Dark magic."

"If you are found innocent, then I wish you a long and happy life," Prue continued.

Sorsha shook her head, bewildered. "If . . . ? You make it sound as though either way, this is goodbye!"

"It is." Prue's eyes bored into her. So cold, and full of malice. How could Sorsha ever have made excuses for them? Ma had seen the resentment festering there, and so had Sorsha, deep in her own gut. Now she would pay the price for not listening. "They've taken pity on me, you see. They're giving me a chance—"

"A chance at what?" Sorsha cried.

"At a normal life, away from the sinners on Torment. I'm living on Crowstone now, the mainland. My father had relatives there who took me in. Ma will stay on Torment. And there is some happy news: it all happened rather quickly, but I am married! My name is Prudence Widdershins now."

"Married?" Sorsha cried. "On Crowstone? How can you leave Ma?"

"We're so different, you and I," Prue continued softly. "You were so wild, so stubborn and difficult, and yet . . . still Ma's favorite. I tried so hard to make her happy, tried to be good. I have been good. And I always warned you your magic was a wicked thing that would get you into trouble."

"Liar!" Sorsha yelled. "You never said anything of the kind! You wanted to be like me, you said it many times!"

Prue cast a weary look at the warders. "See how she will say anything to lessen her own guilt?" She strode toward her, and Sorsha froze as her sister embraced her, leaning close to speak in her ear. For a foolish moment she clung to the hope that Prue had been playing along with the warders and that, somehow, she had worked out a plan to rescue her.

"Goodbye," Prue whispered, kissing her cheek before backing away.

Sorsha lifted her fingers to her skin in horror. Her cheek was tingling from her sister's touch, for her lips had been ice cold. Her mother's words echoed in her head, as clear as the day she had spoken them.

She is jealous of you. She wants what you have . . .

For now she knew what her sister was really telling her. There would be no rescue. All this time their mother had been right. Prue had been waiting, biding her time.

Now her time had come and Sorsha's was over. Sorsha was powerless; her gifts were no use to her. Prue, however, could do as she pleased with them.

Prue had her exactly where she wanted her.

"I curse you," Sorsha hissed through gritted teeth. "To the end of your days and beyond. I curse your blood as long as it flows!"

Prue's eyes widened, but it was with surprise, not fear. "That's enough," the warder nearest to Sorsha said, nodding to Prue. "Get her out!"

The other warder bundled Prudence toward the tower door, but Sorsha was not finished. She lunged against the shackles, the iron cutting into her skin. She barely felt it.

"I curse you!" she screeched. "You want Crowstone? You can have it, forever! May you never leave, and be as much a prisoner there as I am here!"

She thought she saw the corners of Prue's mouth curve slightly before she was rushed through the tower door. Bitterness and anger coursed through Sorsha, bubbling away like witch's brew. She sank to the floor, her mind simmering, plotting.

Sorsha's curse hadn't scared Prue. She knew that no sorcery could be performed within the tower walls. The only person Sorsha had harmed by uttering those words was herself, for they would add to her apparent guilt.

She stared at the window. No sorcery could be worked from inside . . . but outside? It was only a step away and, had she only thought of this before, she could have retained her powers and escaped.

"Sisterly love," she muttered to herself, rocking, eyes glazed. "You're going to pay, Prue. And all the Widdershins sisters after you . . ."

Perhaps there was a way she could have her revenge, even if she couldn't save herself. For while she no longer had her magic, a curse was something different. A curse could only come from darkness.

And what could be darker than death?

Chapter Twenty-Two

Whump!

"PRUE WAS A WIDDERSHINS?" Betty exclaimed. "Or became a Widdershins, at any rate, and . . . and —" She paused to take a breath, sickened. She had wondered if one of her ancestors—a warder, perhaps—had crossed Sorsha, but had hoped that it had been justified. She hadn't seen this coming: that her family was descended directly from Sorsha's traitorous half-sister.

"So much for family," Colton said, his lip curled in disgust. He fell silent for a moment. Betty guessed that he was thinking, as she was, of the Widdershins name scratched into the tower walls. As he spoke next, she heard a trace of guilt. "She betrayed Sorsha in exchange for her way off Torment."

"Sorsha knew she had no way out," Betty whispered. "And no magic left . . . but by jumping to her death, she could create a curse and have her revenge on Prue."

"Trouble was," Fingerty said, "when she invoked that curse, she cursed Prudence's blood . . . which then became the Widdershinses' blood."

"And my family has paid for it ever since," said Betty. Prue had betrayed and stolen to forge herself a new life, tainting the Widdershinses forever. The magical heirlooms had never belonged to them. She felt crushed by grief and disgust. All this time she had thought they were the victims, not knowing they were the villains, too.

Overwhelmingly, she realized she wanted to put things right—not just for the Widdershinses, but for Sorsha. She was beginning to understand what three months in the tower had done to Sorsha's mind. Three months of being twisted by loneliness, only to find out that she had been betrayed by someone she loved. Betty tried to imagine how she would feel if Fliss or Charlie ever did such a thing, and found she couldn't. It was too unthinkable, too poisonous. Because of this, she could only find pity and not hatred for Sorsha. Fingerty's stories had brought her understanding of how the curse had come about, but she still saw no way to undo it.

"If you knew about our family's link to Sorsha, why didn't you say anything?" Betty asked.

Fingerty looked perplexed. "Why would I?" he said at last. "No one ever asked, until you. Even if they had, what good would it have done? I don't know how to break the curse! Yer think Bunny would have thanked me for pointing out she's descended from a traitor and a thief? She's kicked people out of the Poacher's Pocket for mentioning Sorsha's name, she's that proud!"

"Granny . . . Granny knew about Prue?" Betty whispered. It wasn't hard to believe; her grandmother was terribly proud. She'd once thrown a horseshoe at a customer for mentioning their father's prison sentence, even though it was common knowledge.

The journey lapsed into silence. Betty turned Sorsha's story over and over in her mind, but the answers still eluded her. Her worries kept returning to Fliss and Charlie and the abrupt end to their snatched conversation. She could only pray that Jarrod hadn't discovered the mirror's secret and taken that from Fliss, too.

It was past noon when Betty, Colton, and Fingerty arrived in Windy Bottom, and the rasping in Betty's head was driving her to distraction, adding to her growing dread.

After scrambling off the wagon at a crossroads, they

followed the signs to the shabby little town. As they searched the streets for any sign of a mill, Betty got the impression that Windy Bottom was the sort of place no one stuck around in for long. Buildings were crumbling; the streets were sludgy. Once or twice, they forgot they were invisible and spoke when they shouldn't have, much to the bewilderment of passing strangers.

"What if they're not here?" Betty said, trying to stop her voice from rising. "What's to have stopped Jarrod taking them somewhere else by now?"

"Nothing," said Colton quietly. "It would have been the most sensible thing for Jarrod to do, if he meant to cover his tracks."

Betty glared at him. "I was hoping you'd say something to make me feel better." She stomped away from him, finding her way onto a little bridge whose walls were flaking like pastry. If her sisters were gone, there was no way of finding them . . . unless Fliss could use the mirror to make contact. And with no way to break the curse, Betty felt as lost as her sisters. Hope was draining away. Fingerty trudged after her, looking thoroughly fed up.

Colton followed with an apologetic look. "Just being honest. But there's every chance they could still be here. Jarrod wouldn't have thought we'd get past the Devil's Teeth, or across the marshes unseen, without the bag. I don't think he'd be expecting us any time soon, if at all. And there's another thing on our side—he doesn't know Fliss used the mirror to tell us exactly where he'd taken them. If I were him, I'd think I was well hidden."

"That's if he didn't wake up and catch her," Betty said darkly. Had Jarrod discovered the mirror's power? Fliss had vanished so abruptly . . . and not reappeared since.

She felt her face crumple and had to turn away when the tears came, but now that she had started she found she couldn't stop—and she hated it. She had always mocked Fliss for her easy tears, and always avoided weeping herself. After all, it solved nothing. To her surprise, it was Fingerty who handed her a grubby handkerchief. The small act of kindness made her cry harder. Eventually her sobs gave way to sniffles and she blew her nose into the hanky. It was time to be practical.

Colton waited patiently until she had composed herself before he spoke. "Feel better now?"

"Not really," she sniffed. She handed Fingerty his soggy handkerchief. She swayed on her feet as a sudden vision swam before her eyes, something she had seen before: of falling from a great height, the ground rushing up, crows circling above, waiting, cawing . . .

"It's her," Betty whispered. "The last things she saw . . . and heard . . . the crows. That's why we can hear them now." Her heart wrenched as she stared out across the bridge. "Fliss? Charlie?" she whispered. "Where are you?" Tears were threatening to come once more, but she held them back, shielding her eyes as the sun emerged from the clouds.

She moved across the bridge, drawn by the sight of an overgrown merrypenny bush. A few moldering berries were oozing on its branches, but the bush had been plucked almost bare. She remembered a morning back in summer when she, Fliss, and Charlie had picked merrypennies in the fields. As they'd filled their baskets Fliss had regaled them with Granny's superstitions: how it was unlucky to pick the berries after sundown, and how you should never eat them after Halloween because imps would have danced all over them. Granny also knew a recipe to boil them up into a potent liquor, which she did every year while singing the old nursery rhyme about them:

The merrypennies in the meadow, silver by the
    night,
Were hopped upon by midnight imps who
    danced by pale moonlight . . .

Betty would do just about anything to hear Fliss's dreadful warbling again.

A berry bobbed in the wind, like it was agreeing sadly. Betty stared past it, standing up straighter. On a hill directly ahead was a dilapidated building, its once-grand sails useless as broken birds' wings, its windows boarded up. It was so bleached and faded, and its sails so sparse, that at first she had mistaken it for an old water tower or beacon.

She turned, beckoning Colton. "Look, there!"

Already she was scrambling toward it, kicking up dust on the road. Colton hurried after her with Fingerty, who was regarding the eerie-looking place with trepidation.

"Slow down," Colton hissed after her. "We can still be heard, remember?"

"Of course I remember!" Betty retorted, but it was hard to hold herself back, knowing she might be moments away from seeing her sisters again. As they neared, Betty slowed, scanning the windows. The mill was isolated and looked as though it had been empty for some years. The weatherboards were decaying, and the whole place looked like a rotten tooth sticking out of the scrubby land.

The sounds of their approach were camouflaged by the boggy ground. Heart racing, Betty searched the windows for any sign of movement, but it was impossible to see past the boards that had been nailed over them. This was the right place; she was sure of it! But were her sisters still there? This time they were the ones with the element of surprise, not Jarrod. With the dolls' magic she could help her sisters escape, for Jarrod couldn't catch what he couldn't see.

It was here, however, that Fingerty hesitated.

"I don't like this," he muttered. "If the warders catch me with him, that'll be the end. They'll think I masterminded all this!"

"Pull yourself together!" Betty hissed.

Fingerty stopped walking. "I want to go back!"

Colton elbowed him. "Shut up. You'll give us away if you keep wittering!"

"Remember what's in it for you," said Betty. "If you help capture Jarrod, you'll be pardoned. And . . . and if I make it back, I'll see you get free drinks in the Poacher's Pocket for the rest of your miserable life. Deal?"

Fingerty smacked his lips, considering. "Yerp."

They approached the mill in silence. Now that they were closer, Betty could see chunks of wood on the ground where the door had been torn away, and the overgrown grass had been trampled down. Someone had been here recently.

Betty turned to Colton. "How do we get in? Even if we are invisible, Jarrod's probably barricaded the door."

Colton looked up at the mill. "Let's check every window. One might not be boarded, or there could be a cellar trapdoor." He pressed a finger to his lips as they edged around the back of the building.

"There!" Betty whispered, pointing. "Look!"

A tiny window was above their heads. A plank of wood had been nailed across it, but one side had worked loose.

"It's too small and too high," Colton whispered.

"I could look through and see if they're there," Betty said. "If they are, perhaps I can draw Jarrod away from the door and you and Fingerty could break it open. Quickly, lift me up!"

Colton linked his hands, ready for Betty's boot, but before he could hoist her up, there was a loud thump from inside the building. They froze. Maddeningly, Betty couldn't hear much more over the noise of the crows in her head. Silence followed.

"What was—" she began, breaking off as the tiny window came flying open and a tangled mop of hair appeared. Two small hands reached onto the sill.

"Charlie?" Betty whispered, dizzy with relief.

Charlie raised her head, her pointed elfin face confused. "Who's there?"

"It's me, Betty! Hold on!"

"Betty, is that really you?" came another voice, muffled from inside the mill.

"Fliss!" Betty gasped. She emptied the dolls, rushing to make herself, Fingerty, and Colton visible again. "What's going on in there? Where's Jarrod?"

"I tricked him into getting drunk," Fliss answered. "He's sprawled right in front of the door, and the bag is stuck under him. We can't free it!"

Colton held out his arms to Charlie. "Jump! I'll catch you."

"You better," said Charlie, eyeing the drop. She leaped like a frog through the air, and Colton caught her neatly. She gave him a quick hug, then slithered down him like he was a tree and ran to Betty, who scooped her up and squeezed fiercely. She had never been more grateful to feel her little sister's arms around her.

"I knew you'd find us," Charlie said loyally.

"Looks like you didn't need my help to escape," Betty said, stroking her hair. She marveled at how happy Charlie seemed, when escaping from Jarrod was only part of a much bigger problem. Did Charlie understand the curse and what it meant? Or did she simply have faith that Betty was going to figure out a way to somehow make everything all right? The burden of responsibility weighed as heavily as the stone in her pocket.

"Come on." Betty's voice was hoarse with emotion. "We've got to help Fliss." She squealed suddenly as something warm and furry wriggled at her collar. "Charlie! You've still got that bleedin' rat!"

"Of course I've still got him," Charlie replied huffily. She scooped the rat up and put him on her shoulder. "You don't leave friends behind!"

"I'm surprised Jarrod hasn't killed him," Betty said grimly.

"He tried." Charlie eyes narrowed. "But I managed to hide him . . ." She grinned. "And then we got him back, didn't we, Hoppit?"

They moved to the front of the mill, shoving at the door. Thuds came from the other side as Fliss tugged and swore, words that she could only have heard from Granny. Colton's eyebrows shot up.

"It's not budging," Fliss fumed. "Jarrod's too heavy!"

"Wait, it is," said Colton. "I felt it give. We all need to push and pull together. On three: one, two, three!"

Betty dug her heels into the grass and pushed for all she was worth. She was reminded of how heavy Jarrod had been when they'd lifted him onto Colton's prison bed. Had that really been just a few hours ago? It seemed like another lifetime.

Colton used his shoulder to ram the door, shattering the partially rotten wood, and even Charlie and Fingerty shoved. Little by little, the door began to move, and they could hear Fliss more clearly through a narrow gap.

"Just a . . . little . . . way . . . more!"

The gap widened. Betty could see a limp, meaty hand through it, and a low groaning as Jarrod flopped uselessly on the other side. Finally, the gap was just wide enough to slip through.

"Quickly," Colton cried, urging Fliss toward him. "Let's get out of here!"

But before Fliss had even gotten her breath back, Betty had pushed past and was inside the windmill with her, hugging her tightly. There was a thick, sweet smell in the air that Betty recognized. It reminded her of home. It was a moment before she noticed that something about Fliss felt different. She stood back to look at her—and gasped. For Fliss's glossy dark hair, which had once tumbled down her back in smooth, flowing locks, had been hacked away unevenly and was now too short even to tie a ribbon in.

"Oh, Fliss," she murmured in dismay. "Your hair. Your beautiful hair! What happened?"

"Jarrod," said Charlie, who had squeezed through the door with them. "He chopped it all off because he caught Fliss looking in the mirror." She shot a look of contempt at the sprawling body on the floor. Jarrod's eyelids fluttered at the mention of his name. His head lolled to one side, tongue out like a dog.

Betty shot him a look of loathing. How dare he?

"He said it'd teach me not to be so vain," Fliss said in a choked voice. "It'll grow back. If we live past sunset . . ."

"Let's worry about that after we get out of here," Betty said fiercely. She didn't have the heart to confess to Fliss that she was no closer to breaking the curse, but they could at least escape Jarrod and see Granny one last time. "Quickly, the bag!" She released Fliss as Colton slipped through the door with Fingerty close behind.

Together they kneeled by Jarrod. The bag's handles were poking out from under his back, and Charlie tugged at them impatiently.

"Careful, Charlie," Betty warned. "We don't want it ripping."

"What exactly did you do to him?" Colton asked. He sniffed the air suspiciously.

"He sent me out for food," said Fliss. "Keeping Charlie here with him, of course, so I had no choice but to return.

He . . . he threatened to hurt her if I got help. I had no money, so I was forced to steal a few things, but then on the bridge I spotted some merrypennies."

"That's it!" Betty exclaimed, sniffing again. "I knew I recognized that smell."

"I boiled them up with honey, like how Granny does," said Fliss. She cast a scornful look at Jarrod. "The greedy oaf couldn't get them down his neck fast enough, even though it took rather a lot to get him like this."

"Greedy oaf," Charlie agreed. "I stirred in a little something from Hoppit, too," she added mischievously, stroking the rat's nose.

"That's one way to improve Fliss's cooking," Betty said.

"Hey!" said Fliss. She wagged a finger at Charlie. "And that's disgusting, you know."

"He deserved it," Charlie said with a shrug. "Told you we'd get him back."

"What'll we do with him, though?" Fingerty asked, one of his eyes twitching nervously. "I ain't watching over him like this—he's bound to come around soon."

Charlie pointed, bouncing with mischief. A sturdy trapdoor was set in the floor. "Chuck him down there."

"Good," said Colton. "We can throw him in and lock it."

With a generous heave, they succeeded in rolling Jarrod toward the wall. He belched as his head flopped the opposite way. He hit the floor with a thump, landing on his side and leaving the bag free.

Fliss pounced, snatching it up. She had just delved into it and removed the mirror—which Jarrod had evidently confiscated, too—but her triumph ended as Jarrod's eyes flew open and, with a drunken lurch, he seized her ankle.

"You're going nowhere, flower," he slurred, his face alive with rage. "And neither is the brat!"

"My name," Fliss said through gritted teeth, "is not flower, or petal, or"—she shot Colton a warning glance—"princess! My name is Felicity Widdershins!" She lifted her other foot and brought it down on Jarrod's hand—hard.

Jarrod yelped and released her to nurse his crushed fingers. He rolled onto his knees, red-faced, raging and swaying.

"And my name," Charlie declared, "isn't brat. It's Charlie, so there!" She grabbed the traveling bag from Fliss and swung it at Jarrod. It hit him full in the chops with a satisfying *whump*. "That's for kidnapping us, and that . . ." She swung the bag again—*whump!* ". . . is for chopping my sister's hair off, and this"—she brought the bag down on Jarrod's head with a third donk—"is for my granny, because she'd bash you one if she was here!"

"Too right," Betty agreed, momentarily enjoying the small triumph. No matter what happened now, at least her sisters were by her side where they belonged.

Fliss dodged as Jarrod lunged for her again, and yanked the trapdoor open. It spewed out musty air and dust. Jarrod's eyes widened, but he had no time to save himself as his own weight and poor balance carried him forward to teeter on the edge. For a moment there was a flash of victory in his eyes as he regained his footing, before Charlie stepped behind him and gave the bag one last swing.

"One for luck!"

The bag hit him between the shoulder blades, propelling him forward into the dark space. A series of clashes and bangs followed as he hit the bottom, and a cloud of dust and cobwebs flew up. Fliss slammed the trapdoor and bolted it shut.

"Hope you like spiders!" Charlie crowed gleefully, dancing on the trapdoor.

"Well, well, princess," Colton said, gazing at Fliss in admiration. "I never knew you had it in you."

"Neither did I," said Fliss. "But these crows in my head are making me really cranky. And don't call me princess!"

"That takes care of him." Betty took Charlie's hand, feeling a rush of pride for her sisters. "For a while, at least," she said as Jarrod bellowed and cussed from below. Something thudded against the trapdoor from the underside. She turned to Fingerty. "Jarrod's all yours now. That should hold for long enough for you to alert the warders."

Fingerty's face creased into something that might have been a smile. "You Widdershinses," he said, shaking his head. "Yer all barmy as you like. Brave, though. You've got guts, just like Bunny."

"I hope so," said Betty. And was it her imagination, or had a blush crept into Fingerty's leathery old cheeks at the mention of Granny? She decided she didn't want to know. "And I hope you get your pardon."

Fingerty squinted, looking thoughtful. "Yerp."

Fliss nodded to him. "See you in the Poacher's Pocket."

We hope, Betty added silently. Her jubilation was already beginning to ebb. She had her sisters back but was no closer to the answer they so desperately needed —and time was running out. Granny would know they were gone, and so must everyone else, now that Betty and Charlie hadn't turned up for school that morning. Would people already be searching Crowstone's streets, calling their names?

"Betty?" Charlie slipped her hand into Betty's. "I want to go home now."

"Me too," Betty answered. "But even if we get to see Granny again, going home can't save us. By sunset—"

"But it can," said Charlie. "I know how."

"It's not that simple, Charlie," Fliss said gently. She cast a worried glance at Betty. "I told you before. Remember what Granny said, about the curse?"

"Of course I know about the curse!" Charlie roared, surprising them all. She stamped her foot. "I was there when Granny told us, *remember*? And these birds squawking in my head aren't exactly letting me forget!"

"Charlie, calm down!" Betty said, startled.

"I will if you listen to me!" Charlie raged. "But no one ever does!"

Colton kneeled down in front of her and took her grubby hand in his. "Go on, Charlie. We're listening."

"We use the bag to take us back to the start, before it happened. See?"

Betty stared at her, baffled. "Back to the start of what?"

"Back to the Poacher's Pocket, before we ever left. Then the curse won't happen, and we'll be safe and the blasted birds will stop!" Charlie gave Colton an apologetic look. "Only thing is, you'll still be in prison."

Fliss sighed tiredly. "Charlie, poppet, it's a lovely idea, but I don't think the bag can be used to go back in time. We know it can take us anywhere . . . but anywhen? Even if it could, there would still be the other three of us already back in that time, and then things would get . . . well, rather complicated."

"I know," Charlie said seriously. "I thought that when I went back to the church hall to get another bread roll. I was nearly seen by the other me who was getting the first one—"

"Wait, what?" Betty could hardly breathe as Charlie's revelation exploded in her head, momentarily drowning out the crows. Hope and excitement thrummed in her chest. Was it true? Had they really had the means to save themselves all along? She searched her little sister's face, not quite able to believe what she was hearing. "Are you saying you used the bag to . . . to go back in time so you could get second helpings of food?"

"I was hungry," said Charlie, with a shrug. "I thought it was worth a try." Her tummy rumbled loudly.

Fliss gaped. "You mean . . . all that time you were messing around with the bag and practicing with it without telling another soul?"

"Of course." Charlie grinned. "That bag is my pinch of magic, or it will be when Granny's finished with it. It wasn't fair that I had to wait while you two had all the fun with yours."

"Charlie Widdershins," Betty said, sweeping her sister into a hug. "You are brilliant! Greedy, and sneaky, but brilliant!"

Charlie preened. "I told you you'd need me."

"But how can this possibly work?" Fliss shook her head, astounded. "You heard what Charlie said—when she went back there was another . . . another her! Even if we go back, how do we stop—"

"Charlie's idea is almost perfect," Betty said, turning the possibilities over in her mind. If the bag could take them back to Crowstone before they'd ever set the curse in motion, what was to stop it taking them back to before . . .

Before the curse ever existed?

"It wouldn't solve all our problems, and might even create more," she said, speaking hurriedly now. "We'd still be trapped in Crowstone, under the curse, and there would be two of each of us. Not to mention Colton would still be in the prison."

"So what, then?" Charlie huffed. "You said it was brilliant."

"It is," Betty insisted, hugging her. "We need to go further back. Before any of us were even born, before the curse was even made. Back to Crowstone, the day Sorsha Spellthorn died. We're going to stop her from falling from the tower."

Fliss's mouth dropped open. "You really think this can work? Even if the bag takes us back, where could she escape to?"

"We bring her back with us, here," said Betty. After the mounting feeling that all had been lost, Charlie's revelation had renewed her strength and courage. They had had the answer the whole time. They could not only save themselves, but put right the terrible wrong that Sorsha had suffered, too. "Where no one would know her. We have to help her, don't you see? These objects . . . the bag, the mirror, and the dolls—they were all Sorsha's. They were never meant for the Widdershinses. When she put her powers into them, she did it hoping that they'd be used to rescue her. But no one ever did. Until now. Only the Widdershinses can save her."

"And if it doesn't work?" Fliss asked.

"It has to. We're closer than anyone has ever been before. I just know it!" said Betty. "But we need to think first. It's no good going straight to the tower. None of the objects will work there—the magic is rendered powerless."

"It'll be dangerous," Fingerty put in, listening intently.

"There's only one way into that tower, and one way out. And it'll be guarded."

Colton moved to the door, peering outside. "We still have a few hours before sundown. I say we follow Betty's plan, but start off somewhere familiar."

"'We'?" Fliss asked. "Are you coming with us?"

"You three are the reason I'm standing here today. I owe it to all of you, and Sorsha, to help make things right." Colton's black eyes glittered as he reached out and brushed Charlie's hair off her face. "A little girl like you helped me once. Feels like time to pay back the favor."

Betty took a deep breath, touched by this show of loyalty. Hours ago she'd hated not only him, but being forced to stick with him out of necessity. She had never dreamed Colton might grow to be someone she'd call a friend. She gave him a small, grateful smile. "That's settled, then. Let's do it now, quickly, before we can change our minds." She squeezed Charlie's hand. "We need you to use the bag to take us to the Poacher's Pocket, on the morning Sorsha Spellthorn dies. Can you remember to say that?"

Charlie's bottom lip quivered. "Yes, but . . ."

"But what?" Fliss prompted gently.

"What if we went back to the Poacher's Pocket now,"

Charlie asked. "Back to our home, and Granny?" Her eyes filled with tears. "Just for a few minutes. I miss her!"

"We can't," said Betty. "Granny would be furious. She'd never let us out of her sight again, let alone allow us to use any of the magical objects."

"There is a way we can see her, though," said Fliss. "The mirror. Just to let her know we're all right."

"Oh," said Charlie, sniffing. "Yes, let's do that!"

Betty nodded, and Fliss held the mirror before the three of them. Their faces were reflected back at them, dirty and tearstained.

"Let us see Granny," Fliss commanded.

Betty steeled herself as the looking glass began to cloud over. Anxious as she was to see her grandmother, she knew that no matter how relieved Bunny would be to hear from them, they wouldn't escape an ear bashing. She was right.

Granny came into view as the glass cleared, although the image was still thick with smoke. This time, however, it was pipe smoke. It was clouding around Granny's head so densely that for a moment Betty couldn't work out exactly where Bunny was. Then she caught a glimpse of the kitchen window, with all Granny's charms hanging in place.

"Granny?" Fliss said in a small voice.

Bunny's head snapped up. Her eyes were puffy and red. "Fliss!"

"We're all here, Granny," said Fliss. "Betty and Charlie, too. We're safe."

"Where?" Granny shrieked, peering at them as they crowded around the mirror. "Where are you? You girls come home right now, do you hear?"

"We can't, Granny," said Betty, heartsick to see her poor granny looking more beaten down and defeated than ever before. This couldn't be the last time Betty would see her. She had to make it back home. "Not yet. But we will soon. I promise."

"Was this your doing, Betty?" Granny's voice rumbled like low thunder. "Are you using those dolls to stay invisible? Because I've had half of Crowstone looking for you all!"

Betty gulped, unable to bring herself to confess that they were no longer in Crowstone. It would only scare Granny further and make her lose all hope.

"We're so close now, Granny," she said. "Closer than anyone's ever been to breaking the curse."

"And it was me who figured it out," said Charlie proudly.

"Was it, now?" Granny raged. "Well, you'll all be taking an equal share of the blame when you get back!"

"Uh-oh." Charlie was looking distinctly less homesick now. "She's awful cross, ain't she?"

"So, anyway, we, er . . . just wanted you not to worry," Fliss waffled. "And we'll be back soon."

"You'll get back here now!" Granny growled. "You'll—"

"We love you, Granny," said Charlie. She leaned forward and kissed the mirror.

It was enough to make Granny's eyes, which had been narrowed in anger, widen and fill with tears. The sharpness left her voice. "And I love you all, so much. That's why you must come home and stop this madness. I can't lose the three of you, too."

"We are coming home," Betty said. "Soon." *After we set things right*, she added silently. *And home won't be a prison anymore.*

"Betty—" their grandmother began.

Fliss bit her lip. "Sorry, Granny." She turned the mirror over, breaking contact, and took her sisters' hands. "This is our chance to change things. Not just for us, but for all those Widdershins girls before us, as well as Sorsha."

Charlie bit her lip. "All right. Let's do this."

Chapter Twenty-Three

A Friend

A HUNDRED YEARS HAD MADE a great deal of difference to the Poacher's Pocket, and to Crowstone generally. They landed in a tangle of arms and legs in a small alley next to the inn—an alley that no longer existed in the girls' present.

After they'd brushed themselves down and moved to the front of the street, the first thing Betty noticed was how new and smart everything looked. She was so used to the place looking shabby and run-down that it was quite a surprise to see the windows with all their panes intact, and the glossily painted doors displaying no signs of flaking.

We're here, she thought, trembling with anticipation.

We're actually here . . . and our whole future depends on this working.

"What is that smell?" Charlie said. She screwed up her face and pinched her nose. "It's like . . . like the latrines!"

"I think the streets are the latrines," said Fliss as she took in their surroundings. "Ugh, we're right next to the gutters!"

Before she had even finished speaking, a window of a house across the green was flung open and the contents of a chamber pot thrown out.

"It worked, though," said Betty, staring around in amazement as the reality of what they had done began to sink in. "It really, actually worked! We're here, back at the start of it all."

"Wait, do you hear that?" said Charlie. "The birds in my head—they've stopped. They've gone!"

"Mine too!" Fliss exclaimed.

"And mine!" said Betty, realizing her pocket felt lighter, too. The stone in it had vanished. "It's because the curse hasn't been made yet. We've got to make sure it never is."

"Jumping jackjaws!" Charlie exclaimed. "Look at the moon!"

Betty looked up. Though it was broad daylight, the moon was clearly visible, something Granny always said was bad luck. In addition, it was an eerie red, which turned the sky pink, almost like sunset.

"A blood moon," Colton said, spooked. "It must be an eclipse . . . but people from this time won't know that. They'll just take it as a sign of Sorsha's guilt."

Betty gazed at the sky. "If anything, it'd make me think the opposite," she said. "An innocent person about to be executed."

The doors of the Poacher's Pocket opened as someone went in. Warm air and the smell of ale gusted over them, making Betty miss home more than ever. Right away her eyes went to the bar, half-expecting to see Granny there. Instead, she met cold, fishlike eyes. She looked away, heart hammering. Fingerty had described her so well that she knew exactly who this girl was.

"That's her," Betty whispered. "Prudence Widder-shins—Sorsha's half sister, who betrayed her. And like it or not, we're relations of hers." She paused as a man emerged from the cellar. Something about him reminded her of her father, and from the way Prue was gazing at him, the rest was clear. "And that's who she married. The curse and everything that's happened, the reason we're even here, are all because of her." She stared at Prudence, longing to slap the simpering face and sickened to think she shared the same blood as this hateful creature. It was a dirty, uncomfortable sensation that left Betty hankering after a good wash.

"Betty?" Charlie said suddenly. "The bag . . . I can't find it!" She turned to look around, panic-stricken. "I must have dropped it in the alley when we landed!"

The sickening feeling inside Betty intensified as they ran back, retracing their path. The alley was empty. There was no bag, and no one in sight. Then Fliss turned to Betty, ashen-faced and rummaging through her own pockets. Before she said a word, Betty knew.

"The mirror's gone, too," Fliss whispered. "I don't understand! I had it, I never lose things!"

"You didn't lose it," said Betty. A realization hit her like a boat striking a rock. She checked her skirt, already knowing the dolls were gone. "The curse hasn't been made yet, but we didn't think about what else would happen by us traveling back in time."

Colton took a sharp breath. "You don't have the objects because they haven't been passed down the generations to you yet."

"Exactly," said Betty, furious with herself for not foreseeing this.

"But without the bag, we're stuck here!" Fliss wailed, horrified. "And Sorsha will make the curse anyway!"

Slowly, Betty walked back to the door of the Poacher's

Pocket. The others followed, watching as she turned to stare through the window.

"We might not have the bag, but we know where it is."

"In there," said Colton. "With the dolls and the mirror. Prue has them all."

Betty nodded, clenching her teeth. "And we know what we have to do."

"Get them back," Fliss said fiercely. "Then, after we use them to save Sorsha and get home, we return them to her. They were never Prue's to begin with!"

"It's already busy in there," Colton said, frowning. "Surely this place wouldn't normally be open at this hour?"

Betty glanced at the moon; then her attention was drawn to the people bustling around them, some lingering outside to gaze at the reddening sky. Huddling and pointing in excited whispers, their eyes gleamed with malice.

"They're here for the execution," she said hoarsely. "They've come to see the witch be hanged at noon." *Like crows picking at bones.*

"Serves them right that they've had a wasted journey, then, doesn't it?" Colton took her hand, squeezing it hard. "Think we can do it without being caught?"

Betty squeezed back, remembering Fingerty's advice.

"We can if we use a distraction." Releasing Colton's hand, she led the way to the door.

Inside, the Poacher's Pocket crackled with morbid excitement. Whispers of "spells," "sorceress," and "magic" caught Betty's ears. As they made their way to one of the few empty corners, she kept her eyes on Prue, watching her prim, pointed little face taking it all in. A few times, when she thought no one was looking, she gave a secret smile. Betty couldn't wait to wipe it off her face.

"Right," she said in a low voice as they huddled by one of the fireplaces. "Colton and Charlie, you two create a distraction so I can sneak upstairs without being seen. Fliss, you keep watch. If Fishy-Eyes or the idiot who married her look like they're about to come up, then you need to warn me." She flashed Fliss a grin. "Your terrible singing should do the trick."

"I'll do my worst," Fliss promised.

"Ready?" Betty asked.

Colton nodded. "This way," he said to Charlie, leaning in close. "I've got an idea."

Charlie listened, nodding. They approached the bar, where Prue was collecting dirty glasses and her husband was serving. Colton and Charlie stopped by a cluster of glasses ready for washing. Colton leaned on the counter, his elbow sliding nearer to the glasses. Fliss and Betty lurked opposite the door leading upstairs. Betty's mouth went dry suddenly. They were not even at Crowstone Tower yet, and already so much could go wrong.

More people filtered in, crowding around. Betty glanced at Prue, and for a brief moment their eyes met. Betty stared into the pale depths, so devoid of color and conscience, and couldn't help a sharp intake of breath.

A loud smash broke their gaze as a glass shattered nearby. "I'm so sorry!" Colton exclaimed as Prue rushed to sweep up the glass.

Fliss nudged Betty toward the door. "Go!" she whispered. Betty slipped past the hatch in the counter toward the stairs. She climbed them in silence, the murmur of voices below masking the creaks. At the top she paused. Were Prue and her husband the only people here, or could there be other relatives? Hearing nothing, she began to work her way from room to room.

How different everything looked! Plainer, but less shabby. And it was peculiar to see these familiar rooms with no traces of themselves or Granny. Betty began with Granny's room, the largest. Here she found neat rows of pressed clothes belonging to Prue and her husband in the wardrobes and drawers, some half-completed embroidery, and a few books. The dressing table was bare except for a comb and a small pot of hand salve. No mirror, no dolls. No bag.

Betty's heart began to pound, worry rising like the tide. Where were they? Surely Prue would have them here, safe with her? She hurried into the other rooms: Fliss's and the one she and Charlie shared. Both were furnished and pristine, but unlived in. Guest rooms. She left them, searching the kitchen. Nothing.

She paused in the hallway. The only other place she could check was the office downstairs, but it was sure to be locked. Unless . . .

She moved to the cupboard on the landing and opened it, half expecting it to be as sparse as the rest of the place. To her surprise, it was just as cluttered with junk here in the past as it was in the future. Would Prue hide her stolen treasures in this jumbled magpie's nest of buckets and brooms? She was cunning enough. Betty edged in, swallowing her childhood fears to sift through crates, a broken mangle, a cloth bag of pegs. How she hated this damp cupboard—they all did.

She stiffened as shrieks and cries of "Rat! Rat!" from downstairs reached her ears. This had to be part of Colton's plan, too, she guessed. Keeping them busy, distracted. She rummaged further, lifting piles of old newspapers off a trunk. She lifted its lid—and her stomach somersaulted.

Inside the trunk was a familiar wooden box with "W" inscribed in the lid. She lifted it out, heart crashing, hope soaring. The weight of its contents shifted. This was where Granny had taken the dolls from, where they had been kept all those years.

There was no time to search for the key or pick the lock. She considered smashing it open, before remembering the mirror. No. Dare she risk carrying it downstairs and walking out with it? Also no. She clambered out of the cupboard, studying the box. Perhaps with a knife she could pry it open. She ran into the kitchen, hunting until she found a small vegetable knife. It was then that inspiration struck: if she couldn't get in through the lock, there was another practical way . . .

She set about unscrewing the hinges, her hands shaking so much she kept losing her grip. Finally one was off. Betty tugged at the lid, but the other hinge held firm. Through a gap she could now see curved, painted wood and a glimmer of gilt. They were inside! Quickly, she worked on the second hinge. Seconds later it hit the kitchen tiles with a ping, a loose screw rolling beneath the table.

Betty slipped her fingers under the lid, tugging. There

was a destructive but satisfying splintering of wood as she reached in and carefully removed the objects, along with a small pouch of jewelry. A wedding gift to Prue, perhaps. She discarded this, then froze as a familiar voice warbled from below.

"The merrypennies in the meadow, silver by the night . . ."

A faint creak sounded on the stairs. Someone was coming!

Betty darted behind the kitchen door, clutching the objects to her chest. Light footsteps padded past the kitchen, then stopped. Heart hammering, Betty placed the bag and the mirror on the floor and pulled a hair from her head. Quickly, she opened the nesting dolls and placed the hair inside, rendering herself invisible. Taking a breath to steady her nerves, she crept out of the kitchen.

Prue was standing completely still in front of the cupboard. The door had swung open where Betty had forgotten to latch it, and its contents were in disarray. The heavy trunk lay open and empty.

"No," Prue whispered, shaking her head suddenly. She snapped out of her frozen trance and staggered to the door. "No, no, no . . ." She stood at the door, emitting quick little breaths that were like gasps.

A wicked idea popped into Betty's head. She almost dismissed it, but something stopped her. If Prue suspected

Sorsha was behind the objects' disappearance, she might try to contact her and botch the rescue. No, Betty decided. It was safer for Prue to be kept out of mischief.

With that, she strode swiftly and purposefully toward the other girl.

Prue whipped around at the sound of Betty's footsteps. Her eel-like eyes widened, and in them Betty caught a glimmer of fear and understanding.

"Who's there—?" she began.

Wordlessly, Betty reached out and pushed, hard. With a shocked cry, Prue stumbled backwards into the dank depths of the cupboard. Betty slammed the door, latching it fast. Rattles and thuds came from within as Prue clambered over piles of junk. There was a thump from the other side of the door as she found it.

"Who's there?" she repeated, voice shrill.

Again, Betty hesitated. She knew she should just leave, but some sense of honor kept her there, listening to Prue's frightened breathing on the other side of the door. People had died because of Prue. Betty's family and Sorsha had suffered because of her. And Betty knew she had to have the last word.

"A friend," she said in a fierce whisper.

"F-friend? But I don't have any—"

"A friend of Sorsha's," Betty cut in. "Not yours,

Prudence Widdershins! You had a friend. The best kind of friend: a sister. And you betrayed her." Her voice cracked, and she fought to keep it under control. "But you haven't won—not this time."

"I d-don't understand . . ."

"No," Betty said softly. "And now you never will." Silently, she backed away to the kitchen. She collected the bag and mirror, hiding them beneath the folds of her unseen clothes before retreating downstairs.

The Poacher's Pocket had descended into a fracas. Fliss's song had struck up a bawdy rendition with some of the customers joining in, while dozens more were thump-ing on the bar to be served. Shattered glass crunched underfoot, but the cries of "rat" had been drowned out.

She spotted Fliss some way along the counter, having been jostled out of position. Elbowing her way through the thickening crowd, Betty grabbed her sister's arm and leaned close to her ear. "Fliss, it's me. I got them!"

"Betty!" Fliss reached for her blindly, weak with relief.

"Get the others," Betty said in a low voice, spying Charlie and Colton near the door. "And then let's get out of here."

Outside, Betty hurried to the deserted alley and made herself visible before returning to the street, where she almost collided with the others coming the opposite way.

"You did it!" Charlie squeaked, hugging her.

"Only just," Betty answered, handing her the bag and passing the mirror to Fliss. "Come on. We need to move."

"I could get us to the tower with the bag," Charlie suggested eagerly.

"No, not yet," said Betty. "We can't just arrive at the prison—we need to know what we're dealing with and get a plan in place." She cast a fearful look over her shoulder, half expecting Prue to burst out of the doors of the Poacher's Pocket. "Follow me."

Chapter Twenty-Four

Crowstone Tower

THEY HURRIED TOWARD THE MARSHES, weaving around more people coming from the direction of the ferry. Though much of Crowstone was different, with familiar buildings missing or replaced by others, everything was still recognizable. Despite Granny's frequent references to it, Betty still felt a jolt of shock when they reached the crossroads.

A tall gallows stood on a grassy mound. Steps led up to a wooden platform where a heavy rope noose was swaying in the breeze. Groups of people clustered nearby, staring and whispering.

"No wonder Granny hates the crossroads," Fliss said,

glassy-eyed with horror. "She said this was here when she was a little girl and she's never forgotten it. It's so . . . so awful. Dreadful things have happened here."

Betty pursed her lips. "We can make one fewer awful thing happen."

They reached the shore, heading away from the ferry to a small, empty fishing cove. They picked their way through the shingle, mud squelching underfoot. Across the water, Crowstone Prison squatted like a giant toad, eyeing them as if they were flies it planned to swallow.

"Between the three of you, you have all you need to get into the tower unseen and get Sorsha out," said Colton. Though it wasn't warm, a film of sweat slicked his forehead. "You just need to figure out how. The tower will be guarded."

Fliss took the mirror out, keeping it half hidden within the folds of her shawl. "Show us the guards at Crowstone Tower," she whispered.

Immediately her reflection vanished, and a warder appeared at the foot of the stone tower they knew so well. A cluster of keys hung from his belt. Beyond him lay the door to the tower.

"One guard," said Colton. "And one way in. But you need those keys."

Betty nodded. "The objects can help us before we're

through that door, but after that it's up to us to get Sorsha out of the tower room without magic."

Fliss drew her shawl over the mirror's surface, breaking the vision.

"The dolls are the best chance of stealing the keys," said Betty. "After that, we distract him away from the door to get past him. Someone then needs to wait outside to keep watch, and lure him away again when Sorsha is safely out of the tower and down the steps."

Fliss nodded slowly. "So at least one of us needs to stay outside and wait."

Betty looked expectantly at Colton; he had the most knowledge of the prison layout, and the warders. But he seemed troubled, his gaze returning to the prison. She could see the dread in his eyes, feel it coming off him in waves. For the first time she realized how afraid he must be of returning to the place he'd only just escaped.

"I'll do it," Fliss offered.

"Once everyone's out of the tower, it doesn't matter if you're seen," Colton murmured. "The bag will take care of everything else in an instant."

Betty frowned. Something about Colton's words was bothering her, but she couldn't quite work out what it was. "How long until noon?" she asked, looking up. The pale red moon floated like a bad omen.

"I reckon you've got about an hour." Colton took a shaky breath. "But I . . . I—"

"What?" Fliss asked, sensing his sudden hesitation.

But Betty already knew. "You didn't say 'we.'"

He kept his eyes down, unable to look at any of them. Betty couldn't help but think back to when they had first met, when Colton had swaggered into the visiting room full of bravado. All she saw now was a scared young man.

"I don't think I can go back there."

"Where?" Fliss demanded. "The prison?"

"Any of it," he mumbled. "The prison. And back . . . back to our time."

Betty's mouth dropped open. "What exactly are you saying? That you want to stay here? In . . . in the past?"

"Well, why not?" Colton's head snapped up, anger flashing in his eyes. "What is there for me to go back to? Nothing, that's what! No family. Nothing but a life of looking over my shoulder, wondering if my past is about to catch up with me. At least here I can start fresh, knowing I'm not being hunted. I don't belong there."

"But . . . but . . ." she faltered, struggling to process his words and the strength of her feeling against them. *Why should it matter?* the little voice in her head asked. Even if she had come to call Colton a friend, she knew she would never see him again after all this ended. His past would never go away. But if he stayed here, he would be the past, too . . . and the thought filled her with sorrow.

"Maybe not," said Betty. "But you don't belong here, either. You deserve more than this." She gestured to the gallows. "You really want to live in a world that's worse than the one we know?"

Colton shrugged, a muscle twitching obstinately in his jaw. "No. But the point is, I'll live."

The sky was darkening with clouds, turning a bruise-like shade. Betty's heart quickened. "We don't have much time. So this is goodbye, Colton. And good luck." She held out her hand to shake his, but to her surprise he pulled her into a hug.

"Good luck to you, too." His voice was muffled. "I know none of this was really about freeing me, but I'm grateful to you. All of you. Without you I'd still be inside those walls, rotting." He released Betty and ruffled Charlie's hair, then turned to Fliss. "Farewell, princess."

"I'm not—" Fliss began.

"I know, I know." A small smile tugged at his mouth. He lifted his fingers to Fliss's short hair. "It suits you," he said softly, dropping his hand.

"Wait." Fliss bit her lip, then, blushing bright pink, stood on her tiptoes and kissed Colton on the lips. "For luck," she said, her eyes shimmering with tears as she returned to her sisters.

A lump rose in Betty's throat. Perhaps in Colton her sister had finally found someone who wouldn't fall at her feet; whom she wouldn't eventually tire of. Or perhaps this was just another silly Fliss kiss. Either way, time wasn't their friend, so they would never know. It would forever be a kiss of kindness, of lost chances and what ifs.

Betty rolled her eyes, doing her best to sound scathing. "Well, you just wouldn't be you if you went a day without kissing someone, would you?"

"Oh, be quiet," Fliss snapped. "Let's go. Charlie, the bag!"

"Wait!" This time, the voice was Colton's. He jogged to Fliss's side and linked his arm with hers.

"You changed your mind?" she asked, her eyes shining.

"I lost my nerve for a minute there." He smiled at Fliss. "But now I'm feeling pretty lucky."

"I'm feeling sick," Betty announced, but she couldn't help smiling. "Right. Everyone ready this time, really ready?" She took the nesting dolls, reaching for the inner ones, into which she placed the little bits belonging to each of them. She twisted the halves to align, making them all invisible. Stowing them safely in her pocket, she linked arms with Fliss and Charlie, nudging her youngest sister.

"Now."

Charlie took a deep, bracing breath. "Crowstone Tower," she whispered.

I'm never, ever going to get used to this feeling, Betty thought as the shingle whooshed from under her. Briny air bit her cheeks and forced her eyes closed, and she heard Fliss gurgle a nauseous "Oohhh!"

They landed as clumsily as ever, and though Charlie somehow managed to stay on her feet, the rest of them didn't fare so well. To Betty's dismay, Colton cried out upon landing as his left leg gave under him. Though he bit it back almost immediately, the sound echoed off the walls of the stone courtyard they found themselves in. Above, crows scattered and squawked. Betty released her grip on Fliss and Charlie and stepped back, staring up at the tower, whose shadow loomed over them. The sheer distance to the top made her woozy; she had never been so close to it, never realized just how high it was.

She blinked, and a vision of falling flashed before her eyes, dizzying her.

No! She could not let that happen. She was so busy

searching the windows that she failed to notice the heavy wooden door until a warder came charging through it. His eyes darted around the courtyard in suspicion. In one hand he held a thick wooden baton. His other hand rested on his belt, by an iron hook holding two keys. He squinted at a skid in the gravel, then frowned up at the tower windows. Satisfied nothing sinister was afoot, he returned to the tower wall next to the unlocked door, which was ajar. Content he was apparently alone, he took out a pipe and began craftily stuffing it with tobacco, ready to dart back through the tower door if any other warders appeared.

"Fliss and I will go together," Betty mouthed. "I'll steal the keys; then we'll sneak up the stairs to get Sorsha. Colton, you stay here with Charlie until we return. And here." She pushed the nesting dolls into Colton's hands. "Keep hold of these. Once we're through that door, Fliss and I won't be invisible, but taking the dolls into the tower would mean you and Charlie wouldn't stay hidden, either."

Hearts pounding and hardly daring to breathe, Betty and Fliss crept closer to the warder, as quietly as they could over the gravel. With each footstep Betty's chest thumped harder, and for the first time she was grateful for the cries of the crows circling overhead, to mask any sounds of their approach. When they were a mere stride away, Betty reached out and, with a shaking hand, wrapped her fingers around the keys to stop them rattling. With her other hand, she eased the hook slowly out of the warder's belt. She almost dropped the keys when the warder went into a bout of coughing, but somehow kept her nerve. To her relief the keys dropped into her hand.

In a cloud of the warder's smoke, they backed away, glancing back to where Colton and Charlie were watching anxiously. Then they approached the tower door.

Betty steeled herself and pushed the door, waiting for a creak to betray them. It opened soundlessly. She stared at Fliss in amazement and delight as they slipped into the tower, unable to believe how easily they had managed it. Through the open door, they saw Colton and Charlie dancing a silent jig of celebration.

They were standing in a narrow, dank passage with a curving flight of steps leading up. Betty motioned for Fliss to creep ahead and began to follow.

It was then that things went catastrophically wrong, when Betty tripped on the very first step. At the sound of her stumbling, Fliss spun around and made a grab for her, but it was too late. The noise had alerted the warder—and now that they were inside the tower, they were without the power of the dolls to keep them hidden.

They froze on the staircase as the warder loomed in the doorway, the pipe falling from his open mouth in shock. Yet as well as surprise, his face registered fear and confusion.

"Wh-who are you?" he stammered. "Where did you come from?" He reeled as he spied the keys in Betty's hand and took a step back. "Wraiths!" he yelled in a choked voice. "Spirits! The witch has summoned imps from the marshes! Wraiths, I tell you! Will-o'-the-wisps! Send help—!"

Colton hit him at speed, flinging the warder aside. His face was contorted with panic as he bundled Charlie through the tower door. "The keys!" he hissed, slamming the door shut behind them. "Quick!"

Betty threw the keys neatly and Colton caught them, jamming one in the door. He swore, removed it, then tried the other one. The lock clicked in place, sealing them inside the tower as if in a tomb. Outside, the warder continued to yell.

What have I done? Betty thought. *What in crow's name have I done? If we're caught, we'll never make it home!*

"Up the stairs!" Colton gasped, ashen-faced. "Hurry. It won't be long before he raises the alarm!"

Betty grabbed Charlie's hand and began climbing the staircase.

"What will they do?" she croaked helplessly. "How will we get out now?"

"I don't know," Colton said as he started up the steps behind her. His mouth was pressed into a grim line. "All I know is that in a few minutes half the warders in this prison will be surrounding the tower."

Up they went, and up, in a dizzying spiral. Aside from a scattering of tiny windows in the passageway, only a few wall sconces lit the way, sending flickering shadows across the walls as they passed. Ahead of her, Betty heard Fliss's breath coming hard and fast. Next to her, Charlie gripped her hand so tightly her fingers were numb. Behind, Colton's footfall was heavy with exhaustion and dread.

For Betty, too, every step became agony, not only from her burning leg muscles, but from the knowledge that their way out of the tower was well and truly blocked. They were every bit as trapped as Sorsha Spellthorn.

They had made it to the last turn of the staircase when from outside the tower a sonorous clanging of the prison bell began. The alarm had been sounded.

Fliss was first to reach the door at the top. She half slid down it, gasping for breath as Betty staggered toward her, urging Charlie, who had begun to whimper softly.

Colton, too, was rasping for air, and his hands shook as he fumbled with the keys, inserting one into the lock and turning it.

Despite everything, Betty wondered how she would have felt at this moment if the last few minutes hadn't turned out so disastrously. Quite possibly, she thought, she would have felt excited, and a little afraid of what lay in wait on the other side of the door. Only there was no time for that. Time for the Widdershinses had very nearly run out.

Colton gave the door a hard push and stepped inside.

Betty followed, her eyes raking over the vast, circular tower room. It was all she had expected: gloomy, desolate, sparsely furnished. And then there were the words . . . walls scrawled with words that descended into meaningless jumble.

Too late she saw the figure silhouetted against the window, arms wide, tawny hair trailing into the tower room behind her as the wind whistled through it.

Too late, Betty saw she was already falling.

"Sorsha, no!" Betty yelled.

Somehow Sorsha twisted, half turning to look back at them as she fell. Her eyes were wild and bitter, but there was just time for surprise to register, too. She seemed to hang in the air like a feather for a moment, a question forming on her lips . . .

. . . Then she was gone.

Chapter Twenty-Five

Fly

"NO!" BETTY MOANED. "NO, NO, NO . . ."

From outside the tower, horrified shouts drifted up. Betty sank to her knees, unable to bring herself to go to the window. They had been so close, suffered so much . . . for what? Her last hope was gone, and so was Sorsha.

"We're too late." Colton drew Fliss to him with one arm, and Charlie with the other. Charlie was weeping quietly, while Fliss was stiff with shock. "We were just . . . too late." The keys slid from his hand and landed on the floor.

Betty's gaze swept the gloomy, desolate room, taking in the place where Sorsha had lived the final part of her life. *This isn't a room*, she thought. *It's a grave.* Numb, she got up and walked to the wall, her fingertips tracing the deep scratches there. Scratches that formed bitter, hateful words: "Malice." "Injustice." "Cowardice." "Escape" . . .

"WIDDERSHINS."

Betty closed her eyes, but the word remained, like it was etched into her soul. So much hate. How could she have ever thought it possible to undo the curse? How had she ever hoped for such a thing? She thought back to her life in Crowstone, her simple little life that she had scorned for not being enough. Now it seemed it had. And had Betty been a little less bold, less discontented and more like Fliss, she might still have a future to look forward to. And so might her sisters, if they hadn't listened to her.

"I'm sorry," Betty whispered. "I'm sorry, Granny, Fliss, Charlie . . . and Colton."

Her words were lost beneath the monotonous toll of the prison bell. The room was almost in darkness now, the sky outside a hazy orange as the blood moon hovered over the marshes. On the windowsill, a crow landed with an ominous caw, its gleaming eyes on Betty.

"Go away!" she cried, but the creature didn't move.

More swooped in through the other windows, settling on wall sconces, the mattress, and anything they could find. Croaking in eerie unison. Cries from below drifted in on the freezing air. Betty moved to the window, as if in a trance. *Don't look*, she told herself. *You shouldn't look.*

She knew she would have to.

Crowstone lay before her, the Misty Marshes stretching into the distance. The shouts below continued. She forced her eyes down.

The ground below was swarming with warders. Milling around like an army of ants, yelling warnings, trading orders. She couldn't see a body. Had they moved poor Sorsha already? Or were there so many of them crowding around they were sparing her the view? Distantly, she heard a *thud, thud, thud*.

"What's that noise?" she asked dully.

"They're breaking the entrance door down," Colton replied. "Not all of them are superstitious, so it would seem."

Betty turned back to the window. Crows spilled through the air, circling the tower. There was no stopping them now.

It was over.

And then matted red hair streamed out from below the window like a banner. Betty gasped and leaned over the sill. There, a short way down, Sorsha was clinging to the side of the tower, somehow balanced on a thin ledge above one of the passageway windows. Her face was streaked with dirt, her clothes not much more than rags. Betty's shout as Sorsha had begun to fall had been enough to make her hesitate and grab on.

"Sorsha!" Betty cried. A last flicker of hope sputtered back into life from embers. "Don't let go! We're here to get you out!"

In an instant, Fliss and Colton were at her side. Betty leaned over, reaching out. "Take my hand!"

"I can't!" Sorsha huddled into the wall, squeezing her eyes shut. "I'll lose my grip!" Even as she spoke, one of her legs slipped from beneath her, and she scrabbled for purchase. A stone broke away from the wall and began its descent to the ground below. Another followed swiftly after.

"No!" Betty yelled, stretching out toward her. "Hold on! We'll pull you back in. Just don't let go!"

"I don't think I can for much longer." Sorsha opened her eyes, casting a terrified look below. "I was ready . . . It took all my courage, and then you called my name . . . broke my thoughts!"

"You can't do this," Betty told her. "I won't let you! Now reach up and take my hand!"

Sorsha lunged, her fingers brushing the wall. Too far from Betty's. Another stone crumbled beneath her fingers and plummeted below. She shrieked, grabbing blindly, before finding another.

"Let me try," Colton urged. Betty moved aside, and watched, helpless, as he leaned over, straining and stretching. It was still not enough.

An almighty crash and sounds of splintering wood echoed up the stairwell.

"They're in!" Fliss yelled. "The warders are in the tower!"

"I'm not giving up!" Betty grabbed the keys and ran to the tower room door, throwing it closed and locking it. "Fliss, Charlie, help me barricade the door!"

Together, the three of them began piling everything in the room in front of the door. There were woefully few items, and they all knew it would make little difference. Already there was the sound of footfall on the stairs.

"They're coming!" Charlie shouted.

Colton leaned back with a growl of frustration. "I can't reach her. We'll have to try something else!" He straddled the huge windowsill, swinging his legs over the side.

Fliss paled. "Colton, no! You'll fall!"

"I won't." He turned to face the tower room, gripping the sill tightly and lowering himself out. "Sorsha, grab my legs!"

This can't work, thought Betty as the warders reached

the door to the tower room. Defeat was looming stealthily, smothering her last spark of hope. The sound of wood being pounded on reverberated in her skull, in time with the chimes of the bell. *Even if we pull Sorsha in, where do we go from here? The warders have us surrounded . . .* They had only moments before the warders would be in the tower room. Before they all would be doomed.

Crows circled the tower, calling to them, and for a moment it seemed the birds were coaxing them into the air. Not to their deaths, but perhaps to something else . . .

"Charlie, the bag!" Betty cried.

Charlie glared at her through a tangle of hair and tears. "Huh?"

"Come here, both of you. Fliss!"

Fliss's eyes were huge like saucers. "Betty, no . . ." she whispered. "You can't be suggesting . . . we can't possibly . . ."

"It's our only chance!" Betty roared. She grabbed her sisters' hands and pulled them to the window. "We know the magic won't work within the tower walls. But the instant we escape them—" She broke off, nodding to the sky.

"No!" Charlie whimpered. "No, I won't!"

"Yes!" Betty hugged her, hard. "You've trusted me till now. And we know this will work, because of you!"

There was no time to wait for an answer. The door behind them was splitting, sending splinters of wood flying into the tower room. Warders' voices filtered through.

"They're escaping! The sorceress is escaping with her imps!"

Betty swung her legs over the windowsill, urging Fliss to do the same.

Together they squeezed a trembling Charlie between them and wedged her onto Fliss's lap. She clung to the traveling bag, its ugly fabric clenched between her fingers like a stuffed toy.

Betty braced herself and looked down for the final time. Sorsha was clinging to Colton's legs, his arms still clamped over the window ledge next to Betty.

"Take my hand," she yelled. He reached for her with difficulty, his palm clammy, as his weight and much of Sorsha's now hung from his other arm. Sweat beaded on his forehead.

"Hurry," he begged. "I can't hold us both much longer!"

Betty linked her other arm tightly with Fliss's. The wind roared in her ears, sucking at them, willing them to join it. "On the count of three, we jump!" She turned to Charlie. "You know what to do."

"I c-can't . . ." Charlie stuttered. "H-Hoppit's scared!"

"You have to. It's the only way!"

"But—"

"You can do it, Charlie! We know you can. Do it for us, and Granny. For the Widdershinses!"

"Did you say . . . Widdershins?" Sorsha yelled from below.

"Yes," Betty cried. "We're the Widdershinses! One, two . . ."

The splintered door finally caved and crashed open. Warders flooded into the tower room.

"Three!" Betty shouted, and with a battle cry, they launched themselves into the sky. A handful of stones, perhaps four or five, came away with them, soaring through the air. The crows swooped above, dark silhouettes against the blazing orange moon. Faster than Betty could ever have imagined, they were falling.

"Home!" Charlie yelled.

And then, just for a moment, it seemed they really were flying.

Chapter Twenty-Six

Free

THE AIR CHANGED FROM BRINE- to beer-scented, from frost to feathers.

Betty hit solid ground, but it was a curiously soft landing. She opened her eyes and found she was lying on her back, staring at familiar oak beams on the ceiling above. The Poacher's Pocket should have been open and trading, but instead it was deathly quiet and dark, and the windows and doors were locked and barred. Outside was not so quiet; the prison bell was clanging in the distance. Somewhere nearer was the squeaking of a rat.

Betty sat up, rubbing her eyes. Had it worked? Were they really back in their Poacher's Pocket? If it hadn't, then Betty had nothing else to give. All would be lost.

She would be lost. There was no sign of Granny anywhere, and the only movement was downy black feathers cascading like ebony snowflakes. She was suddenly aware that someone was still holding her hand.

"Colton?"

"Am I alive?" He groaned, releasing her. "I must be. Being dead wouldn't hurt this much."

"Fliss? Charlie?" Betty's voice rose anxiously. She leaped to her feet.

"Over here." Fliss's voice sounded from near the fireplace. Betty rushed over and found her kneeling, her arm around Charlie, who was still clutching the traveling bag.

Charlie batted a feather away from her face and sneezed. "Is it over? Did we break the curse?"

"I . . . I think so." Betty looked around. Everything looked as she remembered, and for a scary moment she wondered if nothing had changed. Had they saved any of the Widdershinses before them? "I can't hear the crows anymore . . . and if Sorsha didn't fall . . ." She hesitated. "But where is she?"

"I'm here."

Sorsha Spellthorn stepped from the shadows. Her matted hair reached halfway down her back, glowing like rust in the half-light. Silvery streaks of dried tears crisscrossed her brown face, which, now that it was no longer contorted with suspicion and dark thoughts, had a certain beauty about it. "Widdershins," she said slowly, as if for the first time. The first time not saying it in hatred. "You came for me. You saved me."

Betty swallowed, meeting Sorsha's eyes. For the first time since discovering the horrible truth about her link to Prue, she felt the burden lift. The Widdershinses had nothing to be ashamed of anymore. "Yes."

"Thank you." Sorsha's eyes lingered on the traveling bag. "But . . . why? Did my sister . . . ?" She stopped and blinked, like there was something in her eye. "Did Prue send you?"

Betty shook her head. "I'm sorry. She didn't. But it's because of her that we were able to use the . . . your magic." She gestured to the traveling bag. "The objects got passed down, over time, to us. We each received one and could only use the magic of the one we were given."

"Over . . . time? How much time?"

"Over a century," Fliss answered.

Sorsha nodded, studying each of them. Her eyes lingered on Colton. "And you? Are you a Widdershins?"

"Er, no. Just . . . someone who got caught up with all this."

Sorsha stared at the traveling bag. "I thought I'd never leave that tower alive."

"I know." Betty's voice was hoarse. "All those days you spent in there. All the words you scratched into the walls: 'malice,' 'cowardice—'"

"'Escape,'" Sorsha interrupted. She smiled, sadly but warmly. "That's the only word that matters now. As well as 'forgiveness,' perhaps."

Fliss frowned. "You mean . . . you forgive Prue? For what she did?"

Sorsha's eyes clouded with pain. "If what you say is true, she's gone now. Long gone. And somehow, I don't think what she did would have made her happy."

"But she was jealous of you," Betty blurted out. "Of what you were and what you had. So jealous and bitter she wanted you out of the way, at any cost!"

"Yes, she was," Sorsha agreed. "But jealous, bitter people don't suddenly find that those feelings go away when what they envy becomes theirs. They simply find something else to be jealous and bitter about, because it was never about what the other person had. It's about what they themselves lack."

Betty's cheeks were suddenly warm and wet. To her embarrassment, she found she was crying. Sorsha's words had touched something within her, a deep-rooted guilt that she had been holding in for a long time and trying to pretend she didn't feel. There were times when she had envied her sisters, particularly Fliss for her beauty and charm. But now she smiled and met Fliss's eyes, and they shared a look of love and understanding that only sisters could. They didn't need to compete. Their differences didn't have to set them apart.

Together, their differences only made them stronger.

"There are warders patrolling everywhere out there," Colton cut in. He had moved to the window and was now holding himself so tensely that Betty thought the slightest touch would make him jump like a coiled spring. "So come on, Betty Widdershins. How do I get out of this one? Because I sure as eggs can't stay in Crowstone."

"With me," Sorsha said simply, glancing at the traveling bag.

"You mean . . . it's time to give my pinch of magic back?" Charlie asked, her voice trembling.

"Yes, Charlie." Betty took the nesting dolls out, running her thumb over the beautifully painted smooth wood. "It's time to give it all back." She passed the dolls to Sorsha, then watched in silence as Fliss and Charlie handed back the mirror and the traveling bag. Sorsha held them all for a long moment. Unexpectedly, she handed the dolls back to Betty.

"Keep them."

Betty stared at the dolls, longing to take them. She

hadn't expected that returning the gifts would be such a wrench. "I'm grateful, but I can't. It wouldn't be fair to my sisters—"

"Their power is for you all," said Sorsha. "You've earned it." She gave another sad little smile. "Besides, they're the perfect gift for sisters who look after one another." She pushed them into Betty's hand. "Real sisters."

"Thank you," Betty whispered, stunned. A deliciously warm feeling of gratitude spread through her body, as intoxicating as the magic itself.

Fliss moved toward Colton. "So this time it really is goodbye," she said softly.

Colton nodded, his dark eyes somber. "I suppose it is."

A floorboard creaked somewhere above.

"Betty?" Granny's voice thundered. "Felicity? Charlotte?" The girls froze at the sound of footsteps on the stairs.

Fliss was the first to snap out of it. "Go now," she whispered.

Colton hugged Charlie quickly, then gave Fliss a swift kiss on the cheek.

She touched her fingers to her face. "What was that for?"

"For luck." He grinned suddenly. "But I think you girls have already changed that for yourselves." He turned to

Betty, reaching for her hand. "I'll miss you, Betty Widdershins. Don't ever change." He hesitated. "Friends?"

Betty squeezed his hand. "Something like that. And, Colton?" Her voice became muffled as he pulled her into a hug. "Thanks."

Colton grinned. "It was a pleasure. Well, some of it."

Sorsha tucked the mirror into her clothing and reached into the traveling bag, ready. "Farewell, Widdershins girls. You have your own magic now." Then, linking her arm with Colton's, she whispered something, so quietly that none of them heard.

In an eye blink, they were gone, with only a scattering of crows' feathers floating on the air to say they'd ever been there at all.

"Jumping jackdaws!" Granny shrieked, startling them all. The girls whipped around to face her. A black feather had stuck straight up in her hair, making her look like a cross old turkey. "Just where have you three been? Crowstone is on lockdown—there are prisoners on the loose and you three go gallivanting?"

She peered at Fliss. "I see you took my advice and finally cut that mane of yours. We don't need any more complaints about it getting into the customers' beer. But that still doesn't explain where you've all been!" She wagged her finger at Betty. "This was your idea, wasn't it, hmm? And what in whiskey's name are all these feathers? It looks like every crow across the Misty Marshes has been massacred here!" She eyed Charlie suspiciously. "Is this you, bringing dead things home to bury again? This has got to stop, young lady—"

"No, Granny," said Charlie in a small voice. "I didn't bring anything home this time . . . well, nothin' dead, anyway—"

"Charlie?" Granny said in a warning tone, but Charlie rushed on.

"We were too busy saving Sorsha Spellthorn and breaking the curse—"

"Curse? What curse?" Granny threw up her hands. "You girls and your games, you wear me out. It's not the time for games when that prison bell is tolling, do you hear?"

"Yes, Granny," they chorused.

Granny softened, exhausted by her tirade. She pulled out a chair and plonked herself down, using a wrinkled hand to fan her face. "Mind you, our Clarissa was the same with her games. She always loved the story of Sorsha Spellthorn, too."

"Which story was that, Granny?" Betty asked carefully, with a warning glance at Charlie to hold her tongue.

Granny frowned at her. "The tale of how she vanished

from the tower, of course! Everyone knows that. Why, Clarissa and your father used to drive me mad, making me tell them that story so they could act it all out. Clarissa loved pretending to be Sorsha. Poor Barney had to be an imp or a crow." She snorted. "She's no less bossy now."

"You mean she's alive?" Betty asked.

Granny stared at her in astonishment. "Are you feeling quite well, Betty? You're acting peculiar, not your usual sensible self at all." She held up a hand to Betty's forehead. "You don't feel overly warm."

Betty forced a smile. An unfamiliar feeling trickled over her, like warm sand. For the first time in as long as she could remember, she felt content. Dazed, but happy. "We were just . . . just having a joke with you. I'm fine, Granny."

It's true, she realized. *I really am fine.*

"Hmm." Granny let her hand drop and heaved herself up. "A joke, eh?" She collected a cup from behind the counter and poured herself some tea. "Let's see how funny you think being grounded for two weeks with extra chores is. Perhaps we should ask your father what he thinks. Look, here he comes now—"

"What?" Betty turned as the door rattled and someone pushed it open from the outside. Hope welled within her. It couldn't be, surely . . . ?

Barney Widdershins stood on the doormat, stamping dead leaves off his boots. His cheeks were red with cold.

"You three!" he scolded, closing the door against the wind. "I've been looking everywhere!" He paused, a twinkle in his eyes as he took in their shocked, frozen faces. "I just hope Granny's done the telling-off part so I don't have to."

"Father?" Betty managed, disbelieving. The dolls rattled in her shaking hand. Beyond breaking the curse, she hadn't considered what other consequences could arise from their actions—but here he was. Slivers of ice fell away from her heart. They would never get back the years they had lost with him, but at least now they had time to make it up. "What . . . what are you doing here?"

He chuckled. "I live here, last time I checked!"

"Did they let you out early?" Fliss asked, her voice strained.

None of the girls had moved an inch.

"Out of where?" Their father stepped toward Charlie, sweeping her up into his arms so that she was perched almost on his shoulder. Charlie stared back at him stiffly, then slowly reached out and poked him on the nose.

"Prison," she said.

"Prison?" their father laughed, poking her back. "You cheeky little beast! I'm a respectable man."

"Just about," said Granny, rolling her eyes. "You won't get any sense out of them, Barnaby. They're playing one of their games. I've already told them they're grounded for two weeks . . ."

Before Granny could say any more, Betty found herself walking over to her father. Tentatively, she put her arms around him, half afraid he would vanish like marsh mist. A moment later, she felt Fliss beside her, and her father's breath in her hair.

"You're real," she murmured into his coat. It smelled of crunchy leaves and cold — and beneath it he was warm and solid and there.

"Sweet as pumpkin pie when they want to be," said Granny suspiciously. "But don't think that'll change anything! Grounded — two weeks!"

"S'not fair," Charlie said, glowering. "Not after what we've just done!"

"I'll talk her down to a week," Father whispered.

Betty turned to Fliss and they shared a secret smile.

"A week's not that long," Fliss said, her eyes shining.

"No," Betty agreed. "Not now that we've got forever."

EPILOGUE

"YOU KNOW," FLISS SAID THOUGHTFULLY as she was drying some glasses when the week was almost up, "ever since we came back and saw Father, I've been thinking . . ."

"About?" Betty looked up from the board onto which she was chalking the specials.

"Whether we could have done more . . . to change things, for Mother." Fliss's voice dropped to a whisper. "We had the bag, Betty! What if we'd gone back to the night she died, changed her mind somehow . . . told her not to go out into the fog?"

"Even if we'd thought of it, she'd probably have left even faster, seeing the three of us from the future," Betty said wryly. Privately, she'd harbored the same regrets, but realistically, she knew that nothing else could have been done once the curse was triggered. It was time to let the past lie and plan for the future—now that they had one. "We'd made a decision, Fliss. We had to break the curse and get back to Granny, and we did it. We saved ourselves and nine other Widdershins girls. How many people can say they've done something like that?"

"I know," Fliss conceded. "You're right."

"Not to mention breaking not one, but two people out of Crowstone Prison," Betty added. "I'd say plenty's changed. You've managed to go a whole week without kissing anyone—"

She ducked, grinning as Fliss flicked the towel she was holding at her with a playful "Hey!"

Fliss tossed the towel down, looking thoughtful. "I think I'll hold off on the kissing for now," she said, staring through the window into the distance. "Until someone . . . worth kissing comes along."

"Probably a good thing," said Betty. "You were running out of options in Crowstone, anyway— Ow!" She laughed as Fliss grabbed the towel and threw it at her; then her grin faded. "What we have now . . . it's enough. More than we could have hoped for. Expecting everything to be perfect would be like expecting Charlie to put on a lace dress and play tea parties."

"Eh?" Charlie demanded, crawling out from the fireplace at the mention of her name. "I ain't wearing no dress!"

"Good thing, too," said Betty. "Look at you, covered in soot! What're you doing under there?"

Charlie stuck her tongue out. "Looking for Hoppit."

"You'd better hop it, before Granny sees you," said Betty, nodding to the door. "Here she comes now!"

"Meddling magpies!" Charlie muttered, frantically brushing ashes from her clothes.

The doors of the Poacher's Pocket opened, and Granny came shuffling in with a basket of groceries. Hot on her heels was Fingerty, laden down with a further two baskets.

"Might as well open now, girls," she called, setting her shopping down. "It's five minutes early, strictly speaking. But I'll make an exception for you, Seamus, seeing as you're so helpful these days."

"Yerp." Fingerty nodded, winking at the girls. "An' a hero, too, Bunny." He puffed out his scrawny chest. "Captured the crookedest crook in Crowstone, let's not forget that!"

"Wouldn't dream of it," said Granny. "Fliss, fetch Mr. Fingerty his usual and then the three of you can get yourselves down to the harbor. Your father wants you."

"Father? At the harbor?" Betty glanced at Fliss, bemused. What could he want them for? It wasn't market day; no trading ships would be in. Why was Granny wearing such a knowing smirk? "Granny? What exactly is—"

Granny waved a hand, scattering tobacco from her unlit pipe. "You'll have to find out for yourselves, and . . ." She stopped, glaring. "Charlie? CHARLIE! What is all this soot doing on my floor?"

Charlie scuttled out from under a table. "Father needs me!" she yelled, making a getaway through the door. "Bye!"

"Come on," said Fliss to Betty, throwing down her apron. "Let's go!"

Giggling, they left Granny grumbling and shot after Charlie, through the twisting streets, past the crossroads and ferry point down to the harbor.

"Where is he?" Charlie demanded as they surveyed the fishing boats. She squinted against the sun, her breath misting the crisp November air. "Wait, I see him . . . but whose boat is that?"

Betty shielded her eyes, gazing ahead. Her father's stout figure was visible on a little vessel bobbing on the waves next to the jetty. It gleamed under fresh layers of jewel-green paint. "It's ours," she whispered, her heart soaring. "He did it. He finally fixed it!" Before she knew it, she was running, skidding along the jetty with Charlie and Fliss at her heels until they reached it.

Their father chuckled. "Well, it's about time!"

"I could say the same to you," Betty retorted as they scrambled aboard.

Father unwound the mooring, swaying easily with the motion of the boat. He scanned the sky as they pushed off easily, gliding through the water. "Weather's fine, and it's only just past midday. We may as well make an afternoon of it. So, where to?"

"Marshfoot," Betty said at once.

"Marshfoot?" Father repeated. He shrugged. "Marshfoot it is." Betty settled back in her seat, eyes on the smudge of land on the horizon. Marshfoot might not be as ambitious as some of the escapades she'd been planning, but it was a start. And any uncharted territory, however small, was still an adventure, she decided. Still a triumph.

There was time for bigger, time for further.

There was time.

"All right there, Fliss?" Father asked, shooting Fliss a concerned look.

Fliss nodded, taking deep breaths as she turned a

familiar shade of green. "I've been better," she muttered, catching Betty's eye. "Been worse, too."

"What's this boat called?" Charlie inquired. "I didn't see a name."

She was right, Betty realized with a jolt. "It should have one, Father," she insisted.

"Of course." Father steered them to the left. "I thought I'd leave that to you girls to decide."

"We should call it the *Traveling Bag*," Charlie declared at once.

Their father laughed. "You can't name a boat after a bag!"

"Why not?" Charlie demanded. "Boats are named after lots of things, and most of them are stupid!"

"Charlie's right," Betty agreed. "It was . . . it was from a story we heard once. About a magical bag that could take a person anywhere. It's perfect." She fell silent, realizing for the first time that this was a tale only they knew. For in this life, there had been no traveling bag or mirror handed down—only the dolls, from Sorsha herself. It was a past only they remembered; a secret only they shared. One that had forged their future.

Her hand found its way into her pocket, where a smooth wooden shape nestled snug and warm. She stroked her thumb over the doll's sleek surface, recalling that other journey to Marshfoot, on a foggy, fateful night when she had been so unprepared, and unknowing.

"She who tries, triumphs," Betty whispered to herself. She was Betty the Brave, Betty the Explorer.

And with her sisters at her side, she was ready for anything.

Acknowledgments

The journey into Crowstone was an easy one, but getting out again without a traveling bag was another matter. Perhaps it's no coincidence that as the Widdershins sisters were grieving the loss of both parents, so too was I. Though writing was an escape, I soon became lost in marsh mists of confusion and the problematic time travel that is editing.

Steering me through the rocky waters was my agent, Julia Churchill. Thank you for everything, especially over the past couple of years.

My editors, Lucy Rogers and Mattie Whitehead, chomped away the debris like the Devil's Teeth and devised clever (and greedy) suggestions and solutions.

I'm grateful to you both. Jenny Glencross showed me the missing ingredient that I just wasn't seeing, and Rachel Mann and Leena Lane lent their fine eyes for detail. You five are the Russian dolls of editing, from the outermost layer holding it all together to the fiddliest to find at the center. Without any of you the set would be incomplete.

The rest of Team S&S: Alex, Laura, Olivia, and everyone else—thank you for your support and enthusiasm for the Widdershinses.

It's wonderful when anyone enjoys your story, but praise from writing goddesses Sophie Anderson, Alex Bell, Abi Elphinstone, Tamsyn Murray, Emma Carroll, and Cerrie Burnell sent me giddy with happiness. Thank you all for your time, generosity, and kindness.

And to my family: there are now two empty spaces in our nest, but love keeps us strong. Thanks to creative cuckoo Carlene for the Poacher's Pocket and merry-pennies, and to my kind and practically perfect sisters for not minding being jumbled up and put in a book.

Team Widdershins!